Secluded Mansion Nights

Order this book online at www.trafford.com
or email orders@trafford.com

Most Trafford titles are also available at major online book retailers.

Printed in the United States of America.

ISBN: 978-1-4269-4745-2 (sc)
ISBN: 978-1-4269-4746-9 (e)

Trafford rev. 11/12/2010

 www.trafford.com

North America & international
toll-free: 1 888 232 4444 (USA & Canada)
phone: 250 383 6864 ♦ fax: 812 355 4082

Disclaimer

My Copyright and declaration statement in discernment to the facts set forth in motion that:

This novel is ninety percent fiction. It contains mild-adult and mild-sexual content that may or may not offend you, but it is my right to freely express my literary voice as it is a part of who I am as well as being my right under the Constitution of the United States of America to have free speech, thus if anyone is offended, I humbly apologize, but will not give a refund because this book shall be sold as is, so buyer beware...

Some of the names, places, and dates have been changed, while some have not been changed, and some of the people have long been departed from this life to another realm.

The dearly departed whose names I have used for the sole purpose of fiction was at one time, my living breathing ancestors and it is for their namesake that I foreclose my actual knowledge to you John P and Jenny Q Public this fact and changed their names in part for protection.

Although some of the places along with some of the incidents and some name changes at times are disbursements of this author's imagination by the virtue of reality that stems from my own real life in some places described here in and they too are subjected to fictions content as is to some actual fact and events in the midst of fiction whereby names, places and dates must be changed.

The better portions of this novel are not of reality, but fiction only. Most of these events never took place, but some have, and it's up to you the reader to establish and set apart fiction from reality.

The dead cannot and will not speak out in protest because their names and characters have been changed somewhat so to fit the eras ever so slightly that I have placed them in here because of some relevant relationship and or friendship to myself; solely for the pure purpose of fiction within both actual historical events as well as fictions events taking place in this novel.

All rights of this novel and its contents are reserved, including rights of reproduction in whole, and / or in part in any form by any person, or establishment without any written consent by this author, or this author's editor and the publisher with the exception of, and permission from same to display sections for any promotional public display as deemed necessary with their discretion.

It is further so stated that critics may reproduce only short sections for review, Publishing firms, the media, and authors, and for the purposes that shall be deemed necessary for the retailing and promotion of this novel, and or any book signings to be established at such a time deemed necessary by the publisher, editor, or by this author; and in total binding participation by this Author at my discretion if I deem it a necessity to conduct such a book signing to promote this book.

Dedication

I dedicate this to my beautiful Vera who I adore and will always love. I also want to dedicate this my first book to my sister Letha and all five of my kids, Eddie III, Michael, Kevin, Christopher, and Jennifer whom I love with all my heart, without them I'd be lost and all alone in this world.

To all of the great authors Poe, King, Spielberg, Sterling, Twain, and so many more who have given me so much inspiration that it haunts me to know their spirits still flourishes deep within my wondering existence in this delicate and unknown world that lay beyond reality.

My spirit is filled with heartfelt and humble gratitude for all the help my dear friends gave me with delightful encouragement in my novel achievement of this book and many more hopefully to come.

I thank you all, very sincerely.

Edward H' Wolf

Introduction

Ambers of time flow through the asylums of life. As one embarks on a journey set behind the padded cells of imagination, only those embers of true sanity will prevail in the many adventures to survive the deity of life.

Eddie goes on such adventures through the corridors of time within the chamber walls of the secluded mansion to discover what life is really like in the realm of the padded cells of his mind's eye.

Seeing is believing as he discovers what lay within the nights and days of the secluded mansion in the countryside of Muncie, Indiana where he grew up as a young boy. His friends join him on many of his adventures into the dreary old dark place, and he also has some other experiences that are not becoming of a little boy of age seven. A secret thrives within the woods of Old Hyde Park. It harbors a snare of darkness to all that dare to enter its domain.

There is no escape from the clutches of the evil that hides within the walls of the old farmhouse mansion; the mansion beyond the cornfield where its darkness lures its unsuspecting prey.

The old farmhouse mansion once gave refuge to renegade Indians and Civil War soldiers seeking sanctity away from the unruly war and beyond that stem out of a deeper past era. In addition, it once harbored outlaws, and just plain folk trying to escape reality of the era in the late 1700's to the mid 1900's and beyond if time along with its inhabitants permitted; those of the unseen kind that dwell within the imagery of the mind's-eye.

Secrets still flourish, and they lay in wait… yet to be discovered, in this small thriving community of about two hundred adults and four times as many children. The playful, the curious, the brave; but not so to some of the pure children in Hyde Park that are waiting to float unsuspected into the unknown elements inside of that eerie and disoriented Secluded Mansion on the other side of Old Buck creek that lurk beyond the old farmers cornfield.

At the basement of the old farmhouse is an eerie maze of underground passageways and dungeons you could say filled with its living spirits; from youths looking for adventure to the one's on the other side bringing past's explorers carving out a new frontier to this secret place in time; and to those whom ended their lives with a bloody outcome in an untimely manner not natural to humankind.

This thriving underworld lying beneath the mansion and throughout its many rooms that takes you to a realm of experiences that will frighten the soul right out of even a God fearing and faithful preacher, or the saints of the community's Willow Street Baptist Church. It will penetrate your very existence, and chill you from your spine to your minds eye, spirit, and soul. So beware brave patrons of fiction, beware..

Hahahahahaha…This may be visions of reality looking right at you.

Table of Contents

Chapter 1

Old Hyde Park Indiana

In the early conditions, as you stop, and look carefully at the vastness of the landscape, you will see a ray of similarity so intense to Mother Nature that father time would flow through each tree, bush, flower, weed, stream and blade of tall grass. Every ray of light that shed itself upon each tiny particle in the nature wonderland brought on by the many streams of ripples, waves, bubbles, and swishes of life below the surface of such wonders that they draw themselves toward fictitious truth. They cling to each thought like the sands of time from where they came in the vastness of nature's wonderland of life.

In the seclusion of the depressed darkness there came a sound not like any other you have ever heard, it was a shrill screeching sound in proportion to a freight train thundering in the mystic wind long, long ago.

Ecliptic was the frail dusty moon lit night, filled with the mist of a dense somber fog. Crickets chirped beneath the tall grasses along the crackled white frosty sidewalks as did the shivering bird's way up in the tall oak trees along a quiet Indiana setting in Hyde Park.

Frost and dew covered the grass like quilted blankets; little droplets dangled from bushes, the tall trees were ready to bounce those droplets for a second on the ground before they soaked inside its surface. The sun peaked through the trees as it came up over the back of our little house next to the big oak tree that draped over our tin covered roof.

Now Hyde Park is a friendly little town as far as I remember it way back when I was a very young boy, well at least most of the time it was quiet because of its country roots dug in deep beside a dense wooded area where I played as a child.

Bein' a kid in the country had more advantages than it did disadvantages. It was more the less a sure tradeoff for any kid that had parents who really gave a damn about you. I was allowed to go to Buck Creek, and not allowed to play spin-the-bottle, but done it in the middle of the strange farmers' cornfield or in the hay loft. I was always allowed in the yard of the kid who talked like a human being with good manners, but when it came down to playin' like a drunken sailor with his belly full of rum was not allowed. I could ride my bike anyplace I had a mind to as long as I was careful and watched out for cars, trucks and trains, but I was not allowed to cross the county road 32 because it was way too dangerous for a little fellow like me and my friends and basically I was not allowed to go any place beyond Hyde Park, but sometimes me and my friends went all the way to Selma while walking along the railroad track.

Outside of that I had lots of freedom as long as it wasn't dangerous. Oh, and Muncie was definitely off limits for me to go to by myself but one time I road almost all the way here on my bike one morning real early. it sure was a long, fun ride, but when I got back to Hyde Park, I was so dang tired that I wanted to just lay down and die in Luke's front yard, but didn't cause they'd sure know I'd went someplace I wasn't supposed to go in the first place.

Most of my childhood was spent in and around our quaint community of Hyde Park riding my bike and playin' with my best friends. We'd have lots of fun doing many different things that any kid would ever want to do, even if we weren't supposed to do 'em.

Life was great, and I even ended up having a girlfriend so to speak in a literary since, but in reality her name's Vera U; and her beauty captures me. Oh the adventures she and I had along with my other friends most of the time. If I could do then all over again, I sure would and without hesitation, even with the dangerous things we all done in our country setting. Life was grand no matter what we did; yes indeed.

I remember swinging through the trees hanging on tight with all the strength I could muster clinging to tall vines just like the not so real character Tarzan had done in the old black and white movies in the 1940's that I use to watch on our old 1959 round tube Philco TV in that same year.

Gee I sure do wish I could have kept that old TV, but circumstances wouldn't let me back then and now that I think back so very many years ago, there was a lot more that I wish I could have kept as well, but I got cheated out of all those nice old antiques, I even got cheated out of my inheritance of two large farms. Dang the luck anyhow; If it weren't for bad luck I wouldn't have any luck at all.

The small town that I grew up in as a we child of six years old, Hyde Park lay about ten miles just outside of the edge of Muncie, Indiana where I was born, and not too much went on that people didn't know about, 'cause everyone knew everyone else and all their personal affairs as well.

The whys and wherefores just couldn't keep their noses out of other people's lives; they thought they were justifiably inept. Nope they sure couldn't that's for dang sure. Oh the memories, so many. Ah the twinkling of an eye sparks them back in place. Things way back in the days as a young boy living in the country sure were different than they are now days. Those times will live forever in my mind.

I've lived in the big city since I was 16 years old and it ain't like things use to be. I wished I could relive those days and go back to all those places to see them once again; however relinquishing circumstances this day and age just won't let me loose and make it possible for me to head back and see if all of my old home towns are still intact as they use to be. Gee I wish I could see them one more time. Some day I'll go that's for sure, but till I do I still have my memories of those places, and damn no matter if I don't get back there I'll always relive them in my mind.

I painstakingly remember this huge corn field just below the woods, where I and some of my friends played hid -and- seek, other times we made a clearing just to sit, telling ghost stories, and jokes and so forth. Our little house was put right from the start at the edge of them woods, and having access to the corn field was just a hop skip and jump away.

Below the hill in the meadow, down an old dirt road was our make-shift baseball field where Me, Myself, and I along with my close friends traipsed through the woods, when you come right down to it, I guess you could say that we had a lot of real good times. It didn't matter if it was a hot summer day or a cold snowy one, all we cared about was runin' wild like kids do every day of their lives, playin' silly game of spin the bottle, doctor, or house, depending on who you were playin' them with, hehehehe. Yelp they sure were silly alright. Kids will be kids.

I did so much enjoy going along that dirt road, 'cause there were many berry bushes of all sorts mostly strawberry bushes, there were apple trees, and many other fruit trees in abundance.

While with-in the woods there were hickory nut trees, and black walnut trees galore. Man our bellies ended up so full sometimes that we'd just sit for an hour or so leaned up against some big ol' hickory-nut tree, and every now and then we'd have to unload a pile of our own manure in the bushes.

That dirt road and meadow belonged to the farmer who owned the cornfield. He didn't care too awful much if we played on his property, just as long as we didn't go across the creek to the other side of his property. He was a nice old man, but sometime he could be real mean, especially when it came down to telling' us and other folk to stay away from the east field across Buck Creek.

When he got after a body, you'd think that the devil himself was after ya. No one knew just how old he really was, and it didn't matter to us kids, all we cared about was a place to play away from the grown up folk, and the best place I and my friends could ever think about was that east property that we weren't supposed to go on. Grown folk seemed scared to death to truss-pass on that ol' farmer's sacred field of wonder, mystery and intrigue.

Our community was growing daily, or so it seemed. I knew most of the kids and some of the adult folk in and around Hyde Park, man I went all over the place at my own free will. Most didn't care if a kid cut across their property or not, cause they are basically friendly folk, who help each other when in need. Some seem a little strange and others a little distant in nature at times, but we were a close nit community.

The loop road went all the way from Luke's place down past ol' man Cash's grocery store. It wasn't much of a store, kinda like a mini market for selling candy, and things like that to us kids.

It was in front of his scrap heap junk yard that was his main business.

The road winded in a big loop past the Fuller's place. Tommy, David, his big mouth sister Sally parents place was our main meeting station. When leaving their spread, the road extended past Vera's, naturally, cause she lived across from their house, then it took off to the west past crazy Joe's little shed of a place and all the way to Hill Street. That man Joe sure was a strange fella, he'd ride his ol' bicycle that had a rusty basket attached to the handlebars all over the place; and as he did he would make a beep-beep sound with his mouth cause he didn't have a bicycle horn like we kids had. Joe collected all sorts of junk and his yard sure showed it as did his beat up ol' shed. I peeked inside of it one day for the curiosity of it and it too was so full of junk, that none of us kids wanted to be any where near him or his junkyard of a house.

Hill Street Bridge went way up high over the railroad track so the train could pass under it, that way people were safe enough when it came down to crossing that track, and it allowed that train to speed by at supper sonic speed all the time on its way toward Selma.

That bridge sure took its toll on me a few times, but it was a very fun place for me and my friends to play once in awhile. There wasn't much transportation in our community, and that was a good thing for all of us kids.

I used to ride my Schwinn bicycle down that bridge as fast as I could go, just to see how fast my bicycle really was, even though me and my friends had races all the time, and that bridge was my practice hill.

One day I was speeding down that hill, lost in a one-dimensional realm, not payin' any attention to anything except my speed. Well my pant cuff got caught in the chain sending me flying over the handlebars, hitting the pavement with a thud, bouncing a few times with my little body tangled in my bicycle.

I skidded for about a hundred yards or so, ripping my pants to pieces. I skinned my knees, my elbow, and my whole right arm. When I finally came to a stop, I picked myself up, got untangled, ripped my pant cuff outta that mean ol' chain and hobbled home. I was in lots of pain, blood dripped from my arm, it oozed out of the tares in the knees of my pants and dripped all the way home.

Tears streamed from my little brown eyes, and ran down my cheeks where I smeared them on my shirt sleeve. The front wheel on my new bike was bent, the handle bars were twisted outta whack, and I thought I was gonna die before I reached home.

As soon as I got there, my Aunt Mary, shook her head, and began to patch me up. Good ol' Luke took my bicycle and placed it beside his tool shed, telling' me he would fix it when he had the time and not to worry. I kinda got chewed out a little for wreckin' my bike, but all in all I wasn't hurt too awfully bad. From that time on, when I rode down Hill Street like I was supposed to, I always kept an extra eye on that mean ol' chain, but that didn't stop me from racing my friends on bikes.

That Bridge also had a steep grassy hill on the west side of it, and on real hot days, me and my friends would take big cardboard boxes, cut them just big enough to sit on, and then use them to slide down the grassy slope as if they were sleds. Sometimes we would tumble off, and roll down the hill comin' to a dead stop before we hit a small stream at the bottom. The hill was really long, and it was a miracle that none of us kids got seriously hurt, crippled, maimed or even killed. It was a real dangerous place for kids to play, but we didn't think about all that.

We would go under the bridge to sit on its concrete footing and watch the train fly by us at grease lightning speed, knowin' we weren't supposed to be any place off the bridge because it was property of the Rail Road. If we got caught, we would be in real deep poop up to our eyeballs, and so would our parents.

On a sour note, we had to keep track so to speak of when the train went rollin' down the track. It was hard sometimes, but we managed somehow to keep our eyes peeled. Once in awhile we would get an urge to walk along the rails to see how long we could keep our balance. Sometimes I would go by myself when my friends couldn't come along because they got in trouble allot, but I didn't mind and besides I kinda liked it that way sometimes. The quiet gave me many chances to think of all sorts of tall tails to scare my friends with, beside havin' time at just relax my pea brain without any care in the world. It was just me, the wind, and the tracks, and that made me happier than a pig in slop sometimes.

I wasn't allowed to go beyond that bridge to the north side, because it went straight to the main county road number 32, which was known in Muncie as Andrew Jackson Avenue, and it was a very dangerous place for simi-wild kids like me to play at most of the time. At the stop sigh was another grocery store, which had real food products in it, and the adults would buy some of the necessary food items that they needed to get there from time to time when they weren't shopping in Muncie at Rose's Corner Grocery, or at Mr. Zeno Rosesinisky's food and meat market. I went with Luke sometimes when he went to buy his beer for the many poker games he had at his place, but outside of that I really didn't go to that side of town. Luke and my aunt both told me I'd get my butt blistered if-n I ever got caught goin' there.

They said it was way too dangerous for a little feller like me to ride my bike down because I may mot be able to slow down enough or stop before I speed out into heavy county road traffic. They also said I may even be ran over and killed or something like that, so I'd best mind them and keep on this side of the bridge.

On the opposite side of county road 32 was the old folk's home. And it housed many of our elderly people includin' one of our old farm hands, a blind man we called Bingo had to go there to live when my uncle Bill died in 1956. Bingo was a nice man, who had his strange ways about him. He was in WW1 with my Uncle Bill, and they became good friends in the Army.

Bingo became blind when a mortars shell exploded beside him before he had a chance to put it in his launcher. The blast not only made him blind, but he lost most of his memory, and made him mentally ill on top of it. Bingo thought he was a General in charge of everything around him. He also liked his plug chewing tobacco, and sometimes my Aunt Mary bought a big plug of the nasty lookin' stuff and took it to him at the old folk's home. I didn't like goin' there, but when she went, I had to go with her no matter what. Why? I never did understand.

One day I wanted to get me some pop and candy while at the bridge, but didn't want to go way back to Cash's place to get it. My friends talked me into going to the store beside the county road to buy us all some goodies to munch on. I had my fast Schwinn bike with me that day and thought what the heck, why not, no one would know except for us kids. I hoped on my bike and speed down the big hill as fast as I could go. Several cars had already passed by me going in the opposite direction as I flew down the hill toward the small store next to county road 32. During that time of the day it was the most busy because people were coming and going home from work in Muncie and Selma. Most of the people who worked in Muncie was employed at Owendas Illinois Glass factory, or the Balding Brothers canning factory, those who work in and around Selma were either employed at a food processing plant or at the local slaughter house way out in the country durin' the fifties era. Several of the men who passed by me that afternoon knew Luke and played poker with him once in awhile. I had no idea who any one was that passed me, because I was concentrating on ridin' my bike to the store as fast as I could and get back before I got caught by someone who knew Luke, or my Aunt Mary, or maybe even one of them just may have stopped and blistered my butt royal and then send me flyin home to get more the same. I sure was a takin my butt in my own hands that afternoon thinking' all sorts of punishments were coming my way.

I made it to the store and back in about fifteen minutes of so in my estimate as the crow fly's in both directions. Maybe I was one lucky kid. But at the time I really didn't care. I had my fast bike and my good friends to play with, that was the most important things to me. The thrill of not getting' caught doin' what a kid shouldn't do was the best part of growin' up I recon.

When I got home from playing at the Hill Street Railroad Bridge, all the men who normally played poker with Luke had arrived for their usual nightly card came and lots of drinkin' and chewin' that nasty ol' Union Workman's tobacco. YUCKY, the smell alone would gag a pile of maggots.

As soon as I walked inside to the kitchen, I headed toward the small space we called a living room. We didn't know exactly what to call it, after all that was where we all sat around most the time at night before retiring' for bed; I headed toward the back bedroom to change clothes for the night, and as soon as I walked in the room, one of the men who came to play poker spoke to me.

"Hey kid, didn't I see ya goin' down Hill Bridge toward county road 32 this afternoon." I was stunned, becoming frozen in time, not knowin' what to say. I knew I couldn't tell the whole truth, or I'd get in big time trouble.

"N, no sir, I was playin' by the bridge and wasn't ridin' my bike down Hill street, no sir, I sure wasn't." My lie must have convinced him and Luke because he wasn't givin' me the mean eye, then went on about his business of dealing out the cards. I knew that I had best not say another word so I wouldn't get yelled at by Luke or my Aunt Mary Belle. Yelp I sure was one lucky kid that night as Luke was playin' cards, and my aunt fetchin' those grumpy ol' men beer and vitals the whole evening, it almost made me sick to my stomach. God was sure good to me that was for dang sure.

One winter, Luke made a sled outta wood, so he and I could go down the ol' dirt road at the end of his property to gather fire wood. It was much easier to go that way instead of over the fence and through the woods because of the heavy snow fall. The frozen tree branches were filled with ice-cycles, and lots of white powder at the ready to plop themselves right down on an unsuspecting' fellow. Luke would pull me sown the hill, with our big dog Brownie by our side. He was a good ol' dog, and he reminds me of Old Yeller from the movie of the same name. Anyhows we'd gather plenty of wood, and then Luke would put the harness he made on that big dog, so he could pull the heavy sled back up the hill to his small house. We had to always make several trips in order to get enough wood for a week, and then the next week, we'd have at do it all over once again. The work was always hard, but I sortta enjoyed it, 'cause I always got to ride down the hill on the sled. The only draw back was I had to walk back up the hill through heavy snow. Man was that hard at times.

Shortly before Christmas that year, He and Aunt Mary went to town shopping for presents, and much to my surprise, they bought me a brand new sled. It was a PF Flyer from Se'ers Rosebuck & Company, man that was one of the best presents I'd ever got the whole time we lived in Hyde Park. Bad thing was that when we had to gather wood after that, well, ol' Luke used that sled and it soon got broken down. Sometimes I think he just got that sled for his use, and not mine, even though I used it once in awhile when I had the chance to play in the snow with my friends. My aunt had got a little upset with Luke over the sled being messed up, but soon got over it. She made a special trip to Muncie again just to buy me another brand new sled, and told Luke to fix the one he messed up, that made me so happy that I wanted to cry and laugh at the same time, but not 'ol Luke... he seemed really pissed off 'bout the whole ordeal, but complied with what my aunt told him to do, or he'd have to fix his own meals and we both knew he was a really bad cook...

Soon I was a flying down that hill with the wind in my face, and I didn't have a care in the world, but as winters are in the country back east, it started to get too cold for me to play. The snow got to almost four feet deep that winter, and we were snowed in. All in all we'd gathered enough wood to just barely last us, along with a small supply of coal next to the new outhouse we'd just built that summer.

One of my best friends was a pretty little black girl named Vera U who lived with her mom Ms Capturesme who lived across from my best buddy Tommy Fulkler. We didn't like each other very much at first, but as time went on she became my girlfriend as well as my best friend in the whole wide world.

Winter went by slow, and the snow had its annual melt down session once again. I took Vera U on several sled rides down the hill all by myself. We'd giggle, and laugh up a storm when we fell off my sled, rollin' in the melting snow. We both got into trouble a couple times because we got too wet, and my Aunt Mary blamed me for Vera catchin' a cold that winter., just because her mom got mad at church one Sunday over her poor darlin' daughter getting' sick almost all winter from me taking her out to play in the cold wet melting snow.

As time swiftly slid past us like that big ol' locomotive that always flew down the track under Hill Street Bridge, so did all the bad incidents that took place that disastrously-cold snowy winter. Finally Spring hit us squarely in the face with its pleasant luster of birds chirped melodiously from tree branches, and at night crickets would click their dark black heals to the melodious tunes of the bull frogs down by Buck Creek singing themselves to sleep as the seconds of night drifted into the past, so did their country music.

My Aunt Mary liked frog legs a whole lot and I was more then happy to catch a few for her from time to time. Choirs were few, but sometimes hard, but I did what I had to do with total respect for my elders. The gooseberries came up early and she'd already planted her rhubarb next to the fence in the front yard so when it was completely ready for her to harvest, she'd make her favorite dessert, rhubarb pies and gooseberry pie and some jelly too. I never cared much for any of this type of food and probably never will, but she sure liked the stuff. Yucky.

Spring always brought many wild flowers up all around us, and one of my favorite things was the clovers. I'd always pick them when they first took their tiny purple, white and reddish buds and then eat the buds, they were so tasty. Why I liked them, I don't know, and guess I never will, but that's ok? Me and my friends wondered all over the whole countryside without any cares in the world. The grown folk were always busy with grown-up things and that left us kids to more-the-less... fend for ourselves, except for the essentials of real food like fried chicken, fried taters, cornbread and beans and so forth, my favorite dishes... oh, and of course apple pie... yummy, I can just taste a piece right now. All Luke's crops had been planted in his huge garden in front of his little house. That was one of the things that he was proud of, growing his vegetables that not only helped feed him, but he also sold them to ol' man Cash's for his little grocery store just down the road a piece.

Mr. Cash and Luke were like best buds when it came down to money matters and any type of business. Luke had a head on his shoulders even though he only had a third grade education like most of the folk in our quaint little community had. Education was for us young kids, and the adults were happy with all that they had. They didn't really like fancy - swanky things, only what was necessary to keep them cozy, smillin' and happy, and that's all that mattered most to them. As for us kids we just wanted to play and explore, when we were Outta School. Of course our education mattered to us also, but we never gave anything any real thought except havin' a place to sleep, eat and play. That was our ultimate goal, and ya know if'-n I had it to do all over again, I wouldn't change one single solitary thing about my childhood, no sir, I sure wouldn't that's for certain.

Chapter 2

Old Buck Creek, the Barn-Silo and Mansion

This land is a rich agricultural spread, full of wheat and corn fields in abundance. The broad fields of Indiana have lots to offer a new family, and many took advantage of homesteads and made it a unique place. It is here that Hyde Park was envisioned by the Maxifield family in the very late 1700's.

They arrived here traveling in their ox-drawn wagons, and the view was spectacular; with meadows full of wild flowers, grasses tall in blade stretched far and wide, and the woods so thick at times that it made it hard to see your oxen in front of your cart, or your ass dragging in the backside of it at a steady pace.

George wrote a letter home telling' folk all about the wonderful land they found among the Indian people of the Midwest territory. He wrote to his brother Samuel Maxifield this letter that I have framed in my den at home as a keepsake from my first exploration of this ol' mansion farmhouse.

'Sam.'

"We made it here ok, land is in abundance as far as you can see and then beyond. This is the heartland and it is here that we are in progress of building' our new home. Only heathen Indigenous brown skinned people are in this territory and have welcomed us with open arms since we arrived six month ago. When we arrived, the Indians gave us what they called a long house to live in while we are making our house. Folk back home would like this new territory lots. The main part is complete now, with the help if these nice Indian people. The chief gave me his daughter for my wife. Her name is Waity A. I can't pronounce her last name, nor can I spell it, but she sure is a pretty woman for an Indian, well at least half was and the other half was of the black African descent; and she was a young thing too, about, well Id say, maybe 14 or 15 years of age.

Establishin' a farm here ain't a bit of an easy task at first, but with the proper fertility of soil, proximity to water sources, good drainage, the presence of vegetation and timber, and the right tools, of course a good plow and the use of our strong oxen we're on our way at havin' a wonderful farm and cozy place to live. The good Lord sure has lead us down a good path cause we have all this and lots more.

From what I hear said by our neighbor the so called heathen Indians, who, by the way are really nice folk once ya get at know 'em, the weather is harsh in winter, and hotter than hell in summer times, but we will have more than we need once we get ourselves established amongst them Indian people. They even said that they'd help us with our crops and such if'n we gave 'em some in exchange for all their help.

I agreed and now we are well on our way to success in a new country, with plenty o-land, I'd say about four or five hundred acres or so of the best sod land a feller could have for the takin', and lots more where this farm site lay.

Them heathen have no idea we can just squat and take all we want ta take, but of course we have ta ensure rightful ownership and stake our claim by the registerin' of this land with a government land office back home since there ain't any out here yet. I like the people and land, and even the chief, Muncie gave me this place, he just don't have a clue we'd take it from him anyhows in the beginning' no matter if'n he gave it at me or not, but since he did along with his daughter at wife, then he can't say a dang thing, right? I am all set for riches out here in Indian Territory. The maiden he gave me to wife is a pretty young and healthy thing. She's a sweet, stubborn woman of 'bout 14 years old 'er so and she has good bones for breedin' and farmin' my new lands, yes indeed. I will try and tell ya more 'bout her laters.

Maybe You and Uncle Calvin can pack up yer families and all yer belongings along with bein' a government official and all, get the proper authority and become one of them land assayers out here in Indian territory, build ya a real money makin' establishment in a government land office and make yer whole family and Uncle Calvin's family a nice place ta settle down. Of course since me and my family were the first to settle here and stake the first land claim, I will be the first congressional governor in this new state I'll call Indiana, cause of the friendly Indians here about.

Looks into this for me and let me know in your reply as quick as ya can."

'Regards, your brother'

'George M. Maxifield and Waity A.'

After George and his Indian friends constructed the first three rooms of his house, they started clearing the trees from the land, so he could begin ta plant his first crops of the seasons. He had hopes that his crops would do well, and bring an early harvest, 'cause what was brought with him on the trip to the new land wasn't enough to carry a body over in a short winter, let alone a real long one. It took him just a little over a year to do this then he was able at tillage the soil where the trees and shrubs had been cleared. Much of this began in early mid spring with the deadening and girdling of the trees. This process consisted of stripping the bark off in order ta accelerate the death of the trees; then he was able to clear the abundance of underbrush. Most of the time a fire had to be started in the fields in various different locations to burn away most of the deadened trees. There were plenty of good ones all over the place to use in the construction of the house.

His crop done very well that first year, and over time he expanded the house into a two level place. It was startin' at look real grand like he'd hoped it would, and his dream took shape, time and time again. The log structure was fine at first, but George wanted it refined in saw board features, so he had some of his friends who were in the building industries bring their operations to Indiana, and set up the first mill. He also needed walls to be plastered, but more likely they'd be whitewashed. He had another friend in this line of work also, and commissioned him as well, and he'd promised them that, in due time they'd make all their money back, and in time become very rich in the process.

George was on his way to turning his property into one of the biggest, most powerful farms in the new territory, making his crops a viable contributor to the newly independent state that was just emerging to greatness from his steadfast hands of bein' the very first white settler there and in another letter home to his brother Sam was a real short one. It started lookin' real good for George and his new wife Waity A, but money was in short supply, so he pleaded to Sam to send him more help as fast as he could.

Six months later he wrote:

18

'Sam'

"We've grown several nice crops, 40 acres of corn, or maize as the Indian people call it, about 20 acres of oats, another 15 of wheat, and about 3 acres of the prettiest green grass ya ever seen in yer life. Our house is comin' along just fine and dandy now but we do need more money and more supplies with lots more construction materials so I can complete my home proper; we put up a real nice big barn as shelter for some cows and a horse or two that I seen on our way out here. It has a nice log fenced area for all the livestock that I plan on getting soon. My ambitions are to have a pasture and garden under fence, worm fence or post-and-rail. I am also makin' a big tall silo for our corn, and a couple of new storage sheds fer our other crops.

Well sir, these Indian fellows and their squaws sure are hardy industrious folk, and we're getting lots done before winter sets in and the snow flies. I heard tell it gets mighty cold in this part of the country durin' what some described as bein' fiercely harsh, and causes much death.

Our rudimentary material comforts and essential equipment are somewhat scarce and often inadequate, so send more tools, a wagon load of good quality furniture; a big bed outfit with all the trimming's, a new dinning set, and some sittin' chairs, and other essentials for my new place.

Re-payment will be in a couple years from now providing' things continue the way they are at this time, and it looks real promising.

In the early summer next year I'll make my way back on a four days journey and fetch them critters for my farm. I'm in hopes of tradin' for some 20 cattle. And at least two good strong horses to pull my plows cause them oxen seem to be getting warn out a bit and I'll end up havin' ta make them our food supply for a spell.

There is a plenty o' wild boars, hogs and sows in these y'here parts, and I'm workin on getting nearly a hundred of 'em for further tradin' and eatin' amongst the Indian folk and a few settlers that have already made there way out here on their own accord. Them green horns don't have any idea what their a doin' I'll make me a killin' off-n 'em that's fer sure. Both cows and hogs will get fat off this land, and I won't has a real hard time feedin 'em either, except-n fer in the dead of winter. I'll sure trys-n gets me a wagon and some other farming utensils. I have ta put in a couple wells; maybe by the Buck Creek I'll place an artesian well. It may eventually come in handy."

'Regards, your brother'

'George'

When the simple little log cabin style house was built, they had in mind that a bigger frame houses provided a more comfortable lifestyle than log cabin; so the construction began in the spring time on their dream home, revitalizing the old log home into the eastern Victorian style of the times and set in a place that would withstand the sands of time. There was a lot to be done, and soon old man winter would set itself down for a long stay.

Hardships would soon make prey on the family unless they got some provisions to tide them over until the spring thaw. George sent still another letter back east in hope that it would reach them in time to ship the essentials to tide them over. He pleaded for a speedy shipment from his brother and their acquaintances as the nights began to get chillier amongst the trees that lay in the midst of their huge acreage. Their oxen and other animals needed a place of shelter as well so the big barn was constructed from the near-by wooded area downstream along Buck Creek. A tall rock silo was also built for the corn that they were about to grow. One month went by, and then another and still no provisions were sent their way. George and

Waity knew they had to act fast, least they die. Waity her husband that her people and the Selma tribe would help with their basic needs till shipment reached them. The next day they both went to the Muncie tribe village to ask her father for help. George was a proud man, but had no choice but to swallow his pride, and he accepted the help. The neighboring tribe didn't like it too much that white men were invading their land, but since George was married to a half black and an Indian woman to boot, they too helped him and his wife with the necessities of food, deerskin and other animal furs to help keep them warm enough when the show was to fall on the territory in about two more months or so.

Winter had descended upon them in early November, bringing with it one of the coldest wet snow falls they, the Native American tribes and the white man had ever experienced in all the known times. Many Indian died that winter from the cold heavy snows, frozen nights on the plains took a toll on almost everyone concerned, except George and Waity, who had a semi good shelter to help protect and block the winter chills. The Indians who's cheaply constructed long houses for shelters were strong, but breezy, and they had very few furs to stay warm with, but they had one another to comfort their underfed-malnourished bodies to sustain enough heat as the winter winds, and wet snows extinguished their fires as they slept at night, and many froze to death holding each other in their arms. Food was little in those times and they looked forward to the white mans crops so they wouldn't starve to death along with freezing' rock solid like blocks of ice.

Soon the snow had ended and the whole of winter was over in about early March; some one hundred and fifty Indians died that winter and it almost wiped out the Selma tribe. Many who were left, buried the dead then, packed up all they had and moved the village closer to chief Muncie's village, and not too awfully far from the Maxifield spread.

Since settling in after the cruel winters blazes, another month passed by and things started lookin' good once more. Now they could start plowin the fields in preparation for the plantiin of the crops. The tribes started to flourish once again as they were a hardy group of people, fit to survive the worst and move on as if nothing had ever happened at all. The months rolled past way too fast or so it seemed and on May twenty-third 1813, George saw that Waity was heavy with child. It must have been all those cold nights that caused it, but he and Waity were as happy as pigs in a muddy pig pen about havin' a baby. They now had to make the house even bigger and better than ever so the child could have plenty of room to grow up like a boy or girl should. Another mouth ta feed, meant other crops, like potatoes, tomatoes, pumpkins, onions and rhubarb had at be grown besides corn and wheat, and they needed a milkin' cow so's the new infant could be fed after it was weaned from Waity's breasts. There was pleanty of wild plants in abundance, such as: paw-paws, wild lettuces, and a wild plant sorta like rice. Chief Muncie had a field of his native corn that George named, Indian corn, because of all the wonderful colors of each kernel and it made a nice place at a dinner table when in season.

Waity worked as hard as their ol' mule around the farm even though she was pregnant, and it seemed like there was nothing' that she couldn't do that any man would do himself. Her tall frame along with her bein' pregnant made her wobble and wiggle with each movement. She looked like a slinky cow ready to calf. It seemed funny to George and some of the Indian boys who helped them with the work, and even though they all laughed at her Waity paid them no never mind, and just kept goin' and goin' like there was no tomorrow in sight. She was a strong willed and stubborn woman. Her lack of humor kinda made some fear her short fused temper, but deep on the inside she laughed at everyone else, they were the ignorant ones cause of the way they poked fun at her all the time while she was fat with child in her big belly, and her mother always took her away from the farm so they could have private talks about the many different things that she was to do during her delicate condition and all the things she was supposed to do after givin' birth and besides it gave poor Waity a break away from the work and hideous laughter from the men folk. Lack of experience for any young woman meant tragedy when it came down to bearing and rearing children and her mother knew what was best for her waywardly-stubborn, little-skinny, but pregnant daughter.

Even though winter and spring work was hard; and, the ninth month came very quickly for Waity, the labor was hard was all the more harder on her and it almost killed her to give birth at her young age, but with her mothers help and a few other women from their village she delivered a beautiful set of twins, one girl that she named Sarah and one boy called Calvin born in fall 1814.

George was proud of his son Calvin, but didn't show much interest in his new daughter, and that sort of angered Waity to a point of wantin' ta strangle him to death at times. Her quick temper made her all the more strong despite how tiny she was in her structure, the weight was still on her but even then; a few months after giving birth she became heavy with child once again, and another set of twins slid their way out into the world within the next nine months period. She named the twin boys Leander and Alexander; they were short boys, but strong and hard working all the time. The family kept growing more and more as time went by.

This made George and Waity grow more and more apart from one another for their constant lack of attention to the other; all they cared about was what they wanted to do and the way that they each wanted at bring up each kid according to their own individual merits, and hard work, and from the love they gave to them in a one to one personal basis daily, but in spite of bein' drawn apart, the family all had to live in the same household, and no matter how far apart they all were from each other they all survived as a whole family for some unknown reason. Their lack of respect for others also took hold when it came down to doin' well by others around them. This made Waity's family and the other tribe members slowly pull themselves away from wanting to be around them or even help work on the farm.

Soon word was sent back to family in New England that the land was in abundance out in the Midwest. The family had grown like weeds, crops were doin' good, they were doin' good, and for them to pack all their belonging's and head on out to claim all the land that they wanted.

George's rich brother-in-law Sam Captersome and his sour faced wife Linda Sue took into careful consideration the move to the new territory. In a months time they'd settled a long hard dispute, of which George's wife Waity won., and they soon gathered provisions for not only the long trip, but had enough supplies for George and his wife as well.

The unexpected soon too a toll on their trip and the journey was halted because of a cholera outbreak in the New England area. His wife came down ill, and all indications of the disease were present, but five days later she began to feel and look much better. He decided to wait still another week to make sure that her illness didn't reassure.

That week seemed like an eternity, but it had passed before he knew it. He didn't get much sleep because of worry, and his hair was turning whiter everyday, age seemed to be taking its toll on not only him, but his wife as well.

Once again Sam planed his trip to the new territory of Indiana to meet up with his brother George and his wife Waity; their wagons had to be loaded with the many supplies they needed for a one month journey overland, through sometimes hostile territories. It was way more then they would ever need, but it somehow didn't seem to matter in the least to either of them, money was no object. Indian wars were going on amongst a half dozen tribes along the route, and many guns had to be loaded and at the ready for quick use if they were ever attacked during their journey to the new settlement that George was establishing for them near his mansion in the countryside near the Muncie tribe and Selma tribes, and it wasn't too much longer after that, people from all over the east filtered their way to what the Maxifield family called Hyde Park.

Some settled several miles away in what they called Selma town, others went further west to a place near the white river and close to Muncie, calling it Centre Township. They all had their own private little communities of rich farm land and many were able to make their own businesses, livery stables, supply and hardware stores and even a few saloons sprang up all over the place, and as time drifted with the seasons, the family had a wonderful farm, but in the year 1829 they had a freakish turn in the weather pattern, and a frost killed just about all of their crops. Winter set in early once again and as the temperature fell to nearly thirty below with winds blowing ice crystals, hard powdery snow drifted nearly to the top of their house, and wood was in very short supply causing the inside to be like a refrigerator, and the entire family nearly froze to death that winter.

Many immigrant farmers who cleared land to make way for their homesteads, building houses, and investing all their hard earned savings endured great hardships, some survived and some never made it at all, but most of the time, all the hardships killed entire families, and if it wasn't the bad weather, Indians, or some mean ol' predatory animal didn't claim them it was because they had froze to death for lack dry wood for a warm fireplace.

Waity learned how to write some over time and wrote her husbands dear aunt by marriage, Linda Sue Captersome who was a black woman married to her husbands' wealthy white brother-n-law the banker in the east about their failure as a family, the many miseries and pessimism that took its toll, the lack of self discipline and self respect that spread its way to not only them, but her very own family and her fathers' village.

'Dear Sister Linda Sue

14 May 1829

"Dis' land for our corn and other cropps has bean taken over with crusted dirt, and many weeads and grasses have grew'd to our knees. The past cold's killed knot only most of our craopps, but it also took many of our livstock to their hunting grounds for food and the nourishments necessary to keeps them alife. We do knot have the mooney now to pay fer many of the nesessities lets alone mooney to grew more cropps. Corn in our silho from last seasons will knot take seead to grew tall and take strong ruut. Wheat fields are only rand over by all those weeads, briar bushes and plains cactis.

Da cutworms are cutting our flax, trees are dying right before our veary eyes. After the bad cold came much rain, hard rain, and killed what were left of most our cattles. Sheap in the near by village of Lafayette are not doin' too awefully well and we can knot gets any of them to make breead enough to reaplenish what few we have already lost, 'cause of our hunger we had to kills them to sutain our own lifes. I ask our Great Spirit for much help, and be it his will, he will supply to us the needs, and I ask you fer more of you help allso. Even George and I have grow'd appart as have our chilidrens we are all still together in the same houase, and I do knot knows the reasons why. I must stop my words of worry and knot to bother you with my trubblos any longers, I bid you farewell for now and if the Great Spirit grant me more lives I will try to send ya more words, respectfuly good words the next tyme I rite ya."

'Yers, true full of sin-cerity'

'Sistor Waity A. Maxifield'

This letter I also have back home in a safe place and I memorized every single word of it for some strange reason, I don't know why, but I did; any how before the letter reached Sam and Linda Sue back in New England, they were well on their way to Indiana. When they arrived and settled in with George and Waity for a couple months, hardship had already beset itself on the entire family, but soon they were back on the right track, and life went pretty good once Sam and Linda Sue constructed their own little house on their own hundred acre spread about five or so miles away from George and Waity's place.

In the summer of 1828 George's big mansion had taken on a whole lot more shape. He had plans to make a round tower shaped chapel for worship and soon it was being constructed as he wanted it to look. George gave its look a lavish personality of labor to beautify the big ol' farmhouse. The decorated fixtures made it appear to be out of some foreign church. Its bare spaces were previously painted for a fine triptych and reredos and made the fireplace glow immensely as the night filtered itself away like the smoke that came from the new chimney. A fine mantle gave the new den a quality far beyond the outward scale of other lavish European dens and made the whole room stand out beyond all of the other surroundings in its dominion. By and by George added his collection of heads that he'd obtained on his many African safaris with on of his most treasured possessions, a huge Elephants head with its extremely long protruding ivory tusks hanging out half way across the room. Indeed it was a finely beautiful, very delicate, and intricate setting of exquisite workmanship; it had its hard edges as well from the wild bore's head sitting on a table in one corner with a complete alligator staring at its fresh kill. In its days it was an excellent and perfectly delightful conversation room to escape the hardships of the wild Indiana country settings.

The many optical objects within the confines of the edifice made it sort of a wild west tourist attraction, but George and Waity chased most folk away cause they weren't really the sociable type and high society in the start was mostly all behind ol' George, and as far as Waity was concerned she was all country, mostly Indian. Their wealth came fast after the hardship periods when George's brother-in-law and his family moved to the area, and as time went by they started to welcome more and more people into their home as the township of Centre grew on the other side of the creek in Hyde Park and westward towards Muncie town.

A new tower alongside the house was to be put up that next summer in order for George to make a Memorial to his belated mother and father who passed shortly before he went to the new territory of Indiana. but in order for him to make it accessible from the main house, he had to open up one wall next to his den, and the decision to do that was hard for George, but it was the only place that the tower would fit the rest of the house's constructed style, and was going to be a sort of chapel and would have all the makings of one too, just for private use by his family only.

Plans were drawn out as to its look, unfortunately its cost was not any chicken feed, but upwards towards about fifteen hundred dollars, which was a lot of money for just one room back in those days, but George's brother-in-law Sam put up that and a little bit more, because it wasn't an object for his filthy rich money hungry soul. Soon the foundation was laid and a sub-floor made, then came the hard part, breaking down part of the wall in George's pride den. He almost cried, but when his brother Sam gave him another three hundred dollars, he was able to reconstruct a little more than half of it in a slightly offset fashion that didn't loose much of the original appeal to his pride room.

The round chapel tower was put up in just two months, and it looked Elysian to its surroundings and stood several feet above the rest of the house so George could look out over his new land with ease and peace of mind so his enemies would stay far away because of the out looking statue of winged gargoyle for protection. The two huge winged-gargoyles perched on each side of a golden cross with a single transverse arm; they always had a watchful eye on the farm. Its dormer was laced with red brick overlays of white to look a bit in the rustic antiquity of the old world churches of western European descent and the rustic lifestyle that George and Waity had been so use to. The main part of the chapel had two 4-panelled polyptych installed at for its center piece's for worship, with an amazing second altarpiece executed of panel with gold and tempera, and a long winding staircase that lead from floor to tower top like a serpent all coiled up ready to make a strike at any unwanted intruder that crossed its path.

George used his chapel to sanctify not only purity, but Hope and Faith, calling it cardinal virtues; later on he added Charity and dubbed it the three cardinal virtues.

That made him stronger when it came down to making things work better for him in his quest to achieve wealth as well as to become a powerful community leader and first Governor of his new state of Indiana. He also conducted rituals like Voodoo and black magic from the Indians and from his adventures in the deep dark regions of Africa when he was a teenager going on safaris with his father's Uncle Calvin. In his rituals he used wild prairie chicken and hung them upside down letting blood drip into a small copper cup then he'd drink it so the pure spirit would enter his body and make him strong in mind, body and spirit.

The wild prairie chicken in its piety was a symbol used by Waity's father the tribal shaman, for some of his rituals to ward away evil spirits and was a particularly poignant one. The prairie chicken plucking and piercing its own breast to feed its young with its own blood was viewed as an act of self-sacrifice - an action likened to the blood of the Great Spirit whom through the being put to death upon a ragged tree brought peace and serenity to all human beings. George picked up on this and used it in his prayer rituals for the purpose of receiving purity and to George himself, he was above all who came into his land, and non dare dispute his word. What he said was the law and if any person goes against that law they too would be sacrificed to the almighty the same way he done the wild prairie chicken in his chapel tower beside the house.

Later the Voodoo Princess took what her shaman father done and used it for unearthly and demonic practices as well as a sacrificial tool she preformed black magic with the blood carved chicken hanging upside down and let its blood drip into her mouth and all over her own body in hope that she would turn into a beautiful wild gray wolf and roam the forest to escape all human beings that shamed her as a child when she was growing towards womanhood. She offered herself to an immortal life and brought a reign of terror to not only her tribe, but all who came into contact with her ritualistic conjures, potions and black magic.

"I'm more alone in this world now than I could ever be since one of my wives has departed this earth – more isolated in the confines of this big house than ever I knew any man on earth ever could endure such loneliness ... I cannot say more than this except Dear Heavenly Spirit Thy will be done and I shalt continue my quest for purity here in my chapel."

George had arranged for a wet-nurse to be brought into the house to attend to his two lovely daughters, Nellie Matilda (Mattie) usTuss\y and Sarah Sue Cleavage Maxifield shortly after his wife had died. He then he had his son Calvin prepare his dearly departed wife's tomb. He was a stonemason by trade and was more than glad to work on a tomb for the sake of her memory. His other wives soon realized that the twin girls were starving because of the wet-nurse's inability to give milk. She was promptly let go and two of his wives took on the responsibility to breast-feed Mattie and Sarah back to good health. The girls grew up to be well defined young ladies with well endowed bodies too, but in spite of their qualities of beauty, but both had bad inward dispositions that were of the unusual type.

They had a beautiful residence surrounded by a brilliantly laid out garden and it was interesting to me when I found out that Calvin a stonemason and sculptor created many statues all over the property just for the excitement of carving them. His one sister Mattie turned into a brilliantly creative painter and used some of Calvin's clay models to assist her in painting. Her sibling Sarah Sue took up singing, but felt compelled enough to tackle other worthy projects like sowing and cooking as well as to dabble in Mattie's other secret hobby of Voodoo in the chapel their father made for family worship, but Mattie used to sneak into the cove next to the chapel and peek through a small hole by the fireplace mantel and watch her father in his rituals of black magic, Voodoo and even real prayer sessions once a week and she learned how to do them very well.

Since Calvin was both a stone mason sculptor, it didn't explain his confidence in this trade of making tombs and tombstones for the dearly departed who came to the new territory of Indiana and passed in the processes of trying to make their dreams come true.

At a tender age of seventeen he got one of the native girls pregnant and didn't want to take her as his wife so he decided to run away to a different part of the territory and continue his illustrious stone carvings for not only the dead, but for beautification projects as well. Later in life Calvin did get married to a pretty young and healthy black woman named Willaminia and got her pregnant like he done to the Indian girl who he'd ran away from several years earlier. During his wife's labor she died from the harsh birth of a boy that wasn't as healthy as he expected it to be.

That very month his brother Leander made a visit to Kokomo on a business trip for his father George to start a new pagan church of sanctity and worship and it was there he found his half brother Calvin in the spring of 1836, greatly occupied in carving a tomb for his wife, in a shape approximating to what might be called a pagan church tower like a sandstone pedestal with a huge black rose on a pedestal in front of it with a cross on its top in the same style of the one his father had placed on his chapel in Hyde Park. There were patterns like roses in full bloom carved into the stone separating the sarcophagus what appeared to be a base and cover. It had Roses carved at each end, but on one end he embellish a large bust of himself and on the other end two dove with an olive branches in their beak's to symbolize the account of the top of the Ark of the Covenant.

The entire tomb in its abounds had many symbolic meanings of both pagan and religious scenario's He would end up the rest of his days carving many such tombs for the well to do along with hundreds of smaller stones for the meek and poor. This was his intimate demise in his life. He died in the spring some fifteen years later in 1851 and was laid to rest in the same tomb as his beloved Willaminia.

As years passed his sarcophagus begun to crumble at the corners and in areas which are in contact with the ground giving way to collapse in due time. It appeared to have been carved from some type of limestone and over the past one hundred and fifty-four years over the years has become like a sugary and granular texture from natural erosion, and the elements of time. There had been none other in comparison to his brilliant sculptural abilities at the time of his death in 1851 and none since then have been able to achieve such morbid beauty for the dead as well as the sanctification of the living breathing should who view them while they still exist.

Once in awhile some times things seem to fade in and out for some reason, and it is hard to explain what emotions are going on in my head sometimes. I guess its cause when a soul is in a state between this and reality, this sortta thing happens. Why? I may never know, but at this point it just doesn't matter; I must continue onward with my thoughts or I may never finish my mischievous journey. As I recall and memory short sometimes; on the other side of that cornfield was a part of old Buck Creek that I'll never forget. It was a refreshin' place to go after traipsing through the corn field to get as nice cold drink of water from an old artesian well that someone put in a very long, long time ago, it too was almost like the mystic wind, and ever flowin' ta keep the creek and us supplied with a necessity to sustain life to the 'ol farmhouse mansion on the other side where the only silo stood erect and silent next to the rickety barn, just as secluded as the old farmhouse mansion itself. They seemed to stand alone as well as together beyond the creek and the cornfield. Its construction was made from large stones that were gathered along the creek, mortared together with ancient straw, muddy sand, and lime that they imported from across the great ocean on the eastern port where lots of people from all over the world immigrated and like the creek flowed into the Midwest territory.

Trees lined the creek on both sides as thick as the woods far above and beyond the cornfields acreage. From a distance the ol' house couldn't be seen, but as soon as you got through the groves of thick trees, across Buck Creek, the big mansion seemed to appear right before your eyes as if it were some sort of magical place that had been lost in time; fading back into existence once more. No one knew who put the pipe in the ground to make that ol' artesian well, maybe that old farmer; after all he was a very old man. Non – the - less no matter who or what put that artesian well there, it was just the thing to hit the spot of thirst on a hot summer's day; and, the ol' silo, was just the place to gaze toward Muncie, it had a view like none other that I'd ever seen, and wow what a view as I remember it, 'cause I was the one who'd ever got dared to climb that silo's ladder by my friend Tommy, or any of my other friends that I can remember.

I climbed that silo and I made it back down safely, I guess that it was there just for all us curious kids to use for a short time, well at least for myself anyhow. Things happen for a reason some times now that I think of it. Maybe the people who lived in the huge farm house a short distance away from the barn and ts raggedy ol' corn silo a long-long time ago put in the old well by Old Buck Creek in the first place, and not that it had anything to do with that silo, I really couldn't say for sure, but now that I think of it, every time I took a drink of water from that pipe, it sent a chill all over my body as if to say, "Come on over to the other side the water is better here." The water was so refreshing, oh so cold, and it seems to still flow through my veins.

As a kid, I and my friends use to sneak over there to play in and around that old farm house and it sure was old too, very old, and some times very scary. I have to yet figure out how old that place is 'cause it was so ran down, rickety, shattered. Maybe it was put there in the beginning of time, I really can't say. It was a very tall place with its face a Victorian square style in most of the construction. The red-brick in spots made it stand out amongst the outside surroundings, and it set right smack dab in the middle of a huge piece of property, maybe a five hundred acre tract of rich farm land. Its construction indicated different features I stare in amazement of not only its size, but it's once beauty, that had now deteriorated with time. The style seemed to change with the times of each decade. It had a large wooden-pillared porch added in the classical style of the 1831 period; there were many windows in the huge farmhouse mansion, some very big and tall, others small and long, and they were draped with small etched panes and intricate white woodwork.

On the upper portion above the front porch was a round dormer at the center stage placement for a perfect match of one on each side. They well in proportion to one another, connected by colonnades, supported by glazed galleries and carved mystical stone statuettes as center pieces above each. The two outer dormers indicated bedrooms, in but the center dormer, of which I had no clue as to what its purpose, or use was, intrigued me so much that I sure wanted to find out for myself what sort of room it was. On one side was a tall tower structure that looked like it had been placed there by magic? It was a very creepy thing to look at cause it had two huge winged statues on top of it and a fancy golden cross in the center of the two strange winged creatures.

I sure was anxious to see what was inside that place, but my friends said that they'd never go in there if their lives depended on it now or in a million years from now. There was a burrier of oaks on the left side of the ol' place that reached to the sky and a fenced cemetery in front that extended for about a couple hundred yards outward on the opposite side. It had a large metal cast iron spiked fence that surrounded its stone placements. And a mist that seemed to linger over it all the time. A big weather-vein with a cock atop it and an arrow on the roosters crown seemed to always stand still, even if the wind was blowing all around its tall structure in front of the cemetery; it must have been rusted in time like Buck Creek frozen in the middle of winter. The approach to that cemetery had a cobblestone inlaid pathway leading to the fence, but stopped just outside with no entry. Bushes and more tall trees along with thousands of weeds, blackberry bushes impeded the fence of the cemetery, hindering any form of entry into it, one thing I know is that it sure was quite an impressionistic and curious place, tinted with an air of mystery, serenity and intrigue and I knew I had to explore it with my friends when summer came and there was enough time to do so.

The truth is that very little was known about that ol' mansion, and now that I really think of it, that place was a very dangerous place to play, but we played there with out really thinking about the danger that was involved no matter what circumstances were involved. We all knew not to go there and was told about it so many times that it made our heads spin, but as a kid you just don't really think about danger, you know, kids just don't listen to their elders and parents, and as a kid you just think about only the adventure, and oh what adventures I had with my friends on the other side of the creek.

Well; one day me and my friends went to that old house and explored it real good, and when we reached the hole at the base of that ol' corn silo and poked our heads inside of it, there was a very long rickedy ladder inside dangling all the way from top to bottom, and the small opening led you inside that creaking old silo, it was leaning just a bit too, and as you looked inside; it gave off a musty smell none like I'd ever smelled before, it was a smell of death, and maybe they put their dead farm animals in that silo; and, as my memory serves me right, there was even quicksand in the bottom of that silo and, maybe that was the musty smell, I really don't know for sure. My friends dared me to climb that 'ol ladder to the top and look out over the whole landscape from the tip top of the leaning and dangling steps, my friends were too chicken to go up there, it was very high up especially for young frail little boys my age like I was way back then. But for some in the past that went up that 'ol silo, well they never made it to the ground so I've been told, they fell to the bottom of that old pit of quicksand never to get out alive. I get the jitters just thinking about it now.

To tell you now, as I just look back and wonder if it was true or not about the folk dying in that old silo, well I just don't know for sure, the only thing I do know for sure is that I went up that ladder and made it down safely that's one good thing for certain. Well I and my friends went back to our homes and parents that afternoon and I sure thought about the excitement of that day on the other side of the creek at that old farm house in the hollow beyond the big Erie corn field and dense woods, but man it sure was fun, yelp it sure was. Any way that's not the only time we went there, we had many adventures at that 'ol farm silo, in the woods, in the corn field, and yelp even in that old house, that's another scary place, that old farm house.

Chapter 3

The Tree Climber in the Woods

The woods was a real fun place to play, climbing them tall trees, swinging on them vines just like Tarzan done in the old movies I use to watch on our old round tube black and white TV.

I remember one time I climbed way up in this big oak tree by our very small house and looked all over the whole country side. I use to go up that tree a lot of times even as a 7 year old boy just to look out towards Muncie and the surrounding area of Selma, and all the farmland.

I could see ol' Buck Creek, and the big ol' farmhouse mansion. My imagination took me all over the place; it even took me beyond to far away lands and other countries sometimes. It was a wonderful place to go to gather my thoughts sometimes.

I sure had a blast doing things like that, even though it was dangerous, but as I said before, some kids like I use to be just didn't have any sense of fear in 'em, and just maybe no senses whatsoever. I don't think I would do something like that now, well I just couldn't 'cause of my age for one, and physical condition for another that I have now, but oh I do so enjoy reliving the memories, yelp I sure do hardy har har.

The trees in the woods weren't quite as tall as that 'ol oak by the house, but me and my friends climbed lots of them too.

One time me and my friends were doing just that. Now some of them trees just weren't so strong to hold even a small lad like me, and as I was going up one tree just to try and bend it down so we could bounce on it like a teeter totter (we did that lots) , cause we didn't have such things and had to make our own. Well any how I grabbed on one small branch, snap, crash, pop, boom, bang, and down I came; hard and fast, face down, kerplunk, smack down, right on my stomach, hard, real hard, it knocked the breath right out of me, and man did it hurt a bunch, my friends just laughed., but not me.

"Stop laughing, damn it, that really hurt." Of course they kept on laughing at me, but I told 'em. "One day you'll get the same thing, believe you-me."

To me it wasn't a bit funny. Kids can be mean sometimes, but after I got up off that hard stick, and leaf filled ground I sat for a spell then I started to feel better and went on playing as if nothing had ever happened.

Kids back then didn't have much fear as I said before, and didn't think about the consequences of getting hurt from doing something dangerous but we all had common sense, good values and the like; but, you know something even today kids just don't think.

They know the consequences of doing dangerous things, they just don't care that's one difference from when I was a kid and today's kids, another is kids today don't know how to think because their not taught how in school, and in most cases not even by their parents, and in my opinion most of the parents of today and the teachers in schools don't teach 'em anything about having common sense they only want to push kids right through school and out of their hair and upon society to survive with little knowledge of reality.

When I was a kid the schools taught us common sense and how to think on our feet on the run, sitting, sleeping or even when working and doing dangerous things and dangerous jobs, and the schools back then had good teachers that gave us the right tools like common sense, good morals, values, and with the help of our parents we made it in life just fine. Some kids today don't have a prayer 'cause teachers and parents don't give a dang like when I was a kid.

Chapter 4

The Movie and the Gun

One time I went to my friend's place down the path along side the back of our little house, it was about maybe a half mile or so through the woods.

That path had been there for what seemed to be forever as if it were made by people in the old west times the late 1700 or 1800's, ya know something it just dawned on me that the 'ol farm house may have been built in that era as well, 'cause it was a very old place.

Any how I went to my friends house to watch their TV, we didn't have one in 1956 in Hyde Park, we were poor country folk back then, but my friends parents had one so I was all excited to go and watch that new TV of theirs.

When I got there my friends were playing out in front of their big house next to a pile of wood, the chickens were running around and out in the pasture of their big farm the cows mood slowly in the distance.

Mr. Fulkler was doing something, I think he was sharpening his ax so he could kill one of them chickens for their dinner; he also had his big shot gun there beside him as I recall.

I never minded it too much and just went on inside as I usually done and sat down on the floor with my friends and began watching that big round tube TV, it was nice real nice and I wanted my aunt to get us one some day when we could afford it. We watched an old science fiction movie something new in that day and age not only for TV being a new thing, but movies were real new as well.

My friends wanted me to stay for dinner and also wanted me to spend the night with them, they were able to stay up late as long as all the choirs were all done, so I ran back down that path lickety-split to my house and ask my Aunt Mary if I could please stay at Tommy's house, she said yes, but to be home early the next morning. I once again ran my little butt off back down that path that was our short cut all the time.

We had fun that night and stayed up telling stories after those two movies we watched, it was very late when we went to bed, and I slept in later than I should have, and I also sorta forgot to go home early enough too, and not thinking me and my friends went out side and started playing like pirates, dueling with sticks we made into swords, just like they did on TV the night before. On that Pirate movie they also fired their muzzle loader guns; it was an exciting movie with lots of action.

Any how my friends dad had left his big old shot gun out front the day before, and I noticed it leaning up against the old pick up truck, so I went and picked it up, it was extremely heavy especially for a small 6 year old like me, I remember looking down the barrel of that gun sighting in on one of them chickens, and fired that thing, both barrels at the same time, I went flying backwards head over heals and landed on a pile of hay and wood chips.

The next thing I remember was everyone looking at me especially Tommy's dad. He was yelling at me for all he was worth.

"Damn you Eddie, You killed my ROOSTER." He said, with a thundering tone of voice.

"I'm gonna let your Aunt Mary know about this, but first I'm gonna whip your little butt till it screams louder than I am, then I'm taking you home by your ears and telling your aunt Mary, and I know she'll whip yer butt too." And that's just what happened; I got it twice in a matter of minutes. I couldn't sit for a week, or so it seemed to a little guy like me. I don't think I'll ever forget that whoppin'. As I recall, I seen Vera and her mom come runnin' outside at see what all the commotion was all about as well as several other neighbors, and as I looked toward the Capturesme's place, I seen Vera laughin' at me, but her mom shoed her back inside mighty quickly for some reason. I never done anything like that ever again. To this day I just don't like guns, and never ever will touch one again as long as I live, that's for sure.

Chapter 5

My Birthday Present

Well life went on for me in a more positive way, and for my birthday in August my aunt told me she was going to get me a doggie for my birthday and I could pick from the litter of new puppies that one of her friends was bringing out for us to see, they were Chihuahuas, and boy were they cute. I picked out one of mixed color black and white it was a female and I named her Tammy Sue.

My Aunt Mary told me we were gonna move back to Muncie and that bothered me a little, but I didn't mind too much 'cause I really didn't have a choice in the matter.

I did what I was told and respected my elders for what they did, but it wouldn't be till next year and that gave me plenty of time to say good bye to my friends in Hyde Park and at Selma Elementary school where I was in first grade.

I would also be able to explore that old farm house all of its old run down out buildings even more, there sure were a bunch of 'em to go through and the big barn, wow it was huge, lots of places in it to play around in and hide to scare the living day lights outta my friends, 'cause they deserved me giving them a little revenge from making me climb that scary 'ol silo ladder.

My little dog Tammy Sue and I got to know each other real good, and I spoiled that dog with lots of table scraps and over time she got real fat, but that was many years down the road.

My friends all came to see my birthday present and thought them so dang cute that they all wanted one too, but their parents wouldn't hear of it when they asked them, well when they practically begged them to buy them a cute little Chihuahua puppy like I had.

I recon they were a bit envious that I had something' that they didn't have, but after about two or three days went by, they forgot all about within' a small pet like my Tammy Sue the tiniest dog they ever seen in their lives.

Chapter 6

The Poker Game and the Telephone Pole Shooting

Now my uncle Bill passed away in 1956 and life for us on the farm wasn't easy for my Aunt Mary trying to raise me now that I think of it that's the main reason I guess we moved from our one farm on 23rd street to Hyde Park to live with my Aunt Mary's ex, her first husband who's name was Luke Dillon and I guess that they remained good friends for many years after their divorce, and they did get along good as I recall, but only as friends. They met while working in the Barnum and Bailey Circus and worked together in a shooting act that they performed for folk back then when they were in their early 20's.

Any how I have memory visions of all the things I done and the places I've lived and the things I've seen over my life time. There are so many things that happen in a person's life and as you get older you just start remembering more and more things as time goes by. I some times vision the poker games that old Luke had at his little house and the men would come in chewing their tobacco carrying sacks of beer from old man Cash's grocery store. They come in and sit around this old round wooden table that Luke had made in his back yard some time back, and drink with their mouth's full of chew and spit it in this big old wash tub that was placed there every night for their game.

They would cuss and laugh a lot and tell stories while playing cards. I use to sit in a chair by the old potbelly stove and when they wanted some more wood in the fire I got up and fetched it from out next to the out house.

The smell was awful inside, but I tried not to pay attention to that, I was more interested in the game and the stories they were telling, some were funny and some scared the daylights outta me, but I really enjoyed them.

In one corner Luke had his gun cabinet and a large space underneath with jars that were filled with money, mostly coins from the poker games. There were lots of 'em too, quarters, silver dollars, dimes, nickels, pennies, and a couple filled with dollar bills.

Luke was a good poker player well most the time I guess he was a professional gambler and had grew up in French Lick Indiana on a large farm that his family had acquired from an inheritance from his uncle who was a famous man in his own rights and was a US Marshal from the old west. His last name was Dillon, and his uncle was Matt Dillon or just plain Matt as Luke referred to him as in stories many times over at the card table. Now most folk these days only think about the old TV show Gunsmoke and the character Matt Dillon as being just made up; well let me tell you the fact is that there was a real Marshal Dillon and I'm sortta proud that I knew one of his relatives for real, old Luke Dillon.

Now Luke was quite a character, a tall man about 6 foot 2 inches of lean, a tobacco chewing man filled with a streak of meanness unrepressed by most men in our community. Now don't get me wrong y'here, he was a nice man when he wanted to be, but look out for his temper, cause if someone done something that he didn't like done to him or his property well it would be pure Hell to pay that was one thing certain. His temper got him in an uproar the next day after one of his poker games. Angrier than a mean ol' bull, he pulled himself op outta his favorite chair and stomped outside to work on his big fence and the gate that one of his friends drove his old pick up truck into. Luke wasn't happy 'bout that, cause his gate was broken for one and for another he didn't win too much at the table the night before. He was extremely angrier than he usually got in situations like this. As he worked he looked out across the big garden we had on the front of his property and there was a man climbing up the telephone pole at the very front of his property to install a box that the next door neighbor was having put in for their phone service.

Well Luke didn't like that idea cause that pole was his and on his property to boot. He went bouncing with his long legs as fast as they would carry him right back in the house furiously and headed right straight to where his bed was and grabbed his Colt 45 that he always kept under his old feather down pillow, that gun was his pride cause it had genuine pearl handles on it and that gun use to belong to his Uncle Mathew (Matt) Dillon the real old west marshal of French Lick, Indiana. Hey no jokin' he was… really he was, now ya all know that I wouldn't tell ya any tall tales, lies or any ol' fiction story now would I. Hehehehehe.

He headed for the door pushing it open and one hinge snapped off and that made him even madder than he already was as he headed out the gate towards the pole and the man atop it holding the phone box. I heard Luke yell at him with a thunderous voice asking him just what the hell he was doing up there on his property, and before the man had a chance to say a word Luke took aim and shot that box right outta that telephone mans hands.

Well I tell ya I never seen a man move so dang fast off atop of a pole like that before, it was almost funny, but the man cussed vigorously as he came down and said he was going to report him to the sheriff and to his boss as he got into his old panel truck and speed off. What a sight that was. Man what a sight.

"Wow", was all I could say as I hid behind the gate looking around the edge of that big white fence as Luke came back toward the house to put his gun up.

"That'll teach 'em ta come on my property." He said as he stormed toward the house looking back a couple times ta see if anyone was coming up his long drive then looking at the front door that he'd broke in anger.

Chapter 7

The First Exploration

August 12, 1957. My birthday had come and gone. I was finally 7 years old. We still lived in Hyde Park with Luke and he still continue to gamble on the week ends, but none of that really mattered to me 'cause I had important things to do, like get my friends and go explore that ol' farm house before I had to move back to Muncie with my Aunt Mary.

I didn't know nor understand why we had to move, but we did at the end of the month and I was determined to explore as much as I could while I had the chance to, and be with my friends for awhile longer. I got up early that morning and went to our very small kitchen and fixed me some eggs for my breakfast. My Aunt taught me how to cook when I was 6 years old and now that I'm older I'm glad she did. Luke was getting everything ready for the big game that night and Aunt Mary was out gathering some more eggs from the small chicken coop next to an old round top trailer with rust colored shingles all over it. That was where we kept some of our valuable furniture and other things 'cause while we were away from Muncie we didn't want anyone to steal us blind, so we had moved all we could to Hyde Park.

Aunt Mary came back in with a small basket full of nice brown eggs and after I ate and she was done putting the eggs away I asked her if I could go play with Tommy. He was ten and his brother David was my age, seven, and oh yeah, his sister Sally was almost eight, I didn't like her much at the time 'cause she was always a real mean, and devilish little girl to all of us boys.

Well, I guess I liked her some, but we had to be nice to her, like it or not, cause if we wasn't nice to her then we'd all get a whoopins'. Sally would always tell if we did anything wrong or when we teased her. Guess that's how girls was supposed to act back then cause all of them were tattle tales when I was a young boy full of energy and ready for almost any kind of adventure I could come up with, even going into that ol' scary farm house beyond the corn field. Now Sally knew what we was gonna do and she said she'd tell if we didn't let her come along with us and explore that scary ol' house. So we all agreed and made a pact that if any one of us ever told they'd be made the one who came up with the idea in the first place. All of us boys sure wanted to get even with Sally, and were gonna blame her from the start for coming up with the idea in the first place, and deep inside I didn't want to do it, but for the sake of my friendship, I went along with almost everything that my friends and I discussed.

Aunt Mary said I could go play, and before she finished telling me, lickety-split I went out the front door, and the screen door slammed behind me. I was in a big hurry to go play and explore that 'ol farm house with my friends and didn't mean for the door to slam, but we had a lot of exploring to do. We had the whole day to do it in cause it was the week end and we were Outta School for summer vacation, and what a summer it was, swimming in the creek, playing in the woods and exploring. Country living is great when one is a kid with lots of things like that to do all the time; no boredom what - so -ever.

Little did any of us know what we would find in that big house? It was covered with moss from top to bottom, the windows had been broken out all over and the front door hung off and when the wind blew it would creak and squeak on its rusty old broken and bent hinges and bang against the old cobble stone facing that was attached to its rusty-hinged frame work. I had never seen a metal door so dang heavy and it even had bars on it for some reason and some of them were bent and broken in the strangest way. Maybe the folks that used to live there wanted to be secure and safe in the confines of that once big farmhouse mansion. It was extremely huge, bigger than looking at it seemed from a distance, cause when we all finally got up the nerve to go near it we saw its tremendous size up close, and personal. It was fantastically high, and just as long on all sides as it was tall. I looked up, I looked down, and all around that big place and as I looked through a small broken window in the front, it looked like someone had torn the whole inside completely apart at the seams.

There was rubble every where from broken glass, a wooden table totally smashed into small pieces but recognizable, some broken chairs and man the dust and cob webs, they were all over that basement, and even in places it seemed like they shouldn't have been at all. And the smell! It just man was it awful. It was a very musty odor like a pit of dead animals, but there weren't any animal bones in sight, so I didn't know what the smell could really be from. All I knew was it smelled like dead animals. I knew the smell all too well from the many slaughters of cows, pigs and chickens that everyone butchered for food in our quiet little community and on the farm when my Uncle Bill butchered pigs and chickens and some cows when he was alive and we lived in Muncie. I felt like passing out from the stink of death that surrounded the inner workings of that ol' farmhouse and I almost told my friends that I wasn't about to go in there no matter what they said about me. But I just didn't want to be called a chicken by my friends and more so by a girl with a great big mouth like Sally. We all knew she blabbed all over the community, and at school she would tell every blasted detail and even throw in some lies just to make things sound more awful.

As we climbed through a small broken window with old rusty hinges that lead to the basement. There was an awful smell coming from the inside; we tried our best to hold our breath, but couldn't hold it long enough so we had to just ignore the awful smell that was all around us. The 'ol place was messy every where we went. As we went up the old concrete stairs we thought we heard foot steps but knew that the house had been empty for a very long time so we ignored it and continued. I really think we were all scared but just didn't want to admit it to one another. Sally was the most scared out of us, I think, because she grabbed onto my arm tight. I tried to push her hand away, but every time I did she held on tighter and longer so I just ignored that too after awhile as we continued our adventure deeper into the unknown.

The door was very heavy and it took the three of us boys to push it open, but we did it because we had to prove our strength especially to Sally. When we got inside what appeared to be the kitchen area it was still intact but with lots of cob webs hanging all over the place. An 'ol wood stove stood idol in the middle of one wall and it had a long chimney that extended to the ceiling tall and it was idle and full of dust and once in awhile some dust would fall down on us from our foot-steps creaking the semi-rotten wood floor. The cupboards had drawers missing and doors dangling from rusty hinges, and there were some creepy looking cockroaches crawling all over the floor and from the cupboards. One fell down on Sally and began to crawl on her dress, and several others went up her legs; she let out a blood chilling scream that made even us boys scream. David tried to shush her big mouth by holding it but she just bit him to make him move his hand away. He moved his hand away and he called her a nasty name. I think he called her a little bitch, and we just all knew that the bitch word meant a female dog, cause that's what all the adults called female dogs and sometimes they called women folk bitches too., why I just don't know? Tommy and I just snickered a little and Sally told us all too just shut our dang mouths or she'd tell what we were doing. So we just kept quiet for awhile.

As we wondered about Spooks-Ville mansion we found ourselves in the hallway with mirrors all over the place. They were on both sides of the hall and followed the hall-lit all the way to the end. We never had seen those fancy old type mirrors before. They too were covered with cob webs as well as lots of dust as well. The whole place was in a shamble and it looked as though no one had ever lived there at all; the appearance of the main areas of the house seem to be so torn up like the basement was and that seemed like a good thing to all of us. Well, at least to me it did, and that made me more relaxed than my friends. I was always the one who was dared to do things because I didn't show too much fear when it came to doing things like climbing all the way to the top of those big ol' oak trees and the ol' silo and even coming in this creepy ol' farmhouse. When they dared me to go first, I did it. I guess that made me their leader or something.

The next room we came into was the huge living room, and man was it a fancy place. All the 'ol Victorian furniture was just elegant, a red crushed velvet back to back love seat, another mirror next to a coat and hat rack that was made from deer antlers and several other fancy chairs made from the same crushed velvet material as the love seat. On one wall a huge fire place with a mantle above it and surrounded with what looked like ivory from the very heart of Africa and marble from the deepest part of India. On the other walls there were some big animal heads, a deer head, an antelope head, a small lions head and about half a dozen other heads. As I looked around the room more, I stopped dead in my tracks. I gazed up at a huge elephants head mounted with long tusks on it, that protruded way out over the floor, and as I stepped closer I almost tripped over a lion skin rug on the floor, the head still attached to it. It was a really bizarre place if-n ya asked me?

Wow was my main thought and to me this was just fantastic (even though weird) because I was into things like that and always wanted to go on an African safari and other adventures around the world. Who ever owned this place must have been a big game hunter or something, or so it seemed to me, it appeared like they were rich people when they lived here, but why was everything exactly like it was when the people lived here? No one had lived in this place for over a hundred years or so. There sure were many questions going through my mind about this creepy 'ol house, I didn't know about my friends, but I wanted to find out everything I could about this farm, who owned it and why they moved away leaving all their possessions behind.

Walking slow I gazed around the trophy room, what appeared like another room had been attached alongside the fireplace? It had a strange shape like none I'd ever seen before, and it kinda resembled a religious setting of some kind. I sortta ignored it because of all the dead animal heads and other bizarre things that my small hazel eyes beheld before them. I wanted to look up the set of stairs next to it, but didn't because my stomach was growling at me like one of the lions have attached themselves to my insides and was trying to tell me to feed them, we really had to go cause it was getting close to lunch time and we were all getting mighty hungry so we decided to go home and eat then come back right after lunch and finish our exploration of the creepy farmhouse that to us was now a real mansion and not just a big old house that perched atop a small hill on the other side of Old Buck Creek.

We took our time as we worked our way back through the long hall and back into the messy kitchen area, then down the stinky concrete stairs, and once again we all tried to hold our breathe but couldn't. We then climbed back through the broken window to where we entered in the first place. Sally still clung onto my arm very tightly but as soon as we were outside she let go of my arm. What a relief that was cause my arm sure was sore from her squeezing it so dang tight. I rubbed my arm a couple times to try and get some of the feeling back in it, but it still tingled a little. I knew it would be all right in awhile. Taking one more glance through the broken window holding my noses so the smell wouldn't pierce my nostrils like sharp ice picks, then I stood up to head home. As I did I could have sworn I heard a tiny voice calling us back inside, but I didn't say anything to my friends knowing they'd just tease me about hearing things and I maintained my composure so I wouldn't bringing any attention to myself.

We ran as fast as our little legs could carry us back to our make shift bridge next to the 'ol artesian well took a couple gulps of nice cold water to wash the dust outta our throats then we crossed the log bridge that we had laid across Old Buck Creek and we ran through the cornfield, through our wooded playground and back to our homes so we could get us some lunch.

All of us put out heads together literally in a pact and decided to take a little time when we ate our lunch so we wouldn't draw any attention to ourselves, then we could all meet right after we ate at the bottom of the hill next to our tree that had a really long vine hanging from it that we swung on almost every day just like Tarzan did in his movie and after I ate my sandwich and drank my milk I asked if I could go play back ta my friends' house until dinner, like the good boy I always was.

I was beside myself and I just chuckled. "Hardy har har, yelp I'm a real good boy hahahaha ain't I?" My mouth half full of food, talking and laughing all at the same time, I'd sortta forgotten my mannors and hoped my aunt wouldn't say anything about it to me…

Naturally I knew my Aunt Mary would let me because I always minded her and did all of my chores with out even being told to do them. Heck I even did extra things so I could stay in good standing with her and Luke. Heck what Aunt Mary and Luke didn't know sure wouldn't hurt me or them, that is, unless they found out that I was doing something I shouldn't be, like going across the creek and into that 'ol house that me and all my friends were told to stay away from. I guess that maybe I was a good little boy in my own way. Aunt Mary told me what time I was to be home for dinner and not to slam the door on the way outta the house or I'd get whipped so I walked out closing the screen door slowly so it wouldn't bang, then I ran lickety-split as fast as my legs would carry me to the meeting place.

When I got there none of the others were there yet so I started swinging on the vine acting like Tarzan and trying to imitate his awesome yell as I swung out over the just plowed corn field then let go to see how far I would fly before hitting the ground. It was very soft soil and none of us ever got hurt. Man that sure was fun, I said aloud to myself, and went back up the hill and swung several more times yelling my mouth off as loud as I could knowing no one would hear me cause of the distance I was away from all the houses. Besides, the trees made it almost impossible to even hear your friends yell for you because of the distance, along with the steep hills that we all had to climb.

Chapter 8

The Trip Back

About ten minutes later David and Sally showed up, but not Tommy. Sally said he had to do his chores before he could go play, but just I knew he wouldn't be there to go explore the house this time. Sally and David had all their chores done, and me I didn't have any cause to worry either; I done all of mine a couple days before so I would have my freedom to play.

David and I were best buds. One time I took some of Luke's chewing tobacco, David and I climbed this big ol' Oak tree and started chewing like the grown-ups did. We both ended up getting so sick and we never chewed again; well at least I never did anyways, 'cause I couldn't stand the smell. Got sick and tired from all the poker games Luke and his friends had with their drinking gambling and chewing that nasty smelling and nasty stuff, smelling and nasty tasting Union Workman chewing tobacco, YUCK. I couldn't speak for David and didn't don't know if he ever tried it again cause he never told me if he did. Everything was cool like before. We told Sally that if she ever told we would shove some in her mouth and make her chew it till she swallowed the nasty stuff. She never did tell and we were gonna make sure she never told on us for going into this ol' house either cause we had another plan to make her eat a chicken poop sandwich, YUCK, just incase she ever threatened to tell on us for anything ever again. Sally made a promise and we were gonna make her stick to that promise no matter what we had to do to her, even making her chew tobacco and tell a lie on her on top of everything else to boot.

David, Sally and I went down along side the ploughed cornfield on a path that lead toward the baseball field so we wouldn't get in any trouble. It was a good thing we did cause the old farmer was coming down his dirt rutted road on his tractor to do some planting. We greeted him as we always did and smiled so he wouldn't ask us what we were up to. We always told him we were gonna look for fish in the creek, but even he knew there wouldn't be any fish in it; but he just played along with us and told us good luck. One time, he told us there was this giant carp up steam, and to let him know when we seen it. He never did say why, but we just keep looking from time to time to see if we would ever spot that big carp in hopes that old farmer would possibly give us some money for telling' him where we seen that fish at.

We then headed down his dirt-rutted road to the opposite end where we had our bridge next to the well, just so the farmer wouldn't know we were really going to that ol' farmhouse on the other side of the creek. I guess we always did fool that old man cause he never said anything to us that we weren't allowed to go across the creek. He was the one who had told us about people dying in the silo in the first place just to keep us away from that ol' - ol' place. But we never paid attention to him. My friends said he was crazy and always made up these fantastic stories about the old west days and about him coming to America from some place in Europe called Brussels Belgium or some place like that. We'd all listen to him with his funny accent telling us about not only the old west but his life in Europe as well. His stories were always so dang interesting, and they did keep our attention at least for a spell, but none of us really believed what he said and most the time we'd just laugh and cut up like most kids our ages did and sometimes his stories scarred us kids outta our wits, but like I said we'd just end up laughing most of the time when he finished saying what he had to say, and then we'd all say bye and run away toward the creek so we could cross over to the other side and play.

Today the farmer without a name told us about crops, and why I'll never know?

He started out by saying: "Sit yer selfs right down y'hear now and I'll tells ya hows George took care of some of his crops, come sit." He'd smile through his rotten teeth most had already fallen out, and what was left was real nasty lookin' as well; his big boot lips, a wrinkled scruffy unshaven black face, scrounged uncut hair, and filthy bib overalls made m wanna puke, but I never did and just took it all in like the good 'lil fella I was. It seemed like he was always talking about himself, I think, but was never sure cause he told us so many different tells in so many different ways that we were always confused and amazed at the same time. He'd always start with George for some reason, maybe that was his name, I don't know to this day, but anyway here's what he told us this sunny summer day when we were headed to the spooky mansion beyond the creek.

"George had asked another farmer, old man Otto Layedstillman, who was way more experienced than he was at farming, how to test at see if-n the vegetables were ready for harvest or not. I should say, George my friend, you do have some nice crops, that's for sure, but didn't them Indian fellows show ya how at poke 'em for ripeness. Otto Layedstillman was a share cropper from way back, and he knew all there was about any type of crop a fellow wanted at grow. He looked at George and just shook his head but I just didn't know what it was about that old man, but it really got his goat at times. George just ignored his, um my, or was it his strange ways, I can't remember, but any hows, where were I; oh yea, I were 'bout ta tells ya 'bout how ta tend to his crops. Well sir, yhou too girlies.. hehehe... George looked at Otto and grinned just a tiny bit, and said. "Varmints have also been hangin' 'round here a lot lately. Yea, I know; I have several ways to rid folk of all the different critters and other varmints in these parts. Them there Indians just don't know everything like I do." He, umm I smiled from ear to ear with a shit eatin' grin as I looks at George... where were I, oh yea now I 'member, I've lost count of the times I've caught him in the fields. He started coming around just after I fertilized last winter, then he stopped until I started planting. Since then he's been coming around every few weeks. I'll see him just meandering through the fields. The first crops were ready for him to be a poking at them with the point of the knife before touching them with his fingers. The shards were dry and brittle, cracking and breaking into several more pieces at his touch. He noticed that there was none of the stringy pulp or small seeds that were supposed to be inside a pumpkin. He scraped the pieces to the floor and examined the other vegetable. Well I'd best get back at my plowin' now. Ya kids be careful playin' about that creek now y'hear."

He sure was long winded when he talked, he just didn't know when to stop talkin' sometimes, but us kids would listen to his whole story before we'd rush off to do our own thing and leave that strange old farmer to tend to his field and crops like he always done. We were all so damned glad that he'd finished his story sooner than he usually did so we could get on with our own lives and be happy go lucky and care free kids playin' and a shoutin' like wild Indians on the war path, although it took us a little longer going this particular route, but we didn't mind cause we had lots of time left in the day before having to go home for dinner. Somehow we always knew what time was always and we were never late for dinner or anything else.

The rest of that afternoon would be just as exciting as the morning was and that was what we wanted, a lot more excitement and adventures into the unknown, and that ol' farm sure did provide just some of what we were looking for when we were bored playing Tarzan, we just kept doing it for something to do when we had nothing better to do, but now, we had this spooky 'ol mansion to check out and we were gonna check out every nook and cranny in the place even if it did take us all summer, and we didn't really care about the woods much any more, just that farmhouse, I knew that after the summer was over I would have to move back to Muncie and leave my friends behind. That wasn't a good feeling for me, but still somehow, I knew that I'd make new friends and so would they.

Chapter 9

Did You See That?

Finally me and my friends reached our destination and I was so excited about going back into this old house that it sent shivers up and down my spine giving me goose-bumps all over my arms. Like the first time I went in, first again with Sally clinging onto me like glue then David came in last. The place still smelled the same as we interred the basement, but it looked a little different for some reason, but I just couldn't quite figure it out. There seemed to be more things than before in the basement cause the rubble was even greater than the first time we went in, but anyhow we headed up them stairs once again, down the mirrored hall and back into the living room for a second look see.

We opened the old roll top desk drawers to see if there was any thing of value inside and all we found was some old papers, more dust, and more cob webs to brush out of our way. Sally wouldn't tough anything and left all the real looking up to David and me and some how we didn't mind doing all the looking cause if we found anything valuable we'd get to keep it for ourselves and not give Sally anything just for spite. She wouldn't dare take anything that didn't belong to her, but would take something if a person gave it to her, or so we thought.

I took a letter opener that was on the side of the roll top desk in a little holder that had been made for it to sit in and I wiggled it back and forth in the lock of the roll top to get it open and when I finally got it open I found what looked like some very important papers cause the date on it read 1851, and that was old enough for me to just take that paper, fold it up and stuff it in the back pocket of my trousers.

David nor Sally seen me do it cause they were looking at other things. Sally was shivering for some reason and maybe it was just because she was a girl or something, but I could care less how a girl felt, I knew how I felt though and at the time I felt real good cause I had already found something valuable even if it was a dusty old paper. David took a few tokens for himself, but didn't show us what they were, but Sally was such a snitch that she could be a real sneak on top of her bad behavior and put things in her dress pockets without us even knowing a thing about it, and besides, we just couldn't trust that mean fat girl no matter what.

The letter I took looked like some sort of document and most of it I just couldn't read 'cause it was written in very fancy letters, the same kind that our constitution was written in, but the words were in another language and only the date was half readable to me. I also found an old coin with the same date on it but it wasn't American money and it was heavy and looked like gold with sortta flat sides about six of them to be a fact, and the face on it I sure didn't recognize at all either, I stuffed that in my back trouser pocket with the paper. I had a lot more pocket space in them trousers and I was hoping that I could fill all four of them completely full of goodies like I had already.

I didn't find anything else in that desk that I wanted and David and Sally didn't find anything they wanted in another messed up ol' desk, it was a funny looking desk with what looked like the markings from ancient Egypt scribbled all over it and the legs was made from some sort of animals legs and mounted on top of it were two funny looking birds sortta like dove, but like none that I'd ever seen the likes of before. I told them to follow me into this other room that had a tall stair way constructed in it that lead to the upper part of the house.

Since I was a little afraid to go up them strange stairs cause they were in a different location than most staircases have always been in, my imagination ran amuck just a tad, but maybe that's how they built stairs in the olden days where ever these people had came from in the first place, but I didn't let on like I was scarred, and as always I lead the way, and going up them stairs gave me the willies, but I was supposed to be the brave one I couldn't show any fear what-so-ever.

When we all got to the top there was a fancy made door and walls that just didn't look like walls and like I said this area was very scary and a very strange area. I opened the door slowly and it made squeaking sounds that echoed through out the house. Sally put her fingers in her ear for a couple seconds that it took me to open the door then she quickly covered her eyes in fear. I looked at David, he looked at me and we both gulped looking at each other with our eyes as big as silver dollars, David was holding onto Sally's arm and she was holding onto my arms as we very quietly and slowly crept through the door. It lead into an area that has long narrow hall ways in a square with two rooms on each side and the same fancy doors the same as the entry way.

On the walls were paintings of woman in fancy laced and ruffled dresses with a big hats, a man wearing fancy pants and a top hat in another, and a little girl that sortta looked like Sally, but much prettier than Sally was in still another painting. We just stood there looking at the rooms and the walls and the paintings seemed to be looking right back at us too. There was two fancy candle holders with candles on each wall that all the sudden lit up. Sally jumped sky-high and David pissed his pants when they lit up the hallway. I just covered my eyes for a brief second and then looked at my friends who were frozen solid to the floor and began to laugh at them for being so dang scared. They were speechless as they looked at me with their mouths wide opened and sweat running down their faces as if they were in heat like a couple dogs ready to do the wild thing, their tongues hung out, over the lips and through the gums. That prompted me to say.

"Over the lips and through the gums, lookout stomach here it comes." I let out a big scary sound and then I shouted. "Boo." They looked at me with big eyes, sortta smiled a little and then giggled ever so softly. David turned his head toward me and sneered like the banshee he sometimes was.

"Funny, very funny Eddie, ya just wait, one these times I'll get ya back pal." Sally blurted out immediately.

"Yea Eddie ya butthead, I'm gonna tell my daddy on ya when we get back home." Sally blurted out in her usual rude tone which opened up still anther door of opportunity,

I couldn't resist sayin'. "Gotcha."

"Funny, very funny pal ha ha." David snickered once again, but Sally's face was as red as a reddish after the dirt had been washed off of it...

I turned toward Sally and told her if she did, then I'd say she forced us all to come to this ol' farmhouse with by threatening us with a big fat lie. I didn't yet know exactly what kinda lie it was, but that didn't matter, cause she didn't know either. Ya could say I had her buffaloed a wee bit. Of course I just smiled a real big grin and kept walking down the hallway laughing softly. I was really scarred but I always had something to say to make my friends think twice about sayin' or doin' something' I didn't want them to say or do.

We were so afraid that we didn't know just what to do and was almost ready to boot-scoot n boogie on outta there, but for some reason we didn't scramble to get the heck outta there when those candles lit up all by them selves. We walked slowly down the left hall and went up to the first door that had the painting of the little girl next to it and the next room had the painting of the pretty lady next to it, but on the other side of the hall was the mans painting and all the other rooms has paintings of different women all of which were of African decent. One Painting by each room, and man was that even more strange than the house itself, well in a peculiar way it was.

Looking at one another once again gulping several times, Sally headed for the door and said she wanted to go home, but I told her that we was gonna finish looking in this area of the house first; then we'd go home. It seemed like it was getting late any how and besides we were all starting to show some fear on our skinny little faces. I pulled David in front of me this time not wanting to show him I was afraid so I told him that he'd be a chicken if he didn't open up this door and go in first.

"Why should I always go first, you're a chicken if you don't open this door and go in first, I dare ya"? David said as he trembled in his sneakers like he was in a vibrating machine or somethin'

"No I ain't no dang chicken, I'll show you I'm not afraid either OK, I'm not startin' ta be a scary-cat or something.

"NO, (I told him) but you'll be if ya don't do it".

He slowly reached for the fancy door handle, not a door knob like most houses have, but all the door handles were these fancy brass lion head handles that had buttons on 'em that ya just push down and then pull on the door for it to open. We all peeped into this room through a crack of the open door and it was all clean and very fancy it even had a fancy ol' sofa, a writing desk with photos and other stuff on it, fancy lace curtains and a fancy mirror and even a piano on one side of the room. We couldn't believe our eyes and what we were looking at, so we opened the door all the way and went on inside. As soon as we was inside the door slammed closed behind us, Sally screamed and pissed all over herself. I grabbed her mouth this time and told her to just hush or we'd leave her here. David quickly grabbed the brass door handle and pulled on it but it wouldn't open and he started to panic so I pushed him outta the way and opened the door cause he forgot to push the button down before the door would open.

"Let's just look around this room then get the heck outta here OK". David said with a quivering tone of voice.

I agreed! All Sally did was shake her head in agreement too. I tried not to panic like they were doing cause I was supposed to be the most brave outta all of us, and most of the time I was, but in this case I was just as afraid as my friends and just didn't want to admit it not now nor ever other wise I would be labeled a coward, a chicken, afraid-cat, and what ever else my friends could come up with later on, and I wasn't about to let that happen.

As I searched around in some of the dresser drawers and this time so did Sally and for the first time since we started coming in this house Sally was touching things too. Maybe it was because it was the little girls' room that we were in that caused her to be so curious. Sally picked up several girl things and stuffed them into her little dress pocket, then took them out and put them back saying she

shouldn't just take things that belonged to some one else. I told her
that it was ok cause no one lived here and they wouldn't miss 'em any
way. Sally picked up the things and put them right back in her pocket.
I don't think she really felt right taking those things but she did any
how, and when I looked in still another drawer I found another paper
that had 1860 on it too it seemed to be a letter and this time I could
read some of the words cause they were in English as well as in that
other strange language that the fancy document had on it and was in
the same hand writing as well.

"My Dearest daughter Mattie'

"I want to write you a small letter telling you how good a tyme we
are havin' here in my country and we will be home as soon as your
father fi nish his work in a few day. Tell you other mommys hello and
be good. You daddy say he .love you bunches."

'God bless"

"You mommy Nellie Maxifield"

From what I could read it said that her mom and dad would be
home in a few days that their trip to their country was going good
and for her to be a good girl and that mommy and daddy loved her
very much. It also said that she was to tell her other mommies that
daddy loved them too. This was way too strange and extremely hard
to swallow and believe, 'cause I knew that every kid only had one
mom and dad at a time not several like this odd letter was saying. I
looked the letter over and tried to figure out the peoples names, and
I took several other letters and they all basically said the same things
in them and that made it all the more strange to me and it made me
more curious to find out just who the people was that had this once
nice ol' farmhouse and abandon it in such a hurry leaving behind
many wonderful and fancy possessions.

I picked up just one more letter and on it was, "My Dearest Daughter Mattie" in a fancy envelope with post markings on it from Blackpool and her complete name Nellie Margaret Maxifield scribbled but still readable enough to tell what her name was. Now I knew part of the mystery of who lived here at one time and just had to find more letters and other clues as to what happened for these people to leave everything behind when it appears that they moved back to their home country cause maybe things were too hard here in America especially trying to have a big farm with a fancy house on it. Folding some of the other letters very carefully I put them in my back pocket along with the other things I had from down stairs. David still had nothing that he liked, and I think he was just too afraid to take anything at all. Why I had no idea, but I knew I wanted more and would take what I could to find out all about the Maxifield family from Europe that owned this house once upon a time back in the 1860's.

The day was going fast now and we didn't want to be late for our dinner so; I told David and Sally we should be headin' back so we wouldn't get inta any trouble… they agreed very quickly. They were scarred so much that David was still shaking like a leaf on a fall tree. Sally stuffed as much girl things into her pockets as she could especially after I told her it was OK to take things that no one would ever miss any way.

When we started out of the room and I felt something nudge up against me and I thought it was Sally, but she was in front of me. Turning around quickly, there behind me was the girl in the painting, but what was even stranger was that I could see right through her. I turned back around telling my friends. "Did You See That"? They said no and then I pushed David and Sally out the door quite suddenly. They wondered why I done that. I told them we'd best hurry up and head home so we wouldn't be late for dinner; running down the stairs with them on my heals and a hot breathe right behind me whispering in my ear.

"Stay and play with me please I'm very lonely here by myself, please stay and play with me", but there wasn't any one else except David and Sally running down the stairs behind me. We all hurried up as fast as we could; getting' the heck outta there; running' all the way back home as fast as out small feet carried us through the weeds, cornfield, over the creek, through the woods, and all the way back home where we'd be safe and sound once again.

When we got across Old Buck Creek my friends ask me what I saw in the ol' farmhouse that made me run so scared for. I didn't tell them the truth that I seen a ghost girl or what ever the heck it was, but instead I wanted to just hurry up and get back so we didn't get into any trouble with our folks.

David just said "Oh"; then smiled a little. Catching my breathe for a quick second or two; then here come big foot, big mouth Sally came stumbling toward David and me asking why we left her behind so darn far?

She was gonna tell, but I reminded her that if she did we would make her eat something disgusting and she shut her big mouth as she tried to catch her breath like we were doing. I told them that we'd meet back at our tree tomorrow after church so we could go back and look for other treasures and do some more exploring of the creepy mansion farmhouse on the other side of the creek.

Chapter 10

Church Day

_I_ went my way and they went their way, but all the time I was walking toward home could hear that tiny little voice calling me back to play with her while I kept looking behind me to see if the ghost girl was following me or not. I sure wasn't gonna tell my friends that I was chased by a ghost, especially a girl ghost that was very pretty on top of it.

I barely made it back to the house. I walked in and sat down on the old warn out cushion chair and wiped the sweat off my forehead and took a deep breath in relief that I made it home safe and sound and wasn't followed by that ghost girl.

Luke ask me what was the matter did I see a ghost or something. I almost told him yea, but didn't and told him instead that I was running all day and was just tired. I don't know why he ask me what he did about seeing a ghost or something and further more I wondered if he knew that I really did see a ghost or not.

That night I had a nightmare about being chased by several ghost and just couldn't sleep very well and when the morning came I woke up exhausted from running in my sleep and nightmarish dream that I almost felt sick enough not to go to Sunday School that morning, but I went ahead and took my bath as usual in an old aluminum wash tub cause we didn't have a bath tub like some other folk had, we just couldn't afford it for one and besides there wasn't enough room in Luke's little house for a tub any way. I then got my little butt ready for church.

Aunt Mary and I always walked like most people did in our quaint community of about a thousand folk. Luke never went to church at all but we both dare not even mention the thought to him cause of his anger.

At church that morning we all had out picture taken and I even sang Jesus Loves Me, well I tried as far as I remember in the way back machine of my mind. Church only lasted for about an hour so folk could go about their busy body acquaintances, especially the women; man did they ever like to gossip a lot. Any how I ask if I could go play immediately after service, and as always Aunt Mary told me yes 'cause she was way too busy chatting away with other women folk at tell me anything other than her usual, yes.

Chapter 11

Tag Along Vera

I took off like, pardon my expression a bat outta hell just so I could meet David, Tommy, and Sally, and oh yea she'd went ahead and invited one of her little girl friends to come along this time cause she just didn't like being with us boys for some reason hahahahaha, I just don't know why. Any how her friend's name was Vera U. I didn't know her last name, but I knew she lived with her mom Ms. Capturesme. Vera had just turned seven years old on my birthday, can you imagine someone ya know having the same birthday as you and not know it till ya meet 'em and get ta know 'em a wee bit.

That goes to show ya how bad us kids really were when it came right down to it, cause we weren't adults yet, and we sure did have an extremely long way to go in life before we did come of adult age.

Things happen for a reason some times, but ya never know what kind of curve ball life will throw at ya some times. We tried to convince her that we were going on a dangerous adventure into the unknown and that she may not be able to handle the place we were going to explore, but it was too late for us boys to make a good strong convincing case scenario about the ol' Maxifield farmhouse, Sally the big mouth had already told Vera all about the ol' farm and what we were doing. I piped up and told Vera in a very serious tone of voice that there might be ghosts in the farm mansion, but she just laughed and said that there wasn't any such thing as any old ghost, but I knew the real truth; that oh yea, there really was such things as ghosts cause I'd already seen one and was even chased by it, her, or what ever the thing was, but I told the truth and they all laughed and so did I telling them I tried, but we all know how it is most people would rather believe a lie and not the truth any how. After a brief discussion on the matter of exploring the farmhouse we all headed across the newly plowed field cause we knew that the farmer was in church that morning and would be going into Muncie as usual to get a few things before he headed back to his place in Old Hyde Park.

Sally and Vera talked constantly all the way to the creek and when we got to the creek Sally was quieter, but Vera just kept on talking. I had to finally tell her if she was to go on with us that she'd just have to keep her dang trap shut a little bit cause her and Sally were like two peas in an I-pod, both the biggest mouthed little girls in all of Hyde Park. As we got closer to that 'ol place Vera become much more quiet as soon as she saw the tremendous size of the big house. She was a little afraid to go on, but we all teased her calling her a scary-cat and a big chicken, Tommy, David and me all knew that girls didn't like to be called names of any kind except for their real names, but that didn't matter to us boys we were loving every minute of teasing Vera and Sally as well…hahahahahaha

As usual, I went in first even though I was scared stiff anyways I climbed through the broken window first so I wouldn't show my real fear that I was so convincingly hiding in front of my friends. Tommy came in next then the two girls and David followed up the rear. Each time I went in that basement window things looked different 'cause there was more clutter than the past two times we'd been in there. David noticed it also, but not Sally cause she was still a bit afraid from the last visit she made here. Tommy hadn't been in the place before and almost threw up at the awful smell, and so did Vera, but they held it all inside and didn't Ralph out their breakfast. I even felt a little queasy cause it seemed like the smell was getting stronger each time as well as the clutter in the basement was becoming all the more damaging to my brain.

Leading our expedition once more back up the stairs through the kitchen that looked as though it had been cleaned a little, back through the long hall, and back into the living room, then through the hidden door up the walled in stair case through the other big door and back into the bed room area in the upper crust of the mansion in the field, and it seemed to be getting easier to take the lead each time I was inside, not that I had a god memory or anything g like that, I always put things in their place, knowing that everything was always in its place especially when in such a creepy abandoned 'ol place like this secluded mansion was.

This time Sally held onto my arm just to make Vera jealous I guess, and Vera held onto Tommy's arm as we all went toward the other side of the squared hall way and toward a room a painting of a man next to it. As I got closer to the picture it started to look like someone I seen some place before, but just where I didn't know, I couldn't place his face in my mind what so ever. Once we were at the new location I'd lead us al too, Vera pulled Sally away from me took hold of my arm, but dummy me didn't know her intent at first glance of the situation. Slowly I pushed the door open a little, the smell that came from the room hit me and my friends square in the noses hard, I slammed the door backing away as did my friends, the smell was so strong, like a dead skunk had been in the room for a life time. None of us were even gonna attempt to go in there as long as it smelled like that, even if there could have been a hidden treasure chest filled with gold and other valuables in it we weren't going to put one foot inside.

We then headed to the next room that had a black ladies painting by it, she looked familiar and she also looked more like a Indian person more than an black lady, her flesh tone had a very dark complexion like an Indian woman, but more-so a light black tone, she had very high cheek bones just like that of an Indian woman that I'd seen before in Muncie on the farm we had on 1522 W. 23rd St. and Cowan Road; she was short and well built with a slight muscular volume to her tiny frame and she was a very-very beautiful lady indeed.

This was becoming to be stranger to me as I ventured onward even if I was afraid I just had to find out more about the people who had once lived here. The room was in good clean shape just like the little girls room was and it looked exactly like her room, it had the very same furniture in it also. Sally ask me why we were in the same room as we were in yesterday and I told her that it was a different room and that she was just getting forgetful or something, she insisted it was the same room as she walked toward the desk and proceeded to pick up the very same items as she picked up before. Everything about this place was just too weird.

Turning towards meanie Sal, I told her: "Hey look what you're picking up, isn't this exactly what you picked up yesterday when we were here". Sally took one step backwards away from the dresser and squelched just like a mouse, looking down at the stuff, she then threw it down on the desk saying that she wanted to go home once more and never come here again, but David told her to go ahead and go on home if she wanted to, and to just take her friend Vera with her, that we boys didn't want them with us in the first place. But they shook their heads no saying that they didn't want to go back by themselves and that they would just stay with us for protection. I laughed and my friends laughed with me calling the two girls fraidy cats. That always got to them and that made us feel good to get even with Sally especially 'cause of her big blabber mouth, and we ate it up like chocolate cake and ice-cream on a hot summer day, and it was a very hot day more-so here inside this creepy 'ol place; I knew that my time in Hyde Park was almost finished and soon I would have to move back to Muncie and leave all of this and my friends behind me, dang the luck.

Once again I felt another presence brush up against me and looked behind me, it was just Vera… she'd grabbed my arm and gave me a little smile of being next to me the brave boy once again. Of course I smiled back and thought to myself yea I am a real brave boy all right, I'm so dang afraid I feel like peeing all over myself right now, but held in all my frightened emotions the best I could under the circumstances of where we were and who I was with, my best friends in the whole world, even the two big mouth girls were my friends too, but between boys , well um boys just weren't supposed to like girls much and if Tommy and David found out I really liked the girls as my friends that would sure put some brakes on the things we did as being best friends that was for certain.

There wasn't much in this room, so we left and went on into the room next to it and it also looked exactly the same, but with a different painting beside it that was an Indian woman's painting and on the inside of the closet area the clothing was all Native American clothing as all the other rooms were of African and European decent. The two girls liked all the clothes and started to play dress up with some of the clothes in the closet; I just looked at them and shook my head from side to side thinking; "Girls, they sure are weird, boy I'm glad I'm a boy". I smiled to myself 'cause I liked both girls at the same time, but m ore-so that cutie pie Vera U. Capruresme, and ya know good n well I liked my best buddies David and Tommy who would never know my secret not now nor never, not in a million years unless I gave way to a slip of my tongue which by the way wanted to slobber all over Vera in a sensual adult way at times.

"Hey look at me", Sally said with a big smile. I'm an Indian woman, ain't I pretty?" All of us boys just laughed and smiled saying yea what ever you think. All I could say a second later was; "Well maybe someday you'll be prettier, but I doubt it!" I knew I'd made a big mistake in that statement and my friends looked at me in awe, but I quickly retracted what I said. "Well maybe some day you might be pretty enough for them clothes, but for right now, you just ain't pretty at all, yer just an ugly duckling looking for a place to hatch". I laughed and so did my friends, and that changed the way they looked at me once again and man was I relieved when their suspicious attitude changed so rapidly. Sally and Vera started to get mad at me and I told 'em to just put a sock in their big mouths or we'd leave them here in this creepy ol' farmhouse with all these ghosts, so they shut up, but man did I ever get a harsh look from both of 'em, the kind of look that could kill a fellow.

It was getting close to lunch time and we were all getting hungry so we decided to go home to eat and come back right after lunch. The two girls wanted to not come back with us, but as usual we teased them so they agreed once again to go back with us to Spooks-Ville Mansion as we nick named it.

As we were leaving the Indians room I thought I heard some one whisper in my ear that I was to stay for awhile, and that I was her great grand son or something, it sure sounded weirder than the voice I'd heard the day before; I shook my head vigorously from side to side and looked around me as I turned in a circle a couple times, and kept looking over my shoulders all the way back through the house to our exit and entry window at the basement. It sure was getting stranger and stranger as time went by, but I could care less now cause I wanted to explore all the more and find out what all this meant as well as find out just who lived there a long, long-long time ago. I knew that the letter said that someone named Nellie Margaret Maxifield the little girl in the painting lived here with her family, but all this seemed so dang strange and the name kept bouncing through my brain like a never ending bouncing ball. It made my brain almost hurt to a point of being ill or maybe insane as the adults called it, or something to that effect, and I just couldn't quite figure out this mystery even if'n my life depended on it.

All the while that I sat at dinner that evening I couldn't stop thinking about everything that had transpired so far and I even went as far as asking my aunt for some Bayer Aspirin. She was concerned that I may be getting sick or something, but I reassured her that I was OK, and that all that was the matter was that I had been playing Tarzan to much lately and she told me to go to bed and relax right after I ate my dinner and maybe I'd feel much better in the morning, and if I didn't then she'd take me to see ol' Doc Millersman in Muncie. I told her I'd be ok and not to worry that I would not play so hard tomorrow so she wouldn't worry about me.

That night I couldn't sleep very well and tossed and I turned all night long, I even had a nightmare about the people in who had lived in that Spooky Mansion. In the morning I woke up so darn tired that my legs was wobbly from running in my sleep and knew that I'd better take things slow and not let on to Aunt Mary or Luke that

I wasn't feeling good and that I was really tired so I wouldn't have to go to town to see the old quack of a doctor. So when I went to the front room I was very peppy in my movements and to them I looked all right and could go play after I ate and done my choirs. That made me feel way better and my headache went away as soon as I ate, but I never let on how I was really feeling that morning. Boy I was really tired and just wanted to go right back to my ol' feather down bed and fall asleep so I could get rid of that awful headache once and for all, but I didn't. I finished eating and did all of my choirs so I could go play with my friends and I had a couple of other things on my little mind beside exploring that 'ol farmhouse, and that was, well I was starting to like tag a long Vera U, but I knew I had best be cool so not to bring attention toward myself, so I did my best to keep my big mouth closed as tight as a barn door if'n I didn't wanna spill the beans about liking Vera.

Chapter 12

The Light inside the Darkness

We were lost in our exploration of the ol' farmhouse, and had found a comfortable place to rest before heading back home. Realizing that it was late in the day, we hoped we wouldn't get into trouble for bein' out so dang late. Being tired and growing relaxed we all fell fast asleep. By the time we woke up it was daylight, but not the usual day light; it scared us out of our wits.

Blackness interred the day about noon and the warm summer winds were screaming at us. Leaves from a tall oak tree blew with a fury, fluttering about to the dew covered ground far below their resting places.

There weren't any birds chirping harmoniously with the winds, and the sun wasn't in the sky at noon like it should be with the darkness covering the whole of the earth from one end to the other; night wasn't any different than the day. Little did we know there an eclipse taking place?

As I stare into the darkness from a broken window just inside the basement, the foul smell had somehow vanished, or we were just use to it, anyways Vera hung on my arm tightly; I couldn't shake the clutches of her hands free from my shirt sleeve. I knew she liked me a whole lot and I was starting to grow fond of her too, and I dare not say anything in front of my friends, lest I get laughed at. Taking some wood and papers from the mildew concrete floor, I piled it all in a heap and lit a fire. In the glow of the fire light made her face shine like a jewel; her jet black hair and light-black cinnamon skin glistened with specks like glitter. Her high cheekbones, light black in tone and her cute little nose were a hued rainbow of luster. Submissively her labia smell brought forth an entertaining thought of kissing her. Ah, and her smile too glowed with a ray of bright white beneath the lightly colored tint of slight-pink and blackish-brown lips that protruded below her cute button nose, cooling my black-eyed Vera's pretty face, bringing her deep thick lustrous hair to full measure that also entertained the same thought. Most of the spectrum of colors was present in the fullness of her beauty, and love was in the air deeply as well. Nonetheless we were all scarred stiff. But through the greater light of the fire, at least for a few minutes, tag a long Vera U was my morning star and the light inside of the darkness.

She smiled at me and I at her as the sun finally shone through from the midst of the short eclipse at noon. It was a moment I will always cherish. Silently we stood there together looking at the daylight shining once again through the broken window, my friends put out the fire faster than I started it and we all scurried from the ol' farmhouse once more heading home at last. On the way, Vera and I lagged behind a couple paces so we could talk for that short time; not bringing much attention to ourselves we chit chatted about our experience together in the dark. Before I knew it, Vera leaned toward me as soon as the others had went through the broken window and out of view, then she planted a kiss right on my mouth just before

Sally looked back at us to see if'n we were coming or not. I was beet red from the little kiss and I prayed that Sally wouldn't notice my blush.

"Come on Vera we have to hurry so we don't get into trouble OK." Sally started to ask me why I was so red, but because of my threats toward her, she kept her big blabber mouth shut as tight as the dead fish she was, man what a smelly 'ol fish she was too.

Looking toward the sky, silently I thanked God for Vera. I knew that sooner or later mean ol' Sally would say something to me just because she was now mad at me for the threats I made toward her, but I just didn't care; and as Sally looked at me with her evil eyes, I just gave it right back to her. I knew just what to say back to Sally if she said one word. I hoped that she would forget some things about our exploration of the ol' farmhouse, especially about me and Vera hanging so dang close together.

The farm was truly a place for the dead and dying. The cries of a family who lost their souls interred my mind like the flutter of water upon ripples of sand flowing through time in my ears as we walked closer toward home. Vera and I talked about the bad vibes we got while inside that farmhouse on our journey home and decided to pretend like we weren't afraid of any ghost just so our friends wouldn't tease us. We also had to be careful not to see each other very much, or we'd get heck about being boyfriend and girlfriend from Sally, David and Tommy and our word would be, YUCK, turned inside out if any of our friends ever mentioned it to others. I had to think of something to throw my friends off balance so Vera and I could continue our love escapades.

I finally arrived safely home the next morning. I was greeted by Luke and my Aunt Mary, who chewed my butt out royal for staying gone all night and not telling them where I was. I had to lie to them, telling them that I fell asleep on the floor at Tommy's house because it was late when the TV show ended, and Tommy's mom and dad went to bed early. I reckon that they believed me, cause it sorta faded into the afternoon as time crept slowly by. I wondered what my friends told their parents, maybe the same thing, but I didn't know for sure. I would have to ask them tomorrow, that is if I even seen them tomorrow. All I knew was that for today, I was in trouble a little and decided to change subjects as much as I could so it would confuse my Aunt Mary and good ol' Luke. Sometimes I was resourceful at doing those sorts of things and other times not so lucky, and if my little butt could talk, it would tell ya how many lickens it had gotten over the past several years.

"Dinner sure was good tonight, are we going to have any sweets for desert, it sure would taste good after all that delicious fried chicken". I was really trying the best that I could to make my Aunt Mary feel good about me.

Maybe a little more buttering her up would do the trick. Not telling her where I was at the night before had its toll on me a wee bit and maybe I felt a little guilty for staying gone all night, but those things do happen. When they do, there is nothing a fellow can do except lie through his teeth, change subjects a lot, and fill the air with all sorts of good compliments just to get back on her good side. Luke sure was a different story though, that was one thing for certain. He didn't believe half of what was told to him and the other half he was a bit skeptical about, so I knew that I had my work cut out for me when it came down to putting butter on good ol' Luke Dillon.

Morning came fast! Luke was up at the crack of dawn cutting wood for the soon to come winter. According to the Farmers Almanac, this coming winter was supposed to be a lulu and he wanted to prepare way ahead of everyone in the community. Sawing and chopping sounds made it almost impossible to sleep, so I got outta bed and went to help Luke store the wood in his battered ol' shed. He would soon be working on it as well. I rushed to get dressed and snuck quietly out the back door so not to disturb my Aunt Mary Belle who was fast asleep in her feather down bed; after all it was only five in the morning. I didn't mind getting up early because that gave me more time to play after my breakfast and choirs.

It seemed to be a different world now, but somehow I just couldn't quite put my fingers on it. Things were happening way too fast, and that really bothered me lots, 'cause I wanted to stay in Hyde Park for ever and ever, and all the while that Luke and I gather and store the wood; I worked on buttering him up a little like I did with my Aunt Mary, and maybe he'd talk my aunt into stayin' longer; it seemed to be working well for me too, but somehow it seemed to me that ol' Luke knew what I was doing all along, he pretended by just playing along with me. Ol' man Dillon had a way about him like no other man in our community had, and that taught me how to be a real man over time. He was a real smooth operator in his own way, even with his mean streak, I still liked his attitude somewhat, cause it taught me what life should be like when I eventually grew up ta be a man.

The choir was all done and I had only taken me and him about an hour or so to store the wood and then we went inside to fix some pancakes, eggs, and good ol' jowl beacon for our breakfast, but Aunt Mary was already up fixing all that stuff, and boy were we men folk sure were hungry; I could eat a whole side of beacon and a hen-house full of eggs, I knew Luke was more hungry than I was by the way he piled his plate clean full to almost running over the edged and she knew it because she fixed more than the usual amount of food, and I sure was glad cause I could have eaten a whole skillet plumb full, but I was satisfied with what she fixed for me; and Luke was too, I guess, because he even ask for more, but not me, no way was I gonna ask and besides I was stuffed to the brim with cackle berries and ol' jowl beacon strips.

"I'm stuffed, gee your sure a great cook, and Luke is a good man and your both wonderful."

I stopped short so not to over do it and I knew that I had both of them pretty well buttered up and ask since I had helped Luke put the wood in the shed if I could please go to my best friend Tommy's house to play for a spell. Luke smiled at Aunt Mary Belle with a half grin-half frown sort of smiley face; you know the look, one that if I had said another word would have killed a person. I sat there waiting patiently with my hands in my lap under the table twirling my thumbs slowly not sayin' another word; and, all I done was smile real big with a Chihuahua sort of look on my eyes. It was one that no one could resist. Finally after a couple of minutes she said yes. But she told me that I had better be home by dinner time, or I wouldn't be allowed to play for a week. Smiling bigger than usual I told her thank you, then turned toward Luke and thanked him as well. I started to bounce outta my chair with springs on my feet, but slowed down a notch or two so I wouldn't hit my knees on the table so I wouldn't be yelled at again. I thanked them again excusing myself and assured them both that I would be home by around five in the evening cause that was when we ate dinner.

Turning slowly, I opened the door in a gentlemanly like manner and stepped outside.

Leaping off the bottom step, I took off towards the woods behind the little house. As I hurdled our fence in a hap hazard hurry I almost hit a tree, as I made the left turn toward the dirt path to Tommy's house. I didn't give my aunt, or Luke a chance to say another word when I ran behind the house, knowing they were about to say something, but I was long gone before I let that happen. Lickety-split I speed down the path ducking tree branch after tree branch that hang over it. Breaking some of 'em as I speed along at a lightning pace just like the locomotive going under Hill Street Bridge, but it didn't matter because us kids were always breaking branches from lots of trees in the woods just as the train done on its track. There were so dang many of 'em that by the time the next year rolled around a new branch had already grown back in the broken one's place. It took not much more than three or four minutes passed till I reached the front of Tommy's place from mine, boy was that the fastest I had ever made it to his house, or any other place as far as that went. I sure was proud of myself for achieving the speed that morning even if I was tired from all the work I done.

Mr. Fulkler answered the door and told me that Tommy, his brothers and sister couldn't play. They had to stay home a couple of days because they stayed out all night not telling their dad where they were at last night. They got their little butts blistered or something because I heard what sounded like David, and Sally crying in the background, but not Tommy, was always trying his best to be the strong one, well sometimes he was, but other times I seen him cry his brown eyes almost right outta his face.

I didn't hang around begging him to let them play, so I told him to let them know I came by, that I would see them in a few days. When I left I started to walk down the dirt road instead of going back through the woods when here come Vera running after me yelling for me to wait up. Quickly my skinny 'lil body turned as she approached my back and I gave her a funny look asking her if she got in trouble like David, Tommy and Sally and she said no, because she lied big time to her mom, and she believed every word of what Vera told her, just like when I told my aunt that I fell asleep at Tommy's house, she told an even bigger whopper than I did. Vera had told her mom the exact same thing, except she added that she ate too much junk food, candy, and got sick, so Mrs. Fulkler had her to lay on the floor then covered her up with a blanket; that she would let her mom know that Sunday in church, but that never happened and was forgotten about real soon by her mom, but Vera and I would always know exactly what did happen that night. It would always be our very own little secret.

I guess her and I had almost the same thoughts or something like that when we were headed home the day before yesterday. I don't remember her telling me, or I telling her what sort of lie to say, and it seemed to me like we were on the same wave length when we were together that summer day. From that time on Vera and I seemed to almost always have the same thought pattern during that whole summer. I ask her if she wanted to play in the woods with me, but she told me that she would rather explore that big ol' farmhouse mansion with me instead and that it would give us a chance to be all alone for once so we could talk proper instead of having to whisper or play like we didn't like one another. I agreed with her and off we went hand in hand back toward the woods, past her house that was on the opposite side of Tommy's place, but little did we know that Tommy was up in his room where the dormer hung over their porch and was looking outta his window right at us sobbing like a scolded puppy?

Taking a short cut to Buck Creek and our little bridge, we laughed at the silliest little things as we made our way through the woods toward the field full of sticker bushes, and it seemed as though every time we crossed the field, our socks and shoes filled with those painful stickers; we knew we would have to remove our shoes once we reached the mansion. Finally we reached the basement window where we always climbed through. Sitting down next to the broken down ol' dresser, we took our shoes off to pull out the stickers, as we did, we laughed, giggled and gently pushed each other for the plain fun of doing it. Vera bent over a couple times kissing me on the cheek, causing me to blush. Naturally as any kid would do, I wiped the kisses off my cheek giggling, and inside I not only liked the kisses, I was bewildered with the soft feeling of them on m y cheek at the same time, not knowing what to really think. I didn't have the slightest clue what she was up to, but it just didn't matter 'cause it made me a real happy camper that's all I knew from the shear experience of her pleasurable company durin' the times we spent together as kids.

"Stop that, please Vera." I said as I wiped off the second little peck on the cheek, giggling a tiny bit and then I smiled real big at the same time and kept on laughing, giggling and turning even redder than I already was.

"Alright Eddie, if ya say so. Hehehehehe." She said; giggling at the same time she plucked the stickers' outta her pink and white socks. I looked at her and couldn't resist sending a kiss right back to her, but mine was smack dab on her full plump moist and juicy lips.

"Eddie; wow, where'd that come from?" She blinked her big black eyes a couple times smiling so big that it looked like a full moon, but with glowing white teeth attached to it.

"I couldn't help it Vera, I hope you liked it... did ya?" I asked as I kept pluckin out the stickers from her socks.

Not saying a word, she threw her arms around me and laid a wild wet kiss right back on my lips and I almost passed out, but held my swooning feeling, and when she stopped I just stared at her like she was some sort of magical creature none like I'd ever seen before in my life... Vera was so pretty the way she dressed herself, she always smelled real good too; I didn't know what type of soap she used, but all I knew was that I liked the fragrance; it was a sweet apple blossom smell, not like any other I had ever encountered before. I finally got my senses back and was able to think clear once again.

Yelp, this sure was real nice being with Vera, just me and her all alone! Her dress had the cutest little red and white bow on the back; it accented her little butt to a tee, she had one of them new dread-lock hair styles, short and full of curly waves to just above her stout little muscular shoulders. It was a deep dark black, with a deep shinny dark bluish tent to the under coating in it with highlights of golden brown flesh, and it too smelled real nice and clean. She looked and smelled like a fancy bowl filled with chocolate pudding with an ever so slightest hint of vanilla as a flavorin', and I wanted to clean her bowl totally clean when ever an opportunity grabbed me and put me in the mood to do such a sweet thing.

After I finished plucking the stickers' outta my ol' smelly white socks and from the cuff of my trousers, and then I reached down toward Vera's left foot, gently pulled off her sock, plucking stickers out of it for her; she seemed to be going slower than she usually did for some unknown reason, but I didn't mind one little bit, because the way she was setting, I could see her mid section very clear, she had no panties on and the full Monty of her little thing sparkled right in my eyeballs. Maybe she wanted me to help her, but being a boy, well boys my age just didn't do such things, but since opportunity grabbed me by my happy little brain, I did the unthinkable. I bent toward her planting another big wet kiss right on her soft light brown full flavored lips and almost laid her down for the extreme exploration, but held myself back so she wouldn't slap me... She was sorta stunned and fluttered her eye lashes with the speed of a hummingbird's wing.

"Why... Eddie?" She said with a smiling and shocked look at the same time. Her dark brown cheeks turned the brightest red that there ever was in the color spectrum of crayons, they were almost a bloody barn red with a glow that almost blinded me for a second or two.

"There." I said with a big smeary grin on my face. "Your socks are all cleaned up now, let's go inside and wonder around where we left off in the upper rooms the other day OK."

Vera smiled and giggled at the same time, slobbering a little on the front of her dress. Her mouth was still moist like the flow from the waters of ol' Buck Creeks. I climbed through the window first, immediately she followed me to the point of almost allowing me to crawl up her dress tail, but this time I didn't see anything except her cute little butt wiggle in my face under the darkness of her dress as she shimmied down onto the concrete floor of the basement in the midst of more rubble that was there when we were there the last time. I quickly pulled her dress off my face smiling at her with a want in my eyes that was even un-becoming of even an adult. Man, oh man, I still smell the sweet blossom that came from beneath her dress as my nose touched her butt and private part. Yummy I thought to myself, maybe something will happen, yeah, something real nice I thought to myself and chuckled turning a little redder as I pulled her dress from off my head. I knew that I had a bad mind for a little boy, but damn it, I just couldn't help myself when I was around my beautiful princess Vera.

Trying to take my filthy mind off all that beautiful black flesh of Vera's, I looked at the neatly piled up broken furniture in one pile; a musk smell ol' clothing in a different pile filtered its stink to my nose, but what I had just smelled coming from Vera's behind helped me over come the rubbles musty odors. Vera held her nose for a few seconds along with her breathe but she couldn't hold it very long and let out a big woosh of air as she shouted out with a YUCK so to get her mind outta the gutter as well, I don't know, but it sure seemed that way.

There was some trinkets in still another pile, and papers in a fourth pile, that weren't there before, well at least not in such neatness any way. Vera looked at me and me at her, she looked scared, but smiled at me with her wanting eyes none - the – less, she turned to climb back out the window, but I grabbed her by the bow on her pretty black dress pulling her back toward me questioning her as to what she was doing.

"Eddie." She said as the goose-pimples popped out all over her smooth black skin. "I wanna go home, um, this, um this stuff wasn't here before was it? I'm frightened!"

Goose bumps covered her arms, rap - a - tap - tap went her shivering knees against one another, looking at me and the piles of rubble, she tried to pull away once more, but I clung onto the back of her now untied dress bow as tight as I could. Vera turned toward me and said.

"Eddie, I really do want to go OK, so PLEASE let go of my dress OK, come on now, I said please." She started to climb back upon the box that we'd placed next to the basement window, but I didn't let go of the other end of her belt that had formed a little bow around her cute little slim waist.

"Vera please, why do you want to go home when we just got here a little while ago I'll protect ya, come on now sweetie, stay so we can have some more fun, maybe we can if ya wanna?" Stopping in mid stream of my thought I looked at her still shivering face as I looked at the neat piles of rubble and then deep into her big dark eyes.

"There ain't anything to be scarred of Vera my sweet; I'm here to protect ya OK." Being afraid a little myself, I dare not let on like I was. I reassured her that there wasn't anybody or anything here in this spooky ol' place. I was afraid a little as well, but as usual I didn't let on like I was. In a calm and gentle tone of voice with smiles that looked genuine so I could hide my fear I assured her that there wasn't anybody, or anything here in this spooky 'ol place, because I wanted to spend more time with her alone while we had the chance, but she convinced me to go back outside so she could potty. After we climbed out the window, Vera went behind a bush to take a tinkle, I tried to follow her, but she pushed me back and then giggled a little.

"Eddie, (she heehawed) now d-don't you dare try to peek at me while I go potty OK, I, I have to go really, really bad, don't look. She giggled once again with an invitation laugh and smiled at me and then gave me the ok wink that she really did want me to look at her while she went potty. She then called from behind the bush.

"Now cover your eyes OK, Eddie, ya hear me. (She heehawed once again) Hehehehehe."

"Okay, if you say so." I heehawed right back as she began to tinkle behind the bush and let out a whopper of a fart from goin' poop too. I just smiled with a shit eatin' half smile, and she returned the favor right back to me, this gave me an OK indication to sneak a peek at her while she took a pee behind the bushes, so as soon as she was behind the bush, I snuck slowly beside it poking my head ever so slightly to see what I could see; hehehehehe. I was in awe at the smooth light brown flush that oozed the pee out from below her dress, smiling, I slowly walked backwards to where I was before with a tingling setting itself inside me like none I'd ever experienced before in my small life.

Finally Vera came from behind the bush smiling at me like she wanted to attack me or something, and somehow I felt that she knew I'd watched her go potty, but not a word was said about the incident of her taking a pee in the bush, and I wasn't about to mention that I'd really watched her potty either at least for this time any way.

I kept in my mind that soon I would be moving back to Muncie. I didn't know if I'd ever see her or my best friends Tommy, David, and oh yes even mean-fat little Sally, (the bull-blabber mouth of the community) ever again in my life time. I wanted to make this summer the best I'd ever had in my seven years of life, yelp seven, that was a magical number. I heard folk say that it was supposed to be a good luck number, and at that moment it sure was good luck for me.

We sat there by the bush for awhile so she could get her composure and I my senses back in there proper place. I convinced her that everything was all right and there wasn't anything to fear except the word fear itself and I almost had myself convinced as to what I was telling Vera that morning in the basement of Spooks-Ville, ghost haven, or what ever else one might call this creepy ol' place later on down pathways of life.

I knew what I seen and heard. The image and sounds were in the pit of my stomach, but deep down inside of me I just wanted to spend time alone with Vera at least for this one day anyways; 'cause being alone with her would be worth every moment of being frightened by spooks, ghosts or what ever they were that lived inside the ';ol farmhouse mansion of Buck Creek.

"Vera, lets go back in, everything is okay. We need to go back upstairs again so we can search some of the other rooms that we didn't get a chance to explore when we were here a couple weeks ago OK."

I said with a half way smile. A little bit of fear showed through as well, but Vera didn't notice my worried eyes, they were hidden behind my smile. Somehow she seemed to know that I was just as afraid as she was, but Vera never said a single solitary word to me either, boy was I ever so glad too, because if she ever said I was just as afraid as she was, I wouldn't be able to live it down, and that was a worse fear than being in this creepy place.

Once back inside, we headed back up the stairs, they were as creaky as before but; the atmosphere seemed a little different, maybe it was because just Vera and I were exploring the place together without our friends to poke fun and all, all I knew was that I liked the idea of being alone with sweet Vera U, but none – the -less even with a good air about it, the room seemed to be filled with a presence that I just didn't feel comfortable having around me. It just plain gave me the creeps. Approaching the crest of the stairs, Vera stopped just shy of the last step, turned toward me shaking, as I looked into her deep dark eyes she threw both of her arms around me giving me a bear hug that almost left me breathless. I knew that she felt comfortable being around me and I felt the same when I was with her, but she somehow she seemed a little different at that moment, and I just couldn't figure out why? The next thing I knew she'd taken a couple really deep breathes of air and smiled at me in a sinisterly strange way… she looked deep into my eyes like she wanted to eat me alive or something and it almost scared me to death, but I maintained my composure, because I was the brave boy she grew to know me for being.

"Oh, there, I feel much better now, thank you for being such a good friend to me 'cause I really do like you a whole lot." Vera just smiled once again and grabbed me by my hand pulling me forward up the last two steps. "Come on Eddie; let's play in my room for awhile." Vera fumbled her words a little, then exclaimed. "Um, um, I mean this little girls room that we were in the last time we came upstairs!"

I looked beside me and there was another set of stairs on the other side of a huge fancy door laced with gold trim. I leaned my head toward it to peek inside for a brief moment before she pulled my arm really hard. As I stumbled slightly I shouted with a tiny bit of pain.

"Ouchy, what the Hell'd ya do that fer Vera?"

She didn't hesitate a minute longer and pulled me harder toward the little girls door, quickly opening it. I had a hard time saying anything; all I had a chance to do was gaze at her with bewilderment, but she pulled me still harder, I had no choice but to stumble after her into the room. Bang went the door as it as it slammed behind us, appearing to be in such a rush to entrap us behind its foul play like a thief in the night commin' ta takes us away. The bang echoed throughout the house like a kettle drum in rapid concession with each beat, I stood there looking at Vera as she picked up a hair brush from the floor, and walked to the wall mirror brushing her heir a couple times in front of it. Strange things have happened here, but this was getting' really scary; she put the brush down when she realized that she had just got a new dreadlock hair style a couple days before and was never to brush, or comb it as long as she had that type of style on her pretty little head.

"Do you like me Eddie?" Vera had that always wanting look on her face that she had acquired from the climb-in incident. She stood there just staring into the mirror with a blank sort of look in her eyes as though she wasn't even there at all. I started to walk closer to her and ask her what the heck she was doing, but she turned abruptly really fast.

"Stop right there mister, do not come closer until you answer me, please just answer me OK!" she demanded like an adult about to whop my butt again. I was stunned by her sudden rudeness and the way she calling me mister made me almost pee my pants. Somehow

I felt that it wasn't Vera I was talking to and she acted and looked like Vera, for the most part, except until we reached the top of the stairs close to all those strange rooms. Her appearance seemed to have changed to almost a shadow like, or double type image all rolled into one person.

"I, I, I guess so V-Vera." I stuttered for the first time that I could ever remember. "I, I guess, yes V-Vera, I d-do, I like you, why are you um, looking at me that way?" I just kept on a stuttering some because the way she acted made me a little nervous, I had never acted that way before, in my entire life, but with all of the creepy things that was going on lately in this creepy 'ol mansion, I just couldn't seem to control my actions. I was nervous anyway since I fell head over heals for sweet Vera U.

"Let's just go to a different room across the hall OK, I have never been in there and want to see what it looks like after all this time, come on, let's go, NOW." She said with a forceful tone of tone.

"I'd rather go up the next set of stairs and look inside there for awhile ummm O-OK." My nerves were getting a little shaky and she was really getting to me, making me so frightened that it might show itself to her pretty eyes. Still shocked by her actions, I kept following along. I started to think that she was just playing to see just how afraid I could really get or something. Nevertheless, I started to smile again as the fear slowly faded away.

"Hell No Mister you'll do what I wanna do." She shouted even louder.

Her rudeness was appalling to my ears, and I wanted ta just slap it right outta her so we could get on with just exploring and maybe later we could conduce a different kind of play if the opportunity grabbed us again. She grabbed my hand once again, pulling me from the little girls' room running ran out, dragging me right behind, almost on her heals and dress tail. I almost fell a couple times in the whole ordeal, but didn't fall to the floor like a newly caught fish to flop around and eventually be eaten by some big 'ol monster or some little girl-woman so to say.

"Hey, slow down Vera. Why are you in such a hurry to explore those rooms across the hall?" I asked as I put on the brakes of both feet on at the same time skidding about a foot or so before we both came to a sudden stop. At the second bend of the open top hall way that went in a square beside an open pit in the middle. I was looking down one side of the hall that had a very light reddish rain streaming through it from the inside. I gulped a couple of times swiping a small amount of sweat from off my forehead and then proceeded to fling it on the floor beside me, but it sotta splattered on Vera instead.

"Sorry, um, just that I, um well, I wanna really see what is in that man's room on the other side of the hall, I thought I heard some sort of funny sound coming from that direction when we first came up here and I'm curious OK. Are you starting to be afraid of being with me?" Vera asks with a pouting look as she gazed down at the floor.

I too looked down toward the floor as well, telling her I wanted to look in there as well, but we needed to take a little more time in doing it, because it was so spooky here, and I reminded her that I wanted to look in the other stairway to see where it led to after we left this area. As we stood there for a few minutes, I watched the winds whip the hair about her shinny brown face. The wall had a small hole in it letting the wind whisk inward toward the hallowed hall way. Somehow things almost felt like we were deep in the Amazon basin of Brazil, or maybe in the deep dark jungle's of Africa someplace, our setting was almost like a tropical breeze flowing all around us with a very humid atmosphere as if we were in a rain forest that we somehow discovered with a Mayan, or African style fence of stone that had inlaid marble tiles on the floor of some ancient pyramid right there in the midst of the ol' farmhouse mansion. It was the wildest thought and one so mysterious, but I always thought of strange things at strange times, more so when I was tired and so afraid deep down on my insides., but what on God' green earth was it doing there was anyone's guess. I thought, and shook my head in order to clear some of the strange cob webs from my mind in order to clear my little pea brain of imagination.

"What the Hell?" I sort of shouted out loud in a burst of frustration. Vera just looked at me, and it seemed that she was looking right through me, beyond my essence and deep into my very soul.

"Eddie!" Vera said as she just gazed at me with puzzlement in her voice. "I, I, I thought you never said such words like hell, where did that come from?" She asked me with a shocking look. I responded to her with the exact same answer as she blinking her eyes a couple times, she smiled telling me it was just so creepy in here and that it made her uncomfortable to be with me and in a way I wanted to sort of stay away from her, but on the other side I couldn't for the obvious reasons that filtered inside my devious little mind.

Our exploration and taking small tokens, not salvation, was our quest and saying such words as hell just somehow didn't seem bad at the time, but we both knew that we would have to repent when we went to church that next Sunday for saying such bad words, and stealing things that belonged to the folk who lived here, telling lies, and having nasty thoughts of making the wild thing inside a spooky ol' mansion farmhouse, but hey, we didn't know any better, we were just kids. This time I grabbed Vera giving her a bear hug, I really tried to encourage her to take a little more time exploring this ol' house with me, but all she seemed to want was my love. I guess her hormones were kicking in just a tad earlier than most girls, man oh man I sure wanted her as well, but I'd have to wait till I was older, much older to have that kind of fun with a girl cause at my age and hers it wasn't possible to engage in that sortta activity, but it sure could be one heck of an extra-curricular activity if you'd want to call it that?

All that huggin' and kissing among other stuff in our other exploration felt good but at the same time Vera was scarin' me all the more with her adult like attitude and mannerism, but I somehow didn't mind too much bein' a kid and all... hahaha.

As we walked slowly toward the room where the painting of the man was hanging, approaching the door, feeling another presence, a different presence than that I'd encountered next to the little girls door. I had to use my personification of qualities traditionally associated with my male sex, including: courage, strength, and aggression in order to engage in the unexpected. This one made me shiver and produced goose bumps all over my entire body, and they tingled like nothing I'd ever felt before in my seven years of life. It was almost like something interred into my body trying to take control, but what ever it was that made me shiver all the sudden left my company, as I looked at Vera, and she at me as we stood silent in front of that big oak door with a small door knocker on it that looked like an Indians head or something close to that effect, but I couldn't quite make out the image because it was so faded as though something had been knocking on it for centuries causing it to slowly wear out with time.

At that moment the door opened all by itself as we stepped close to it. We hesitated for a couple of minutes looking straight at the open door, then we both turned our heads ever so slightly glancing inside the huge room that lay dormant before our silver dollar sized eyes and quivering knees. Knowing how I was feeling, but never looking at Vera's expression I stepped one foot closer to the room and poked my head just inside a little to see if anyone was inside the room or not. My eyes were still huge and almost ready to pop their sockets.

"Um, Um, uuumm is any, anyone there." I asked with trembling tones of fear.

My lower lip quivered and my knees shook like a newly made bowl of Jell-O; stepping closer around the corner, and thinking I had a hold of Vera's hand, but instead it was just the door knob that I had my hand on, walkin' inside I pulled the door closed behind me leaving Vera outside the room with silence all around glaring at the room with emptiness inside my head. As I looked around the room, it was almost empty, but a presence of something wicked surrounded me like the Devil himself was in the room. My body shook like an earthquake had grabbed me. It was pitch dark except for a small faint glow by a table in one corner, the light seemed to be emerging itself towards me with an ireful display of being invaded upon… straining my eyes to look closer at what was coming my way, I almost jumped outta my skin, it was extremely unattractive, ludicrous, and grotesque, and I almost froze right to the smelly, dingy and slimy moss covered floor beneath my wet feet I turned slowly, but slid with each motion I made trying to escape the horror that bestowed my hazel eyes.

"Vera, V-Vera." I muttered, stuttered and turned towards her, but she wasn't there.

I turned to grab the door knob, but it wasn't there. I tried desperately to find it, but it still wasn't there; panic set in like the light was after me or something, and then my body started to sweat, and a cold chill interred me like frozen Buck Creek in the dead of winter.

Here in Hyde Park, winters were extremely cold and snowy. Ice cycles seemed to be forming all over my frail little body like those that had hung from our house in the middle of last winter here in the forestry countryside. Not one single thing had ever felt like this, except being next to Buck Creek, and the cornfield that had zilch growing in it in the silence of the snowy season. Frozen platelets were forming on me and I felt wet clear down to my bones. Death seemed to be all around me, and as I turned around, right right in front of my eyes was a man with a sword in one hand, he was dressed in a black butler type suit with a long ruffled shirt that was buttoned all the way to his fat little chin, his eyes bulged outward with insanity, his tongue hung out like a dog in heat and he seemed to be coming right toward me ever so slowly. My eyes peered right through him, and all I could see was the cracked brick wall that stood behind him, glancing to his right there was a beautiful woman dressed all in white with a white hat on her full head of dark-dark coal black hair that was blowing ever so slightly with a breeze that was coming through the blood red curtains behind her and faint reddish rain was still flowing through the rickety walls like in the hallway.

I tried to scream like the whistle on the locomotive, but something seemed to have a choke hold on my vocal cords and wouldn't let go of it, turning around with the speed of my hero and western movie star the Lone Ranger, I grabbed for the door knob once more, my hands seemed to know where that door knob was the whole time, even in the pitch black I was somehow able to pull the door open way too fast that it hit the wall bouncing closed behind me as I leaped out of the room, Vera was just standing there laughing her fool head off at me for some strange reason, pee trickled down my leg and spotted the front of my pants next to my zipper, not enough to notice a whole lot, but it was enough to flow down my leg enough to make my right sock wet with a pissy smell that I had no choice but to live with at the time.

My breath was steaming like a tea kettle atop of Luke's ancient wood stove in his tiny kitchen, and the more I panted, I felt like the locomotive engine that used to pick me up behind our place on 1522 W. 23rd and Cowan Road, that was one of the two farms we had in Muncie, but not the one we were going to move back to at the end of summer. Sweat rushed down my face as though I'd fell into Buck Creek once again. I grabbed Vera's hand at last and pulled her with all my might, but she didn't budge, she just laughed at me even harder than previous and the more I stare at her the harder she laughed and that it made a trickle of pee pop out onto her pretty dress as well and as I looked at Vera with horror and ask her in my shivering voice that went up in tone just a bit.

"W-what the S-SAM HELL ARE YOU LAUGHING AT, L-Let's get the heck outta here, there is a man in that room with a sword, and he was coming right after me, and I think he killed the lady that was in the room with him." My voice was beginning at get weaker inside from all the yelling, I grabbed her by the hand and pulled her with the force of a hurricane, once more, yanking her a couple feet behind me, but she kept on a laughing all the louder scaring the, pardon my words here, but the holy shit right outta me so much that I almost crapped my pants on top of pissing them for real.

Vera stopped all the sudden and screamed at me in a different voice than hers.

"WHERE THE HELL DO YOU THINK YOU ARE TAKING ME, I BELONG HERE WITH ALL OF MY MAMMAS."

She toned her voice down a little bit as I pulled her another foot or so. I stopped dead in my tracks for some odd reason and my voice seemed to change as well, but it didn't seem to bother me in the least.

"Your right, Mattie, we do belong here. I belong with you, and you belong with your five other mommies."

My face was a paler than pale white and I had no expression whatsoever, nor did I know what the hell I was even saying at the time. I shook my head a couple times so hard it gave me a head ache. I shook it once more; turning toward Vera and done something that I had never done before in my entire life and that was slapping a girl in the face for the first time ever in my life, Vera looked at me and returned the favor and as we both stood face to face for a brief moment and rubbed our faces we came back to our senses from the ordeal of being possessed by some sort of entity that had taken control if our minds.

"Why did you slap me Eddie?" She said with tears in her eyes.

"Why did you slap me Vera? I just want to get the heck outta here, let's go now, OK."

"No, we must stay and look in some other rooms, there must be some reason for our strange behavior. I don't know what it is, but we best try to find out what happened in this ol' place, all right?" I was rude to her for just a few seconds, but I just didn't really care one way or the other how I treated her that moment.

Vera wiped the tears from her pretty deep-dark black eyes and sortta smiles outta the corner of her mouth, it was watering with saliva like a mad dog and it ran all the way to her cute little, half dimpled, soft black button shaped chin dripping on the bottom of her dress along with the already snotty covered hem, somehow there was an imaginary line of uneasiness pulling us to the edge of our wits as if the devil had his clawed hands on not only Vera, but me as well with his deep red burning eyes so full of tension; a Hell-red grin had pierced our very souls with thoughts unbecoming of two young and innocent children as we both were… or so we thought, this time there was no child's play, but that of the beast from the depths of Hell itself.

His scene lay in wait for the both of us as we continued to explore the ol' mansion of creeps. This was his home and the graveyard was his neighborhood to play in with the unsuspecting who dare inter his domain and as we lingered apprehensively in the midst of demonic spirits who were trying comprehensibly to gain all the poor souls they could, including ours if we'd let them, but we fought them off in our struggle for survival. Our parents as well as the other members of our community would be shocked to absolute death if they knew what danger us kids were in, so we swore to each other that not one single solitary word would ever get back to our parents, or our friends parents and all the nosy neighbors in Hyde Park.

In that mansion there was no Halloween party, and for certain not any Trick or Treat candy to be sought subsequent to and considered by Vera, or me, but the quest for sanity amongst the imaginary realm of Voodoo, witchcraft, demonic spirits and the provoked, ridiculed - tormented souls that had been ravished at the hands of just plain bad vibes of life that was a part of our inward thoughts and only means of escape back to reality, not that of the insanity state that we were in at that instant. Skeletons with a strong liking, taste, or tendency for something especially for fire and a pronged farming tool with a long handle and three widely spaced, slightly curved prongs, that is used for stacking, turning, and moving hay were all around us. This was the extraordinarily scary thought that went through both our little heads, but we had to be brave, at least I did, I knew it deep down inside my guts, and I had to snap outta the spell the devil had a hold of me with so I could protect not only my soul and life, but that of Vera as well.

In this past's creepy residency, our sounds of psyche-scarring nightmares would not be heard until some century in the future if we lost our battle to save our souls from Hell and the Devil himself. Even the smallest glimpse of him would carry our spirits away on a train of fire to place them in the very pits of brimstone and thick pitched black smoke that lay in our path if we didn't come back to our senses really fast. Vera and me was the few and the brave who dare to make the journey through this big house by ourselves and if we survived and was able to tell about our experiences, then we'd be dubbed as either heroes or locked away in some asylum for the rest of our natural born lives, and not see daylight ever again, as well as to not be able to collect one piece of delicious chocolate candy handed out in those devilish little baskets standing in front of the soft and dark glow of a strangers doorway that up and coming Halloween. Flirting with Vera was one thing, but flirting with spooks and death was still another.

It would be a night when children would dress up as witches or ghosts and go from door to door asking for candy and threatening to play tricks on all that if refused to give way to a wonderfully delicious candy treat. It was back in a time that only Celtic peoples celebrated the childish holiday, but now popular in the United States, Canada, and the United Kingdom.

My mind wondered how the people living back in the late 1700's and 1800's took all the pressures of life and death while living in the same house for years under extenuating circumstances that were beyond their control. Most families had only poverty and lots of kids to contend with, but when they brought other relatives as well as once in awhile a stranger or two into the household that needed a place ta stay, even if for such a short period of time must have been very difficult in the least and by takin' food and bedding space away from the original families survival in a strange wilderness land full of many dangers like wild animals, wild savage Indians, outlaws, and the latest trend that was filtering its way to the new territory, prostitution amongst the black slaves as well as the white' and Indians of the 1800's era and the new territory of Indiana sure did make it difficult on the new settlers, that was one thing for certain. Life was hard enough and when death hit a family of community, it took its' toll on everyone around with much depression and stress, and to make an effort to live normally in conditions so malicious, that not even the world beyond would have one sterile thought of contentment for those who enter therein, and when a stranger with bad intent invaded the privacy of a home and its inhabitants, that meant real danger and disaster.

The house was not only a dwelling for the Maxifield family, but a stronghold and safe haven away from the many Indian wars and the Civil War as well when it took place for all who needed help in times when things wasn't what it should be for them? The Maxifield family would always welcome any stranger no matter what or who they were even if they were on the run away from what little law was chasing them across the territory through the sometimes hostile environments of the old west.

I had to keep selective ideals and occasionally clever thoughts so imaginative that even they would entertain the ghosts, ghouls, mean ol' Gray Wolf, Voodoo Princess and what ever else that occupied this spooktacular place.

"Vera this family must have had a circus here at one time by the way all of those wild animals were scattered all over the den and other areas. I wondered if they had clowns to make funny faces like this back then." I made a weird smiley face with my fingers in my mouth and stuck out my tongue making a bluulala lala pllllluts sound, and then giggled like an idiot just to make Vera laugh so neither one of us wouldn't be so scared any more.

We walked still further through the creepy place and looked in several other rooms before we decided to stop and eat some wild field snacks that we'd gathered along the way; Vera and I wondered through the corridors of time and horror time and the winds flew in all directions except to direct us to head back home, and as we sat there, I told her a joke that some of my friends had told to me in the cornfield clearing we'd made the fall before. It sortta cheered not only her up, but me as well.

"Your so funny Eddie, how do you come up with such funny things like you do all the time, even when your afraid."

I crinkled my eyebrows a tiny bit and looked at her and wondered how she knew I was afraid, and then I giggled still another silly noise that made her really ease her tension and mine and didn't let on like a scary-cat or big chicken, but she knew somehow that I was just as frightened as she was the whole time we'd been together while exploring Spooks-Ville mansion.

The next room we went into was one that sent cold chills up and down my spine. It had the atmosphere of where the devil himself lived. There was a throne that had two cauldrons, one on each side of its cold trimmed back and seat of what looked like blood red crushed velvet. There was an alter made from imported black and white marble in front of a huge fire place that must have held its chimney up to the tallest part of the house; I walked over to it and held my hand over the area where the fire was once lit, heat still radiated from a mound of ashes, wood logs and a couple lumps of charred coal that seemed to be smoldering beyond the mantle's wire-screen grate in a pit of darkness. As I looked closer into the char of ashes, there were several bones that looked like a human arm and leg and the lower part of a persons jaw bone with most of its teeth intact in their blackened sockets.

We left the room almost as fast as we entered it, and continued our investigative journey into the great unknown of the mansion.

Summer was going by way too fast and I didn't have much time left to spend with her and wanted to make the most of it while I had the chance to. She told me that she would try to slow down some, but all I wanted was to see as much of the house as I possibly could, before I left for Muncie, but at the same time I too wanted her.

As we hugged, our bodies clung to each other like plastic wrap clinging to some leftover chicken from last night's supper. It felt real nice hugging her close like that, the closeness felt like a phoenix rising inside of me, my whole body wanted to turn me into a bull fighter that had just received a tremendous gore from an angry bull's horns and my mind was gone for a moment into ecstasy sending me into ecstasy and almost out for the count, conversant with wonderful feelings like I'd never felt before, but incapable of action. I knew that I'd best stop indulging in fantasies about Vera U and me, so we could get on with our exploration before it got too late. After all, I had to be home at a certain time and only had a couple more hours of exploration left before we had to get back to reality and home.

"We'd bettet get goin' 'cause I need ta get home before 5 for dinner! I exclaimed to Vera in a breathless nature.

" Yer right Eddie, me too, but next time we come here alone again ok, so' we can pick up where we left off."

The day had gone by way too fast and luckily for us both, but we'd made it home right on time... thank God.

That next day Vera and I got together again knowing that our other friends were still bein' punished, this gave us more time together alone once more. Our route was always the same when we were with one another and not with our friends, and it was our secret and we wasn't gonna share one single solitary thing with anyone period.

We were soon at the mansion once again and deep inside of its darkest places that we could find.

Chapter 13

Dead under Glass

Vera was still crying, but I stopped the flow of tears with my shirtsleeves, and she followed suit and just wiped her tears and her snotty, runny nose on her dress tail. Like a chalk mark it ran all the way across the bottom of her pretty dress as well as her wiping the yucky stuff from the top of her cute, soft little hand all the way to her shoulder. Man was it ever gooey. But for myself at least mine was contained on my cuff just above my hand and not that noticeable to the naked eyes.

As we explored the darkened corridors more strange feelings crawled up and down my spine causing me to shiver just a little, and Vera noticed my frightened look.

"Hey Eddie are ya getting scared?

"Heck No!" I exclaimed with a smirk as I wiped the sweat from my brow trying my best to maintain the composure that I had before I cracked a few jokes to make us laugh.

"Well I am too." She said with a half smile on her cute little moist juicy lips that have the taste of paraffin candy pop bottles and licorice.

"Yummy" I thought with a whisper from beneath my own quivering lips as I looked at those juicy lips of hers.

I really wanted to kiss her again, but because of the fear that made my body tremble, I really tried to hold my lustful composure for the right time, but nonetheless it kept playing on my sinister little mind.

We walked for what seemed to be a good half mile down a long corridor that was damp; with slimy moss covered walls and a slimy slippery moss covered cobble stone floor that had little tree roots protruding from beneath the goop of the muck and mire that lay beneath our damp cold feet.

Right in front of our eyes was an arched stone door with two skulls on the pedestals of each side and there upon the door were words that seemed to be written in blood that said.

"W I C A Keep Out Lest Ye Die."

A slight smell of musty air protruded from beyond the old wooden door that smelled like a dead animal was buried someplace inside. Its rusty hinges were held tightly in place. It was that kind of smell that really bothered me lots of times that I watched my Uncle Bill butcher hogs for trade in Muncie before he passed away in 1956. It was a smell that a person always remembered no matter how long they were to live upon this messily little planet called earth and to top it all off there wasn't no lock on the door and no place for a key hole either and that made it even creepier.

Vera and I looked at each other, we couldn't say one solitary word, and all we could do is gulp our Adam's and Eve's Apples like we were drinking something hard to swallow. Shivers went up and down both our spines like millions of sewing pins penetrating our bodies. She then grabbed hold of me like there was no tomorrow, and maybe by the looks of things there just might not be any tomorrow, well at least down here in this place that looked like some sort of ancient dungeon straight out of the middle ages or maybe it was Hell itself standing in our faces. Somehow this eerie place seemed to all the sudden come alive with strange moaning sounds or was it just our stomachs growling, I didn't know, it could be our stomachs snarling back at us because of the lack of food, speaking of which I sure was getting hungry and very thirsty even though I was scarred to the point of pissing my pants.

I know that Vera must have already pissed in her little pink panties by now, and I would have every opportunity to check that out for myself after we get outta this creepy place, that is if we ever did get outta here alive and in one piece, not a million all torn to shreds, chewed up and swallowed by a mean ol' devilish beast or placed on a rack and pulled apart from all four limbs or have our head cut off by a guillotine, leaving our torso's to rot in this stinky, murky, and slimy ol' dungeon below the mansion to rot and weather away to bones and eventually turn to ashes and be blown away in the winds that creep through these hallowed chambers of horror.

There was a trace of glass shimmering in spots beneath us from the small light that was coming from the small holes in the ceiling just above the door. This seemed strange from the place we were in, and there was scratch marks lurking on the murky cobblestones as well. Moaning sounds that were alarming to the ears seemed to flow from beyond the creepy door before our dollar sized eyes. My ears rang with a buzzing as if I'd been in front of some sort of machine that squeaked immensely loud, more shivers surged and caused my body to shake as if I were a leaf caught up in a winter wind storm with cold freezing ice crystals covering my whole being as I stand in front of its horrible noise that play deep in my ears and scurried into my head making my thoughts to wonder mindlessly with imagination. My encounter of the sounds stretched my imagination even farther than before and I was as wide-eyed as a wombat that had been hung out for a predator in the jungles of Africa. I told Vera that we may end up being confectionery treats for the devil or one of his imps if we entered this room. She held my arm tighter than she ever did, and buried her head as deep into my back as she dare to. My body felt numb and my blood ran as cold as the water from the artisan well next to Buck Creek in the freezing dead of a snowy winter's night.

Bravery, and shivery seemed to be going hand in hand inside of me as I protected my sweet Vera U. from what ever it was laying in wait behind the huge door before this frightened 'lil scary-cat boys popped out eyeballs. The neighborhood seemed to be getting more crowded as I drifted my hand ever closer to what may be my last stand at the battle of the Bighorn River in Wyoming and Montana territories out in the wild west, with me being general Custer and the predatory wild savages headed in for the final kill. I could almost see the greasepaint from the devils face on top of me ready to strike a deadly blow to my throat with some sharp dagger like weapon, but I soon became a milestone of strength and bravery and placed my hand on the door handle so we could see what ghost, beast, or demon was playing a game of hide and seek in the dark room. I was doing it not only the both of us, but for all the youth of our quaint little community of Hyde Park.

I always wanted to be the hero in some scary Lon Chaney, Boris Karloff movie, or even a good western hero like the Lone Ranger and maybe I could be my jungle hero Tarzan and slay the beast with my bare hands, yea that's what I'll be just this once if'n I don't piss my pants again in the process of doin' it. Reaching my trembling hand outward toward the rusty slimy door handle and Vera grabbed my arm before I got three or four inches from it.

"Eddie," she gulped several times. "Eddie please, d, don't open this door, p –pp pretty please, I'm so scarred and really want to go home so I can change my panties, I peed all over myself. I, I really want to take a bath too, I, I, I, Let's get the heck outta here OK, p-please, Eddie lets just g-go, (Gulp) now ok." She had the look of seeing death in her dark tear filled eyes and I knew that I wanted to go home too, but we come this far to see what lay beyond that my curiosity over came my fear.

"Vera, I am too scarred, but we come this far lets go the rest of the way and just pee inside OK, (gulp) then we'll just run the hell outta here and not come back for a long-long time OK."

Of course I was lying to her and opened the door all the way so we could get a real-real good look inside this dungeon's room of horror and it maybe death that is standing right in front of our faces; hopefully of some poor soul, and not our death waiting for us behind yon chamber's door. The door creaked as I slowly pushed down the handle and forced the hinges to slightly move a half of an inch at a time till the door opened all the way, and as I creaked the door open the smell that came from the room was like a ton of rotten eggs and dead animals all mixed into a frying pan of hot boiling oil that had been cooking for centuries without end. This could be the end of both of us I thought to myself so not to make poor Vera piss her panties any more than she'd already done.

"Go ahead V-Vera, ladies f-first." I tried to joke under my quivering lips with a tiny girl like voice that sounded more like a mouse than a frightened little boy who thinks himself the bravest of the brave and a true hero amongst hero's. I just smiled, and was about to piss my pants as well, but I didn't want Vera to know cause she would surely let it be known no matter what I said or done to make my friends back off from such a terrible teasing subject.

"A-are you joking, I - I, I sure d-doooo hope s-so Eddie, you are joking right." (Gulp). She shook all over as little trickles of pee ran down her goose pimpled legs and molded to the cobble stone and moss covered floor beneath out feet.

"Yes, Yes I am just joking V-Vera."

My words were getting fewer by the second and my voice became as a horse's voice with tones of nay, and Winnie, with slobbers like that which comes from an animal in heat, or one that turned rabid from being bitten from a mean ol' Gray Wolf, wolverine, or mountain lion that wondered down from its predatory terrain to search for food in the thick woods down the way from the mansion along the creek and I sure did wish at that precise moment that I could choose to skip the devil's lair in this dreary dismal ol' house, and in despite of my freedom to leave I went inside the lair for a look see; and, to me it was more of a cultural demon, so ta speaks of, but even more so for me to fear what lies within, seemed more of a hari-kari than the death which may lay beneath the cold ground waiting on hell to keep me warm in the dead of night from bein' torn ta shreds from some wild beast, or even a frozen winter's furry than fear itself could have done to me in the long run of bein' frozen ta death.

Our confrontation would be a conquest to a haunted life if we were to die here so young, innocent and not knowing what it would be like to be an adult, fall in love, and have children of our very own someday that would play silly games of spin the bottle, truth or dare, and then set around some spooky place like this and tell tall tails so bizarre that they'd end up in an asylum for many years because of some childish freight-night of horror amongst the rituals taking place in a realm of the living dead. I too swallowed my Adam and Eves Apple both together ever so slightly.

Vera starred me right in the eyeballs, as if to say... if I ever get outta here alive I will tell the world all you have done to scare the heck outta me, then I'll kill you. The tension was almost too much to bear and I could almost read her little pea brain literally as if my thoughts and hers were in some sort of space mind melting machine that joined our intimate thoughts into one existence; I was scared to death so to speak, and I sure didn't want Vera to know just how sacred I really was, but I went ahead and stepped one foot after the other toward the spook filled and smelly door of the devils image inside its den and crypt that seemed to be starring right back at us with its inward cold steal piercing eyes.

My thoughts immediately stretched to its outer limits, maybe, just maybe lurking behind the door was some sharp claws, or nail piercing teeth of a giant animal of some kind, ready to devour our souls, and just rip us to shreds like confetti at a ticker-tape parade when we stepped into the realm of its dark rotten egg smell filled domain; I just stood entwined in trepidation, siphoning the last bits of courage from my body ready for end of the road to come if I took one more step in the direction of that room it may be the end of me and Vera. I was also at the ready to throw in all the towels of all my silly childhood fears and look forward to a better life with safety and security far-far away from this place as humanly possible.

Once inside the tan-stone room, the devil seemed to be crouched behind its moldy black mattress throne, hayfork for teeth and grinning like a hungry beast. I heard it cry, and then it belched what looked like flames coming from between those big hayfork teeth.

Gloom seemed to follow us through our every endeavor while our distained journey pathway was lit with chills and thrills from beyond the unknown of our inward thoughts, never the less our only thoughts were that of our own deaths. I for one was making sure I kept my sanity as much as possible. Nothing was standing in our way except the word fear, there was lots of that lurking beyond what our eyes couldn't see, which was hardly nothing at all except the slightest light peeping through a couple of holes from above the dungeon door in the ceiling of cob webs, with the muck and mire flowing beneath our already filthy feet, pokin' my head ever so daintily through the cracked door, my teeth chattered with a fierce clatter like that which comes from the pinging of an old beat up machine on its last leg of existence. My eyes got as big as a new silver dollar shinning on old Luke's poker table beneath the glow of dim light from his dark dingy smoke filled living room; I couldn't say one word as to what my eyes beheld in front of them; the entire room's alcove illuminated with a red glow that brought Hell right there to our hearts and I could already hear funeral music playing in my ears that was more the likely coming from another room, or some old radio show in my Aunt Mary Belle's bedroom. It boomed from behind the ol' mattress with an eerie them for a black mass at our church one funeral day that summer.

"Eddie." Vera shook my arm as she whispered my name. I stood motionless with my head buried inside a tomb of death, none of the likes that I'd ever seen in my 7 years on Earth. "Eddie, what d-d-do y-you seee i-in th-there?" She hesitated a second and shook my arm once again this time I felt her touch and almost jumped out of my skin as I pulled my head from inside the tomb of the devil, and slammed the door closed. I furiously turned toward Vera with my chattering teeth still clanging away from fear, my eyes still as big as silver dollars. With the last bits of courage from my body I yelled at Vera words that I thought I'd never hear myself say.

"V-V-VERA, VERA L-Lets get the-the HELL OUTTA HERE NOOOOOW." I grabbed her arm pulling her behind me as I ran slippery back down the corridor the way we came into this dismal place of death.

Soon we were at a stairway and I just kept on trucking till I reached the top of them stairs, down another hall, fleeing as fast as I could with Vera still on my heals screaming at me all the way. She kept trying to pull my hand from her arm, but it clung on tighter than the vice in Luke's old shed, I simply would not let go of her arm for any reason period, and I just had ta protect both her and myself from the beast that was snarling and nipping at our heals.

"What, what, what the Sam Hell did y-you see down there, COME ON EDDIE, tell me now." Vera done all she could trying ta catch her breath and just screamed at me with her tiny voice all at the same speed of light and sound.

I thought that I was running from hell itself; and ran like I'd never run before in my entire life knowing that I was fast, but not as fast as I was that awful day when me and my sweet Vera was almost killed by the likes of that hideous beast from inside of the mansion's chamber of horrors.

"Aaaahuuhhh, ahhhhhhhhuuahhhhhh." Vera panted louder and harder than I'd ever heard her pant, or was it the beasts that was panting in its stride of trying to keep up with my speed. Not knowing for sure if'n it was hot on our tails for sure I kept on trucking like a high-baler on his last run with Vera flopping right behind me before we was even retired to a nice cozy place in the country and far as he could be away from the dangers of running his rig like a madman down the highways to make his living to just survive the stress of not being killed by a maniac of a beast or the devil himself.

"Slow your ass down Eddie. Come on please slow down?" Vera panted like she was outta breath and exhausted from the brisk run away from the dangers of the mansion's chambers. Her breath was still blowing puffs of cold white smoke like substance from behind her soft juicy wet and slobbery lips.

All she could do was to keep trying her hardest to screaming the same thing at me until we reached the outside of that creepy old mansion farmhouse, and as soon as we got outside, I told her the horror that was in the dungeon tomb. She couldn't believe what I told her, but I warned her of the danger if we were to go back down, down to the place that time must have forgotten about a hundred years or so ago, finally I told her that we'd best run home as fast as our slimy feet could take us, and that we shouldn't come back there ever again, but Vera acted more brave than I was acting, telling me that the next time we came we'd best come as a bigger group, bringing Tommy, David, and Sally and that she wanted to see what I'd seen.

It was way too scary for me now, but I was supposed to be the brave one of the group, but now I was exposed to the girl I liked so dang much, that I didn't want her to blab my fear to our friends, so I agreed to go back that next week end after my friends got off their punishments. By the time we reached the cornfield we were both outta breathe, the evening was getting a little chilly more-so because of our wet feet and all from crossing Old Buck Creek and from the slime of the dungeon of that awful, creepy Mansion.

Chapter 14

Night Stalker

That night I just couldn't sleep. I tossed and turned all night and may have drifted off once in awhile; the red glow of the piercing fiery eyes penetrated my very soul causing me to roll over in bed, and pull the covers over my head, and then threw them off in a nervous panic from not being able to breathe while buried beneath my quilt and fuzzy wool blankets, I awoke slowly, but there was a ringing in my ears that startled me, it rang so loud and wouldn't stop, it hurt real bad and it felt like my head was coming off just above my eyes. I must have slept like a bump on a log, and was all alone in my bed... God, how my small life felt like it was a bad dream even while bein' awake, just a sittin' there on my feather-down bed that was all clumped up in a ball right below where my pillow had been layin', it was all I could do not to keep from shivering and quivering and not wantin' ta ever close my eyes - ever again as long as I lived.

Strange thoughts kept fillin' my mind, making the panic even more troublesome. My breathing kept a fast steady pace with every tick of the ol' grandfather clock in Luke's very small living room.

That big 'ol Gray Wolf was imbedded deep in my little head and it just wouldn't go away. I sat on the edge of my lifeless bed several times during the night just so that wolf wouldn't come in and eat me alive. Once in awhile I'd look out the window through a tiny part of the heavy white ruffled curtains to see if it was next to the house and then I'd lay back down closing my eyes and covered my head with my Indian print blanket; the sweat dripped off my eyes, running down my long nose and into my mouth a bit, the taste of sweaty salty flesh was awfully bitter and it reminded me of the taste and smell from the 'ol silo, the smell was that of death, and the more I thought about it, the more I shook under my covers.

"Sleep, why won't sleep come, it won't leave me alone, ahhhh, go away." My thoughts drifted in and out as did my eyeballs from lack of sleep, redness flowed through the veins inside the whites of my cream puff eyeballs, and all I done was just toss and turn all night long.

All the sudden, from one corner of the room, I seen those fire piercing eyes, they stared at me and I at them. Near by was a carved tombstone made out of wood, it was rotten in spots, I couldn't hardly make out the name that was written on it too well, but it looked like George M Max----- or something like that, the date was for 1820 something, and there was another inscription below that was also not clear enough to make out; my main focus was on that mean 'ol wolf showing its blood stained white fangs, it was growling at me as cold red saliva slowly ran down its tangled misty white fur, its head was down ever so slightly as the saliva dripped onto the slim green carpet beneath its huge paws.

"What do you want? Go away." I said with more panic in my tiny little vocal cords.

My body quivered and filled with sweat. I tried desperately to drive it away, but it kept creeping ever so slowly toward me, snarling with every step; exasperatingly backing up away from it was a bit of a pain in the butt, turning around to run and without realizing that the wall was at my back I thumped head first right into that damned 'ol wall, bumpin' my head I fell down onto the soft carpeted mossy concrete floor. Flying out the door I went, zooooom, swoosh, just like a jet taking off as fast as I could with that meaol' beast was snipping right square for my heels. "Feet don't fail me now" was my main concern; and the higher I kicked my legs behind me I wished that my feet would hit it smack dab right in the jaws with each stride I took, but that big ugly, fierce-looking beast just kept snapping at my small skinny 'lil butt with such force, it sounded like one of the huge punch-press machines from the canning factory in Muncie trying to send me into oblivion. Its vicious powerful fangs snagged my socks a couple times and I thought I was a goner. I ran through the meadow like a speedin' train, leaping with such a bounce over every underbrush and tree branch that stepped in my way just like Superman. The field seemed like a hard bear plot of land. The underbrush, cactus and tumble weed that got in my way seemed to magically move outta my way as I speed by them. I wasn't about to be part of the food chain for that big predator. Its claws clinched each stride, and the powerful legs were almost too much for me to outrun. Chilly air rushed by my ears like the wolf's hot breath was as close to my head as it could ever be.

I could hear it say, "YUMMY, WHAT A TASTY DINNER THIS ONE WILL BE ONCE I CATCH IT, AHHHHHH, AHHHHHHHHHH, AHHHHHHH." Its breath kept coming into my ear faster and faster, and I almost tripped several times trying to run even faster than I already was.

"Feet don't fail me now; carry me away from the jaws of this death machine to the safety of my home; Ahuh uhuh, ahuh uhhhh, uhuhh", my short whisks of breath was finally dragging me down to a snails pace, but I kept thinking' hard to myself I must escape, I have to go still faster, I must flee, I must or I'll die right here, right now."

All the sudden it happened, I finally tripped and fell to the cold wet ground, several small cacti stuck me in one leg, and I scrapped my left arm as I went down hard, flat on my face. As I landed, the wolf was jumping straight for me with its mouth wide open. I covered my eyes with my hands and as I peeped through my fingers a bit and looked around, I found myself setting on the edge of my bed once again, my hands were still over my eyes, but I seen that I was still alive. I wiped the sweat from my face and gave a sigh of relief as I just sat there stunned by the wolf following me home.

"Wheeeeeeeew, man oh man I thought for sure I was a gonner and was so relieved that the mean 'ol beast had departed my company... thank you Jesus, thank you for saving me, I promise to be a good boy from now on, I swear I will, thank you, thank you, thank you dear God."

Once inside the tiny bedroom that was no bigger than the bushel basket my aunt Mary carried her clothes in while doing her laundry on the ringer washer they'd picked up at a hog auction last summer... I plopped my skinny and sweaty body down on my feather bed, and rested my head on my goose down pillow, starring at the ceiling for a spell was all I could do while tryin' ta catch my breath from all that furious runnin' from that wolf, and as I lay there it dawned on me that it was only another ghost, but a very vicious one at that. Over and over I thought how nice I'd be from now on; still all of those creeps just kept filtering into my head from Spooks-Ville farm, as did the thoughts of having to go back to that weird and sinister place on the other side of Buck Creek when I woke up, but after all I did promise my girl friend Vera that I'd go back with her, and our friends. The whole of that night I couldn't sleep, and just lay there planning out what I was going to do when we got to that mansion. I had several things in my mind, and somehow I'd sortta forgot that I promised Jesus that I'd be a good boy, and I fell fast asleep from being exhausted as if I were a cars muffler.

"Leave me alone you mean 'ol wolf, I'll hit ya with this big stick, go away and leave me be, I wanna live, my friends will miss me, and so will my aunt and 'ol Luke. I have to move back to Muncie in another month and I have to help my aunt move our things, so please go away and leave me alone ok you bad 'ol wolf." It was still in front of me, snarling and growling like it had been doing when I was in the basement dungeon of that creepy house. I looked at the door and made a run for it, and as I ran right for the door, the wolf lunged itself right in front of it. Luckily for me the door was open all the way and since I was a fast runner, and great jumper, I ran like a bullet and flew right over that mean growling 'ol Gray Wolf and headed down the hall faster than any human could have ever ran in their lives and by the time I reached the broken window that was the entry way into that creepy place, the wolf had vanished,, sweat beaded down my face and made my bedding soakin' wet and I woke up restless.

A smell of the coffee filtered its way from the kitchen to my bedside and up my tiny nostrils, and boy oh boy did it give me an appetite. Although bein'as tired as any kid could ever be from a nightmarish adventure, I sat there for a few minutes on the edge of my bed and thought about my life; rubbing my eyes and the sweat off my face, knowing that I'd best get my clothes on and try to stop shaking so dang hard so not to draw attention to myself when I walked to the table to eat my breakfast, my head shook fiercely to overcome all the stress, but the wolf was still in my mind and I quickly jumped into my old blue jeans, threw on my blue plaid shirt, slipted my new Buster Brown shoes on over my new white socks, and flew outta the bedroom past the green arm chair, past the gun cabinet where Luke kept his money hidden among with all his guns, all except his big 45 caliber revolver that belonged to his dad the famous Marshal Dillon, and jumped down the one step into the small kitchen and plopped myself down on one of Luke's very old hand made kitchen chairs, grabbed my fork and told my Aunt Mary I was really hungry.

"Hey boy, slow yer self down now y'hear... hahaha." Luke chuckled, which he hardly ever done and looked at me as if I were some sort of freak or somethin', but it just didn't matter to me in the least at that time.

I recon life wasn't so bad after all; at least I was still alive, thank God. I even ask my Aunt Mary if I could have a small cup of that delicious smelling black coffee that was brewing on top of the ol' wood stove next to where she was sittin'. She hesitated for a minute and then got up and purred me a cup of that Joe. Man was it good, and was just what the doctor ordered at just the right time too, even though I burned my tongue on the boiling hot black road mud, and chewed robustly at a piece of dark crusted toast, my stomach didn't make too much of a protest from the breakfast I was shoving into its tangled and somewhat nervous pits as I ate like there was no tomorrow.

My nerves felt much better as I sat there sippin' on my coffee. Aunt Mary and even ol' Luke were shocked by the way I was plunging down the harsh, strong-black substance.

"Hey boy, slow yerself down now ya hear, that aint milk yer drinkin." Luke said as he took another sip of his coffee starring me right in the eyeballs with his somber morning' look as he usually done any way. I paid him much never mind as I finished the hot strong pitch black coffee.

My doctor didn't say too much as he listened intensely to my every word and said" Was that Luke's favorite expression?"

"I recon?" I said in the epigrammatic of the moment.

"Continue" Said my doctor.

Anyways I went on as if that short moment had never happened.

"Thank ya that sure tastes good. Can I go play now? Please!" Setting my cup down in a hardy fashion just like Luke always did, I stood up from the table like a man, and looked at them both with my puppy dog and bedroom Hazel eyes. "Please." I asked once again. "Can I go play now, please, please?"

"Oh stop yer wimperin' and a yelpin' like an ol' hound dog, go ahead, but don't stay gone all night again y'hear me and be home by dinner young man!" Aunt Mary said yes, but as she usually done, I turned around and didn't look back as I headed outta the front door like a gentleman, telling them both thank you.

"Yes-um, I sure will... thank ya... c'ya at the dinner table." I said as I walked like a good boy as the hands of the kitchen clock stretched towards 8:00 a.m., I was outta the door, but once outside, my feet took to flight once more, and it seemed like I'd gotten my energy back all the sudden and a lickety-split I speed off to the back fence and leaped it in one healthy cat like leap. Zoom, I was gone down the path to my friend's places.

I was really too young to practice my own destiny and if I didn't do it now at my age, then I may never have a destiny at all, or so it seemed at times, wanting to take over my entire life and not have adults control almost every aspect of my life was always one of my dreams and I wanted to just skip ahead of my friends, oh how

I wanted to become an adult, at times my regrets penetrated deep within my mind's eye to make that decision of wanting to become an adult, but at the time being all I really wanted was to be a kid without any problems, especially like the ones I was experiencing from all my nightmarish encounters of dang ol' ghosts, skeletons, and yes even that mean ol' gray wolf that was haunting my very soul.

The slight wind from my speed sent leaves fluttering about my size 5 feet with the sound of a dozen bones clattering together as I continued flying down the path towards Vera's house. As I ran, the mean ol' wolf's spirit dwelt deep inside of me as it does even right now… "ooohh", it made my bones shiver with every breath I took, and at every breath it blew at me., I felt as though I was still being chased by it, and when it leaped with such a bound right in my face, I peed my bed during that horrible night just thinking about its hideous face, with those big white fangs, the straggling hair all tangled with saliva so thick that not even an axe blade could penetrate its heavy cream like foam.

"So you use to pee your bed?" Asked my doctor as he raised his left eyebrow? "Go on" He said as he usually done.

Not really hearing what he'd said I continued even at the same time he had spoke

"This is where it gets really hairy. I tell ya things couldn't have been any worse. My teeth are still tingling and my bones as cold as the clay we are standing on; they are making the same sounds as when it leaped at me, my heart is pounding like a thousand Indian drums ready for a war dance and chant."

As I stood there entertaining my thought with the events that took place while in the basement and in my bedroom at Luke's place., sweat and cold chills slid across my forehead and made my shirt cling to my body. When I reached Vera's place I was outta breath as if I'd ran a marathon. Where was I, oh yea, I was about to say! Anyways Vera came to the door as I stood there still sweatin' like a stuffed pig in heat.

"Hi Ms. Capturesme, how are you today is Vera ready to play yet?" I asked and smiled as I looked into her eyes trying at act like nothing was wrong, but somehow it seemed like she knew I was worried about something, but she never asked me what?

"I'm fine Eddie, and you." She smiled as Vera and I walked off toward Tommy's place side by side and about a foot apart so not to draw any attention to our love affair we had goin' on at such a young age.

"Vera… Eddie's here." She shouted as she looked towards the stairway. Vera flew down it as if something was even chasing her and was at the door in a matter of mere seconds.

"Hi, Vera how are you this mornin', lets go?" I said

"I'm good Ms. Capturesme; we'll be playin' tree climbers today, down by the plowed field, just so ya'd know ok; bye." I turned and waved at her and her at us as we speed across the dirt road to Tommy's place.

We all came together in a group and headed to the woods through our usual space between the woods fence and the pasture gate where Mr. Fulkler kept his cows and bulls, but one of the big bulls was standin' right next to the gate and gave a loud bellow as to say this is my territory, stay away or I'll gore ya to death. David stamped his feet at the mean ol' Bully, and just laughed.

"He's harmless, dad hit him between the eyes with a two-by-four one time and ever since he's been like a chicken, and just bellows, that's all." He smiled real big, and we all laughed at the bull, and knew it was only full of bull shit tryin' at scare us kids away from the pasture and its territory.

Walking through the woods I told all of them, not just Vera, some of what happened to me the night before. Several times I tried to change the subject so I wouldn't tell them too much till we reached the farmhouse where I was gonna tell them the best parts of when I was chased by the mean ol' Gray Wolf, but they kept egging me on to tell them everything that happened, but my fiendish 'lil mind kept on changing the subject as much as it would allow me to do… man that was hard, cause I just liked to stay with one subject when I got on one and having a one track mind most of the times like all kids didn't really dawn on me at the time. Somehow a thing like that comes easy for most kids at age seven through twelve, but not me, I thrive on bein' different… hahaha.

We wasn't paying any real attention to where we were going, and made a wrong turn, ending up further down stream next to Buck Creek than we usually we did. It all looked the same, even our makeshift bridge was laid across the creek, but somehow it seemed different to me, paying it no never mind as I sometimes done we continued across to the field where the mansion was supposed to be standin, but it wasn't there just an old out-building stood erect, forgotten, and rundown. It was once a little shack used by the Voodoo Princess in its hay-day. As soon as we saw it, we knew we were about a little piece away from the farmhouse, so we stopped and sat down just so I could tell the rest of my nightmare story to my bugging pals.

The ran down shack was as gray as the mean ol' wolf that chased me from lack of gray and its white-washed coating, and just about as big as Luke's ol' tool and storage shed. A twisted metal pipe stood limp, and swerving toward the gray cloudy summer sky, on the ragged wood shingle roof, and a couple knotty birch tree planks held up the sagging shack with its a small weed laden porch in a harsh dirt area, and there my tale of horror unfolds to frail little unsuspecting minds.

What I'd told my friends to this point wasn't anything as to what was to come next. They were already shaking in their shoes, and that made them more afraid of goin' back to the spooky ol' Mansion that lay several hundred feet north east of our current location by the Voodoo shack. A small little wild cur dog was barking in the background. I recognized the bark; it was one of the female bitches that chased me from time to time when I went beyond our baseball field playground, but I kept on talkin' as if I didn't hear it, because that dang ol' bitch bite me on the ankle one time, turnin' quickly I kicked it in the teeth before it had a chance to run away yelping like a cry baby puppy, well sir that dog never came near me ever again, but somehow it knew when I was in its territory.

I'd finished most of my tale and then we headed on to Spooks-Ville. We'd walked about another two and a half blocks through the field and up a dirt road there was a cobblestone driveway that led to the farmhouse's cemetery. We didn't want to ever go into that place 'cause the house was spooky enough, and so we tried our best to stay as far away as possible from it and the contents that dwell within the confines of the huge spiked cast-iron fence.

It was said that during the Civil war a rebel soldier took up residence in one of the out buildings on the farm where the Voodoo princess lived after he killed one of the mansions maids in the dungeon below the basement, where George Maxifield kept his torture devices that he collected for the museum he would construct once his house was build, and the farm was well up and running. Stories had been told that the soldier went mad from the Voodoo Princess' potions and that he stole dead bodies from the graves in the cemetery, took the parts to the Voodoo woman where she made them into evil potions.

It was also said that she was an insane Indian shaman's wife who practiced her shamanistic and demon Voodoo rituals in villages, but when the tribe she was a part of found out she was desecrating their dead for such madness they banned her from all tribes, and no one knew where she'd went to. Just shortly before each winter bodies end up missing in several cemeteries around Hyde Park, Selma, and other near by small towns. Not even the authorities have a clue as to where they'd been taken or for what purpose, except from all the legends and other roomers that were always spread through-out the countryside. The Mysteries are still unsolved. Most of the taken bodies have been female children, why no one to this day may ever know?

As we entered the cemetery, a smoke like figure came towards Sally and the closer it got, the more features she and the rest of could see as clear as I or you and it had stained gray pants, a gray shirt with yellow stains with black buttons and a crumpled up torn gray collar, dusty brown shoes, and dark, wrinkled skin on his hands and face, it was the soldier arising out of the past and floating slightly above the ground, and as I looked closer he had grayish-white hair like cob-webs that streamed down the back of his neck and alongside his bony head; huge bags under his blue piercing soldier eyes and his deep-dark lines scarred his see through cocoa-black face like cracks on a rotten piece of wood, and as I kept glairing at him, I noticed he only had a few remaining teeth in the mouth, black, yellow and rotten. A weathered blackish and tinted pink tongue sortta filled the ridged and crooked gaping holes between the few remaining teeth in his prune like mouth, or what was left of it.

"Goin' ta git ya little girl and yer puny little friends too!" His cracked voice shivered with each word. Sally tried to say something, but had a little difficulty achieve her words to warn us there was a ghost by the shack the whole time and that she'd heard him speak his awful gibberish to her mind. Sally was on my right side and reached for my arm, clinging onto it, almost tearing from my shoulder outta its socket and Vera gave her a real mean look and she let go really-really quick.

"I'm a gonna git my big gun, and blast ya right in yer little behinds if-n y'all don't git off my property now." I heard as he passed by a shadowy figure of an ancient black woman standing near a tomb, one of which I tried not to read, she stood alongside the confederate soldier, and we ran like creased lightening, and our shivering, clattering teeth, that seemed to be shaking loose with each click in our mouths and stride we took.

Continuing running up the road, a little faster than we were, Sally let out a blood chilling scream that penetrated our very souls with fear. The two figures faded in the distance far behind us.

"W-what h-happened S-Sally." Vera sak with sweat and tears shiverin g down her face.

"I-IT T-TOUCHED M-ME, I-I FELT I-IT PULLIN' M-ME T-TOWARDS I-IT." She was shaking so bad that her whole dress was almost completely wet from pissing al over her self.

Well, we went on anyway, but this time we approached the mansion with great caution, and at the same time we maintained a brisk pace until he turned onto still another dirt pathway just off the main dirt driveway leading to what looked like another big spooky cemetery, but it was still the same one, but on the opposite side of the mansion, and in the distance we could hear the woman laughing as she went inside the a hallow tomb, that echoed like the chambers of my beating heart was at that frenzied moment inside the cemetery...

When we went inside the big mansion we sat on some wooden crates to catch our composure and our breath, hopefully allowing

Sally, and her piss filled dress to dry out a spell, and as we sat there, I told my friends the rest of what happened to me the night before.

"I looked and just about halfway across the field there was a sudden movement of bushes rustling against one another, but there was no one around but me, the bushes, and no wind to move those bushes. I stopped and looked for a second, fire red eyes glared at me, its standing figure was crouched at its behind amongst the bushes. That Gray Wolf was a big one big mean beast, and it must have stood three feet tall at least while on all four legs and weighed about two hundred pounds. It had a big bulging stomach while it crouched on bowed legs. The breathing both relaxed and tightened its stomach muscles with each breath; all four paws had razor sharp claws protruding out and downward like a farmer's cycle ready to mow you down to the ground; its powerful legs and head poised in the ready position, and those fangs; big, white and pointy shown all its fierceness behind those fire red glowing eyes. Its wild hairy -pointed ears were bent back like lethal hearing machines, and twitched at each little sound, even the slight breeze made its hair and ears twitch. It leaped out at me once and stopped a short distance away, then crouched in the ready position once more as it growled at me, foam like saliva dripped down its hair puffed jaw bones and then to the cold ground below its tremendously large paws. It let out a howl that shook my whole body with fear, so much fear that I dare not move least I die right there on the very spot I was standing my ground. I done the only thing I could and as the wolf leaped at me ready to tare my throat to shreds, but I jumped outta the way just in the nick of time and began running as fast as I could, but I fell flat on my face when I tripped on a tree branch. I gasped in pain as the monster pounced toward me. It couldn't run as fast as me because of its huge belly; cause I knew it was pregnant by the way it wobbled with each stride. I tried to get up, but kept slipping on rain soaked weeds and leaves. As I finally stood in the runnin' position the wolf took hold of my arm by pulling on it just below my elbow, but her teeth had a strong secure secure-fixed and unlikely to give way hold. The beasts' claws held my body down as it shook my flesh, leaving me with bloody scratches. Struggling hard I finally freed my arm, and somehow escaped the jaws of the death machine. That big ol' Gray Wolf shook its head; because I must have injured its face somehow and stunned it enough to escape and run like a tornado's winds. The wolf chased me all the way home. I was breathing so hard when I woke up in my bead that I didn't know if I was really alive or not, sweat covered my bed from top to bottom and I realized I was out of harms way at last ands safe in my room. It was just awful, and I pray I never have another Hell filled nightmarish night like that ever again in my entire life."

Once I cleared my head and rubbed my eyes as we sat there glairin' deep into one another's eyes. Every word I said made my blood and my friends blood run as cold as ice-cycles on a winters night and I could see the whole scene all over again in my mind.

I had to take a breath of air and regain my thought from talking too much and then I continued to tell them the rest of my story.

"I could smell the filthy odor from the wolf enter my nostrils, and the hot breath right in my face as I escaped the beast. I could see all the blood on my arm and legs as well as the bloody saliva drippings down the wolf's tangled hairy face. It just wouldn't leave my mind. I could still feel my arm drop to my side and dangle limply with pain and the blood dryin' as I ran through the fields and woods towards home. Havin' a couple scratches and both puncture holes on my arm and legs as well as the bloody saliva drippings down the wolf's tangled hairy face. It just wouldn't leave my mind. I could still feel my arm drop to my side and dangle limply with pain and the blood dryin' as I ran through the fields and woods towards home. Havin' a couple scratches and both puncture holes on my arm and both legs, but at least I lived through the ordeal and am able at tell ya all about it. I still have a little pain in my arm once in awhile from it, but I just don't pay it no never mind most the time." All that talk about my nightmare sure seemed to help me overcome some of my fear for some unknown reason, but ya know how it is with a 'lil fella like me.

"Wow, Eddie that was quite a story." David said as his big brown poop filled eyes glared into mine.

Some how maybe deep inside himself, he thought me full of crap too, but as always not too much bothered me 'cause I was supposed to be the brave one of the bunch, but I knew that I had scarred the crap right outta David 'cause he too peed his pants, but I didn't say anything about it and knew the rest would notice as well and if'n they wanted to say somethin' to him… well that would be their choice, not mine.

"I'm happy you're ok Eddie." Vera told me with a slight quiver in her accent. "Can I see your knife, please?" She smiled under her fear, and tried to maintain her composure as best she could, but it came forward with flyin' colors from deep down under her goose pimpled brown skin.

I showed the knife and scars to my friends as I tried to come to grips with my senses. I stood and walked to the broken window, gripping it tightly. Shaking my head a few times, taking a deep breath of air, I kept wondering if the wolf was still around the farm, or what was even more frightening to me was what if it were on the inside here hiding in wait to kill us all as we explore the depths of hell, but we walked back through the place like we owned it, and we knew almost every inch it or so it seemed, at least the parts that we'd already explored, but me and her still had a whole lot more to search than we'd ever have time enough to do while I was still in Hyde Park, hardy har har... hehehe... before I moved far away from my best friends and my little black beauty, sweet Vera Capturesme.

The deeper we went inside our haunted palace the more dismal it got and we'd reached still a brand new part of the ol' house we'd not yet explored, and as we got close enough to one room we heard heavy breathing and winning coming from beyond the dark. I hesitated outside the door, but the rest tip toed inside. I was shaking in my shoes, 'cause I knew it was the mean ol' wolf waiting for us to enter so it could rip us into tiny little pieces and devour our bodies into non existence.

Takin' a hold of Vera's hand I pulled her to me, giving her a big kiss, like we'd never see each other ever again. She returned the favor as we both crept inside the dark room behind David, Tommy, and mean 'ol Sally. and as I suspected, there in one corner of the room hiding behind an old mattress was the big gray wolf. Its womb burst with pain, she yelped a shrill yelp that went through-out the chambers of the mansion like the snowthunder and roar of a fast speeding train that is tryin' its best at stop in a hurry, but her pain was too intense to bare her brood of babies. The sinister appearance made her almost human like in her actions, but like the ripeness of her stomach she couldn't take the pain any longer.

As I watched, she took her back paws and placed them on her bulging ripe for the picken' plump belly, then she began to scratch as fast as she could with her sharp claws till blood oozed outta each claw mark, the time was very close and the pain worsened with time and her dark yellowish-green eyes were now dollar sized puss-filled globs ready to burst like a dam with a large creek ready to flood the whole room. The tips of her claws would soon break through, but that wasn't enough. The cur bitch wolf knew she had to do the unthinkable, and rip her stomach apart with her sharp fangs like she was devouring a human victim, and the creatures look intensified as she bit into her painfully delicate belly to free her babies from death. She knew deep in her mind that she too would soon die, but why should her pups die too.

Soon they would all be set free from her womb. She oozed with guts, blood, babies and blackened after-birth, its bloody skin still had several lighter patches on its rough surface, cracks made dark veins on places where the wolf lay giving birth to its pups, and it was completely ripe as it burst wide open, spilling everything out onto the floor beside her. She growled at us several times, but couldn't move because of her stomach bein' torn apart from the harsh delivery and it was all we could do but to just stand there horrified watchin' the pups being born. They were hideous, not yet fully developed and not like their big bad mother, who was hideous in her own rights. But some how we all felt sorry for the mean ol' gray wolf, even though it had attacked me the day before in the field. As we all turned around, that wolf turned back into her original human female form. She lay there naked on the floor with the bloody mess next to her now skinny black-body. Some how I knew it was the Voodoo Princess from the way Luke and his card playin' pals had described her appearance at the poker table many times. It had burned deep into my head to stay for ever. She was free at last.

All those stories I heard had been placed right before my eyes. They'd come true and buried themselves in my mind along with all the other tales I'd heard over the summer at Luke's place. Yes, I must admit, it was hard to take, but I swallowed my fear and shed a couple tears for that big bad bitch werewolf who lay still to both this world and the one beyond, well maybe… after all she was a ghost werewolf from out of the darkened past.

We just looked at those six half human and half wolf pups, three white, one red, and one black, but one wasn't moving, and had died in the birth process. The woman let out a major scream and one last growl, and then she was gone. She vanished into thin air from death. We all turned and walked outta the room cryin' our eyes out. After viewing the mess we then headed back toward the basement so we could go home once again. Our day had come to an end, and on a sad note, but left us all with a good feelin' of bein' safe at last from the mean ol mother gray wolf of the mansion, that just so happened to be a big bad werewolf, half human and half Gray Wolf. I wondered if the pups would ever make it in the midst of the mansion with no way out except through the basement window. They were so small and helpless, and we all wanted to take one home with each one of us, but we couldn't in fear of bein' found out for exploring places that no kid should ever be playin' in- in the first place, let alone bringin' home a wild animal like a gray werewolf pup to keep as a pet.

I recon that the bodies which have been disappearin' from cemeteries were now in a new form, their spirits had been transformed into the Voodoo princesses werewolf form from the potions shed made from their female organs. The rest of their body parts she and Samuel Rosebud had eaten in order to survive in all those harsh times many years ago, but what bugs me now is why and how are the new bodies from these days still bein' taken from graveyards all over the place? Maybe those werewolf pups did survive after all, somehow. All I did was pray that their ghostly spirits would stay away from me and my friends so we too wouldn't take on the fate of death at an early age in life, like those who once lived in and around this spooky ol' farmhouse mansion in the meadow near ol' Buck Creek and Hyde Park here in the Good ol' Indiana countryside.

Chapter 15

The Horror' Inside the Mansion' Chamber'

A red haze engulfed the very essence of our faces, fear raged deep with in our trembling souls as to the horrible sight of the dungeons torture chamber penetrated our dollar sized eyes. This brought to mind a story I heard from the men playing cards with ol' Luke one night.

Legends have it that the people who owned this house let Confederate soldiers hide in their basement so they wouldn't get captured by the Union Army.

One night while there was a party going on in the upper part of the house. A slave girl named Matilda Sarah Cleavage (Mattie) for short who was the niece of Linda Sue Captersome with who she left New England with to come out to the Mid-West and start a new life in spite of all that she had back East. Took a walk down to the basement to get a few things that they were running out of at the party, and at the same time she snuck some food to a soldier and never came back. Of course it was said that these people had many slaves, and one wouldn't be missed whatsoever. Well as the story goes, Mattie was more than likely raped by the soldier, and then tied some sort of torture devise, beaten unmercifully with the soldiers buggy whip, then he pulled her apart from every limb and her remains are still in the exact place she had been found as a reminder not to take in any m ore strangers to hide, they'd just have to fend for themselves or fight on the battle field to die like they deserved, and the basement door was locked and boarded up for a long-long time.

We'd walked through several corridors till we reached a big door that had once been nailed shut; some of the boards had been torn off and taken away but two were still dangling from the door untouched for who knows how long, so I pulled on one and it came off real easy, David tried to pull the other one away but wasn't strong enough, so Vera grabbed hold of it as well giving it a big yank causing both David and her to fall on their butts, of course we all laughed at them.

"Are you ok Vera?' I asked as I helped her up and left David to help himself back on his feet.

"Hey pal hows about helping me too?" David asked, but Vera and I just opened the big door and he got up saying: "Meanies I'll pay ya back." He whipped his butt and gave a tiny smile.

Walking in was creepy enough by itself, but when we seen all the weird contraptions and the skeletal remains, we stood there glazing at those very poor ol' souls that was strapped to one of the biggest things ever created, we didn't know what it was, but her body tied with shackles and chains to some sort of wooden lookin device, her arms and legs were out - stretched in painful looking positions as far as they could possibly be stretched in all four directions, her head hung downward, her bosom shown through the torn clothes, her flesh, what was left of it dangled from every limb of her shattered body lash stripes were scattered through-out her dress in random directions.

Her soul seemed to have been released everywhere during the course of the lashings while her limbs were torn from her bodies sockets after what looked like she'd been raped by someone who was extremely strong. It was the most horrible thing I had ever seen in my life; of course mostly all that was really left were bones beneath that raggedy ol' torn dress, but we knew it was once a woman.

No one knew how long that soldier stayed in these chambers, or what ever happened to him, but I could almost picture her in that old fashioned blue dress, the once beautiful teen-aged looking black maid with long dark brown wavy hair flowing down her back almost reaching her butt, 'cause a painting of her was hanging on one wall of the upper part of the house that we'd already explored a short time back.

Well anyhow as it had been told to us by that 'ol farmer... she, that black slave girl kept mostly to herself when not performing her duties for the house all the time. My mind drifted back in time and I could almost hear her voice, so soft in tone, it should have frightened me, but for some reason I wasn't scarred at all.

There in a darkened corner of the chamber, cowering in a corner was a tall, slinky man in a gray Confederate uniform with a knife drawn and lying beside him was a bull whip. As I watched the soldier shivering, Mattie came in with a tray of food. She walked toward him, but he jumped up all of the sudden and grabbed her, flinging her down on top of the torture rack, and ripped her blue dress up over her head holding her down with one arm. He told her not to scream or he would kill her right there and then.

Mattie being naturally quiet and obeying almost every command that was given to her, she lay still while he had his way with her. After he was done, she lay there almost naked, and crying till he finished doin' the adult thing to her young and beautiful body, I closed my eyes, but could still see everything that had happened in that chamber. It looked like to me that the soldier couldn't stand her crying and took his whip off the floor in one hand, his knife on the other. He walked back towards the shivering Mattie and held his knife to her throat, and then he bound her hands and feet to the rack, and gave the wheel a couple cranks to stretch her body in a gruesome position. She let out a scream from the pain of being stretched, but n o one heard her because of all the noise from the party above. He took off his bandana and gagged her mouth shut, then gave the wheel a couple more turns. Her bones snapped from her arm and legs sockets and she fainted. He wasn't satisfied so he took his bull whip and beat the living daylights outta her., then the mean cowering soldier ran outta the chamber right through the closed door, down the hallway toward the stairs and vanished in thin air.

I covered my eyes as I watched her die a horrible death. When I realized where I was, I snapped outta the visionary trance, tears were streaming from my eyes. I took my arms and wiped the tears from my face and held Vera close to my chest, and then I quickly let go of her and bent over towards the floor. A sour vile rose out of the pit of my stomach and enter my mouth.

"AERRRRUUUUCK." I wiped my mouth after the vile was hewn from inside my stomach in one large swoop and strewn all over the moss covered cobblestone floor.

"YUK." Vera and Sally both said at the same time. "This is gross."

Sally then threw up in response to my vomit being hewn outwards in every direction.

"WHY THE HELL'D YA HAVE TA GO AND DO THAT FOR, YUCKY? YUK, THAT'S JUST HORRIBLY DISCUSTING!" Vera said as she covered her mouth at the sight of the vomit as well as the shattered body of what was once a woman of possibility great beauty when she was alive, and walking around in the halls of the upper part of the 'ol farmhouse mansion far above me and my friends in what appeared to be the pits of Hell where we now stood in the midst of vial, and all the grotesque corps in the corner of the room.

Sally's sweat, and her vomit that she was standing in, and her brother David's mingled together at the same time as they clung tightly onto each other. Tommy shook his shoes so hard it seemed to cause a ripple effect like that of an earthquake trenching the 'ol spooky place as he flung the vomit from off his shoes causing some of it to splatter on the woman's torn body that lay on the torture device.

Vera grabbed me like she wanted to climb inside of me and hide for ever and ever, even though I threw up all over the place as did Sally and David, she didn't seem to pay much more attention than the gross comment. I didn't seem to mind her body tightly wrapped around mine comforting my inward fear, and I giving favor to her in return, even in the after effects of just throwing up all over the place.

I looked in another corner of the dark, but somewhat misty filled chamber room, and there right before my eyes was a guillotine from the middle ages standing tall with its sharp blade still shinning as if it were new.

I stood there with my small mouth wide open, almost as soon as I realized what I was looking at, something came over me like a magic spell or something and I was in a trance of some sort. Immediately I started seeing more weird and bad things from the past coming alive as if I was actually there witnessing the execution of Matilda Sarah Cleavage (Mattie), and to all the other horrors that had taken place early in the afternoon on that hot July day in 1894.

The past was alive inside my head and I couldn't get it out for some reason, maybe I was possessed by some entity, and a voice inside me said in a lowly wooing tone: "It had been only ten years after the purchase of this house that I am standing here looking in horror after he tied my dear wife's hands behind her back and gagged her mouth with his red bandanna, then tied her beneath my newly purchased guillotine for the museum I'd been constructing' in Muncie town. It would have been a grand museum once it was finished and it would house many such torture devices for display to show the good folk from all over this region what had taken place in merry 'ol England just before I made the journey to this horror ridden territory that had been established several years before out in the mid west part of the America's." The voice went on saying: "He then triggered the blade' mechanism, causing it to fall at a fast and furious pace, chopping off her head to let it fall into the block basket at the outer edge of that awful death machine and lay there in a pool of blood, with her eyes wide open. I ran out of that dungeon as fast as I could, covering my mouth in horror, crying in despair over the loss of my beautiful third wife Mattie the elder… ooooooohhhh my Mattie… my dearly departed Mattie had passed at the hands of an untiringly vicious renegade Indian outlaw named Samuel Rosebud of the Muncie tribe who's been a staying' here as a boarder in one of our upper rooms and he'd taken Mattie, my third wife to the dungeon to make passionate love to her, then brutally killed her in cold blood and there was nothing I could do about it because if I was to even try, the law would suspect me of committing such a horrendous crime of and convict me for doing it without hesitation. After he killed poor Mattie, the half black, half Indian had vanished into thin air without a trace of him, but why was he even in my house in the first place..

WHYYYYYYYYYY?" It shouted causing me to shake my head so hard that it gave me an aweful headache.

"Where am I…. bloooowa, what happened?" I asked, but no one said a word, all they did was stare at me like I'd went totally crazy of somethin'

"OOOOOOOO… what a horrible way to die." Vera finally piped up and said as she covered her big dark beautiful eyes with her soft delicate hands.

Not another word was said at that point as we keep lookin' at all the bad things inside the chamber of horror. Things like this just didn't happen in this part of the country and since I'd never divulged my intent for this awful machine of being displayed in the new museum that I'd never told anyone about from day one of the construction project, I wanted it to be a surprise for the town, but now this. What was I going to do now; I kept it to myself and went on about my life thinking that no one would ever find out, not now nor ever.

I had came totally out of that trance and was just a sweating' like I'd been running for a million miles, and I was shakin' in my shoes so fast that when Vera shook my arm, I let out a loud shrill that would haven woke up even the dead, like the woman whose bones and small pieces of what seemed to be petrified flesh still attached to her horrified headless body, her skull still in the basket as it had been for all these years, and that other p;oor woman on the other thingy-ma-bob that hadn't been touched or discovered till us kids came down here to this creepy dungeon basement beneath the farmhouse mansion we now called Spooks-Ville.

"Eddie, hey, Eddie, w-what are you lookin' at?" Vera ask me with all her curiosity as she looked at me, then to the corner where I'd been stairin' with the intensity of a flaming campfire, then she too let out a scream of the same effect and it sent more chills through my body and bounced off into David and Sally' bodies causing what seemed like still another small earthquake to rumble the dungeon so hard it caused me and Vera to fall flat on our butts as we just kept gazing at the horrible death machine and the dead body still caught in its clutches, but this one appeared to be fresh.

This was indeed a dreadful experience and all I wanted to do was to get the Hell outta there as fast as I could, but at the same time I wanted to stay and look some more. I decided to stay cause I didn't want my friends to see me as a big scary-cat or even worse a big chicken and a coward that I really was, so I got up and went closer toward that big guillotine to see how it worked, but didn't want to touch it so I just poked my head slightly toward it so I could view all the gears, the sharp blade, and yes even a closer look at the dead body in its midst. As I looked closer at the body, I gazed at her left hand, and in tightly closed fingers was a piece of paper that was still in almost perfect shape. I leaned forward to see what it said, but I could hardly see a thing, so I ask David if he had any matches, and of course he did as he usually did, 'cause he was the one who was taking cigerettes from 'ol man Cash's store so we could all have a puff now and then, even though at the time they made us all cough, but already knew that from him smoking cork weed even before that as did the rest of us, all except Vera and Sally, those goody two-shoes...

I took one match and tried to light it, but a small breeze blew it out as soon as I lit it.

"Damn it. Give me another one of them matches David." I shouted as I looked at David, Sally and then at Vera, and smiled slightly as thought to say, its alright, nothing bad will happen as long as I'm here, but deep inside my inwards were still shiverin' as my heart pounded with the beat of millions of native drums. "Come on David, just hand me that Damn match OK buddy."

"O-ooo-k-kay Eddie, h-here y-ya are p-p-p-pal." He was still looking at the horror with his silver dollar sizes eyes as was his sister Sally, but Vera was in sort of a calm mood all the sudden, and started to giggle a wee bit. I didn't know what was so dang funny, cause I'd just pissed my pants a little more than I'd already done when we'd initially went inside the chamber's room. I looked around for a lantern, and remembered that when I was in that trance, I'd seen one in my viewing of the beheading of this poor unfortunate soul of a beautiful woman. I tried hard to ignore Vera's cause I knew that all she was giggling at my pissy pants.

I remembered that the Lantern was hanging just inside the door and I turned telling Sally to go get it, but she couldn't seem to move one inch, so I shouted at her to just go get it or I'd give her a good spankin' when we got outta here. Sally looked at me as if I meant what I said and headed toward the lantern and a big whoosh of wind blew up her dress and exposed her nice pink panties, and as the light from the small hole in the ceiling just above her shown down on her exposed cute little butt, I smiled real big, but Vera just gave me a real dirty look and I glanced my head down toward the cobblestone and moss covered floor turning a little red in the face in embarrassment from lookin' at another girls behind among other things she was showing. Sally quickly grabbed her dress from both sides with her small hands and pushed down her dress as if no one was even looking at her southern exposure.

Sally finally brought the lantern to me in slow motion and placed it in my hand. I looked at it with amazement, and it too looked as new as if it had just came off the store shelf. It was still full of coal oil and the white wick had never been burnt one tiny bit. I took a whiff of the lantern drawing my head back from the smell, and knew it was still good because of its strong odor of just coming right out of the plant that had made if. I looked at the name on the bottom of it and it said George M Maxifield Sr.' Lantern Company, Est. 1815 Centre Township; Muncie, Indiana. I thought to myself that maybe these folk were the first people to settle down in Muncie, and I sure was going to do some research about all this, even as young as I was. Maybe I'd find my heritage, or something else interesting when I done so. That I just didn't really know, but the thought did inter my mind a time or three.

Taking another match from David's match box, I took off the globe from the lantern and struck the match gently and slowly moved it towards the wick that was full of coal oil, and it lit immediately at the first touch of the match. All I did was smile, as the glow grew bigger and brighter in intensity. It lit up the chamber room to a brilliant brown and red brick sparkle with the blade and other hardware from the guillotine shinning its horror all over the room. As I went back towards the death machine holding the lantern in my right hand, I tried to read the paper, but it was upside down, and in order for me to retrieve that paper, I knew I had to get closer than I really wanted too. The blade was in the upward position and looked like it was locked firmly in place, but to get to the paper, I had to do a little climbing because of the position of the dead woman's hand, it was placed beneath the blade just enough that it and the paper was a little bit out of my reach.

My adult mind kicked in on the inside of my kids pea brain and I thought to myself, "How could anyone be so induced to a measure making the infliction of capital punishment on a wonderfully once beautiful woman as this one once was, or anyone else as far as that went. For within these prison walls lay a private solemnity of unjust law and unwilling death, and here lay proof positive of, God only knows just what all went on in the confines of this horror chamber outside of those who done these atrocious deeds?"

Leaning still forward al the more just to get a hand hold on the death instrument, I had to touch blood splattered spots, but just didn't care, all I knew was that I had to get that paper from her fingers so I could read it, then stuff it in my pocket with the rest of the things I had gotten earlier that morning.

"Please, Eddie, please be careful. I won't know what to do without you in my life." Vera was scarred so damn much that she even pee'd her panties a little bit, but it wasn't that noticeable, and she felt so embarrassed that she held the rest way too long and had to slither to one corner behind one of the machines and finish her job.

Vera most of the time showed her affection to me more often now that it had been brought out into the openness of mixed company so to speak.

"Ya bet I will." I said gas I got ever so close that I could almost feel breath coming from the woman's severed head in the basket, I glanced back, and didn't see Vera, but quickly gained my focus on what I was doin' so I too wouldn't end up the same way as that poor unfortunate woman here on this Guillotine. My body was trembling with intensity and my heart still pounded like all those Indian drums in one of their dance ceremonies or something.

"Yea, Eddie be careful or else we'll have to try explaining where you are and how you got yourself killed by a dang 'ol Guillotine here in this creepy 'ol place. We'll just have ta explain a whole lot, yelp, we will, so please be careful ok buddy." Sally stated with a fearful tone of voice!

She was always blabbing her big mouth with one thing after the other most of the time and Vera had to make her be quite. By that time Vera came back from taking her piss and had heard all that was said.

"Damn it Sally, would you just shut up your big mouth, or I'll tell everyone that it was you who talked us into coming here in the first place, ya hear girl." Vera gave her blabber-mouth friend a shake from her fist like she was gonna pound the hell outta her, but just stood her ground with an attitude toward Sally like none that I'd ever seen before in my life. Damn I was proud of her! She finally had a strong stern voice of authority in this matter more-so now than in the past just because of all we'd been through while exploring this place, and I was glad that I had power over mean 'ol Sally at last. That made me thrilled to death, well I guess I'd best not wish for that right now, at least not while in this position that I was in tryin' ta get that dang 'ol paper for another trophy of a ancient relic to put on display in my room when I got back to Muncie at the end of next month when I had to move and start life in a new environment and new school. No sir, death was just one thing I needed for myself right now that was for dang sure.

I was right at the edge of getting that paper and almost slipped and fell to my death, but I held on ever so tightly and the mechanism didn't trigger loose to make that blade come crashing down on my head, cutting it off like this poor woman's was. My hand grabbed the paper and pulled it free from the fingers of her left hand and as it interred my fingers, a big whoosh of wind came through that hole in the ceiling and blew that paper up into the air and tossed it around like a whirl wind from a tornado high above us all. I tried to grab it as it went up, but couldn't reach it, and was forced to jump off that guillotine and tumble onto the cold hard moss covered and damp floor. I rolled head over heals a couple times backwards, the blade wasn't jarred loose one bit as I looked at it as I rolled to safety.

"Wheeeeeew, that was close, too close for comfort. Am I alive? I started sweattin' really bad, and the combination of both sweat and pee started to make me gag slightly, but I was so happy that I fell safely, but scraped my arm on the death machine as I came falling down off that awful thing. I looked at Vera as she flung herself at me, grabbing me, giving me a big hug and planted a wild wet kiss right on my lips in front of Sally and David.

"Are you ok my love, my wonderful - sweet Eddie?" Vera asked as she threw her arms around me and gave me a real big squeeze, she even started kissing me all over my face, and I ask her to stop in a gentle whisper into her ear, I gazed at her and she at me as she withdrew her beautiful body away from me and stood up holding my hand at the same time, and I came up with her, I smelled her pee'd panties, but didn't asy anything, I just smiled and gave her a wink that everything was ok.

"Damn the luck anyhow, just look at that paper, its still floatin' up there in midair, now how am I gonna get it now." I started getting' just a little pissed off at the whole situation, but gave my best to maintain my temper.

All the sudden my fall must have forced the womens hand to let go of that paper and it came swiveling down toward the floor, but as it swerved towards me, it all the sudden made a turn and landed right under the blade, right in the middle of that dang thing.

Vera thought herself brave now and lunged herself forward toward the wooden basket and jumped right in it with the woman's partially hair covered skull and reached her hand in toward the paper and as she snagged it front under the blades shadow and had it in her hand when the blade came crashing down right toward her arm and head, but just in the nick of time she got out of the way. Vera seemed to have flown right out of that basket as fast as she went in it and had the paper in her hand and boy I was happy she had it, but more so, I was extremely happy she too didn't get herself killed or even hurt in her daring and gallant effort to retrieve that paper as she plopped herself right in front of me, I grabbed her like she'd done to me and I then started kissing her the same way she did me, and I too enjoyed it equally as much as she did. Finally I was able to get my hands on another treasure from Spooks-Ville as well as to read its content. It was sort of strange writing, but I was able to read every bit of it, except one little corner that had been torn off sometime during our attempt of either getting it, or sometime during the struggle between the man and the woman during her rape and beheading. The paper was some sort of poem and my friends were as anxious as I was to hear what it said. Sally started to grab it out of my hands, and Vera slapped her hand real hard.

"Ouweeeee, now why'd ya do that for Vera, all I was gonna do was take and start readin' it since Eddie didn't wanna read it." Sally started to cry a little bit, but could only hold her cheek where Vera slapped her.

"Damn you Sally; Eddie was about ta read it ya little bitch, now keep your damn paws off my boyfriend now y' hear. Go ahead and read it OK Eddie, I'll keep Sally in line." Vera just smiled at me and her beautiful black eyes glowed from the small light of sheer happiness, but not in my life did I know Vera had such a temper and found out she was just like I was, and that was a good thing that we were so much alike in almost every way, except she was a girl and I was a boy, that was the major difference and man was I glad too. Most boys my age hated girls, why I had no real idea, but as I said, I sure was glad she was like me in everything except being of the opposite sex and all.

"Thank you Vera; Yea Sally just keeps your paws off -n me always, y'hear. Now can I just read this blasted paper? It's a poem of some kind… it says."

I started reading it slowly and handled it very carefully so not to rip it any more than it had already been ripped; it has a few splotches of blood on it in spots, and a couple words were sort of hard to make out, but nonetheless I was able to read the whole thing.

With-in the Chambers of My Lonely Heart
With-in the chambers of my lonely heart,
Where-by the walls have crumbled from the emulate start.
Its cracked and broken door is rusting,
And it is engulfed with cob-webs, idle and dusting.
The corridors are long, dark, and narrow,
And they echo with the silence of ghostly flaming arrows.
For my lonely heart is like a solitary prisoner placed,
And there upon cracked walls the only image etched is your pretty face.
The chambers have no iron to brace their ragged walls,
And there is not one burning candle-light hanging from its ceilings tall.
The rooms are empty, but also filled with despair- no one to care,
And the floors are deep pits that have only musky air.
Shivering, quivering veins like twisted pipes do slowly flow,
It's filled with murky blood all dried, and scaly in chambers above and below.
The foundation is shaky, flakey, always crumbling and cracked,
The roof is made with powdery imbedded cloth-like gunny sacks.

It's weak, and weary pounding-throbbing beat, is a burning aching lonely heat,

It's not always kept up, and it's thundering tone, never neat, a fiery beat.

The loneliness there is pitched with empty desperate fading sounds,

And it is built upon a trembling, quaking rocky ground.

There is only one window, broken, molding, and always nailed closed tight,

And its dormer is an eerie, creaking, hallowed freighting sight.

There are no furnishings, nor drapery hanging upon bent curtain rods,

And the concrete is sinking on quicksand with-in this torrid lodge.

But there is only one thing that can renovate the chambers of my lonely heart,

And that is for only you to fill it with real true love from the emulate start.

Love eternally, yours fur ever.

Edward H' Wolf ... 9 August '94

"This sure is a sad letter Eddie. What do ya think it means?" Vera asked with a saddened sortta look, and just half way smiled at me as if she'd already figured it out all by herself.

David asks in a normal voice. We looked at him in surprise, maybe all this scarred the stuttering right out of him once and for all, at least I hoped so, cause I sure was tired of hearing him stutter like he did, it was so annoying all the time. I prayed. God let it be so, please. Well I got my prayer answered, or so it seemed, cause for the rest of this exploration of the mansion he never stuttered not even once period. Man what a relief that was. Sally and Vera just smiled at me with a tremendous joy in their little pea pickin' hearts, and started to giggle just the way all girls their ages done.

We all took one last look at that dead woman's body entangled with rope around the clutches of that big 'ol guillotine, then looked at the other torture instruments in the other corner and wondered who the Sam Hell all these people were in the first place to do these awful murders in our quaint little community of Hyde Park Indiana deep into this back woods country setting that we all loved so dang well.

"Wow, this stuff is deep, I don't know what it really means, but it sure was sad and sortta pretty too at the same time. This Edward H' Wolf must have been a writer or somethin' I recon, but who was this George M Maxifield Sir?" My curious mind wondered for a brief second about how someone could write such things, but then I realized that this woman must have had a lover outside her marriage to this George guy who was the maker of the lantern and must have been a wealthy business baboon, or was that tycoon, anyways who cares?

"Goofy kid that's Sr. is senior not sir dip-stick. Sally blurted out in her usual rude manner.

"I KNEW THAT YOU LITTLE FEMALE DOG." I just had to tell her in mild words that she was just a real little bitch.

I looked at my friends with an evil eye, and with my other one I winked at my princess Vera as if I really knew who that Wolf man was, and maybe I did in my mind somehow. I laughed…"Hehehehehe." But I had no clue as to who the other feller was, or deep down inside maybe again I did know who he was as well… somehow. I continued to smile the whole time, but frightened too at the same time.

My tone was soft and gentle as well as being quite calm all the sudden. I couldn't believe the serenity that surrounded me at the time, it was almost as though I was surrounded by an assembly of boys and girls ready to raise their voices in a chorus of parodies of magical negro songs all strung out in shrillness amidst the cries of native American Indians ta helps 'em gets themselves outta a difficult situation by taking stock in this character by use of some special insight of powers yet undetermined; the howls of wolves, and the atrociously dismembered body of the dead woman' screams as she tried to yell out for help just before her head was cut off its beautifully shaped body, as well as our on looking assembly to the gibbet of horrors with-in the chamber of the very pits of Hell itself here inside Spooks-Ville farm and its house of the ghostly insane.

These murderers out of the old west that lived here must have been a real wild bunch of men and women in their days. The black magic that some of the women practiced was taken mostly from the shaman witch doctors in and around the area of neighboring Indian tribes, and no one wanted to come around the mansion for fear of what might happen to them, so the majority of folk just stayed away along with their tall folklore tales and such, including most Indians who knew what was going on within the confines of the farm of horror.

We turned and walked out of this atrocious place of death and made our way down the hall to still another room. As we walked I thought that this must have been the most heathen land under the heavens back in the 1800's era.

What dreadful events might we to discover in the next room and the next after that one, only God knew for sure what lay ahead in our explorations.

In the next room we found more dead women' bones, some were chained to the walls, most of their clothing was intact except that their dresses were disordered just a teeny weenie little bit, exposing some of their private body parts. They seemed to be sort of in a petrified state outside of some death deterioration that had taken place over the years, but that seemed to me as being some sort of wild west type of entertainment of a some fashion, giving it an engagingly provocative power of arousing a sympathetic response from Vera and Sally, but for David and me it was a little bit stimulating. You might say it was some more of that good 'ol southern exposure in the minds eye of being in the appealing realm of sexual arousal. Hahahahaha. My laugh was sharp like a dagger.

Both girls covered their eyes, more so Sally as she shook her head from side to side in a dischargeable fashion at the atrocities that lay before her frail and somewhat aggravating little bird brain inside her big fat head, but Vera quickly uncovered her eyes with both hands and walked over to one of the women and began to weep a little.

"Why, why did all this killing happen to only women? There ain't been any dead men so far in all of our exploration, this is just horrible, and it appalls me something fierce. Why did someone daunt these women in such a gruesome manner, I'd best tell my other mommy's when I get back upstairs." she bowed her head in a moment of prayer for the dearly departed poor soul who was so brutally detached from life in such an awful manner as what our eyes were beholding. It was simply horrible.

I was having a hard time trying to understand Vera's strange way of talking, it also took a shocking toll on David and Sally as well.

"Vera, what the hell are you talking about, I can't understand a single damn word your tryin' ta say."

"Yea, V-Vera, me either." Sally blurted out, interrupting me in her usual rude manner.

"Shut the hell up will ya puss face Sally, I was trying to talk, you know better than to interrupt someone else when they're talking first." My temper was startin' ta get the better of me once more, but my voice was firm and I too showed her my rude side also and she quickly hushed her big mouth so I wouldn't really chew her out. Sally needed that once in awhile, but when she stood there as quiet as a church mouse, I knew that I was truly in charge of her, and that made me feel more like a leader than I already was.

All the sudden something brushed by my arm, it had a chilling feeling, and I knew it was another apparition trying to get my attention. I didn't realize that Vera had been taken over by one of the mansions ghostly presents from earlier on in this exploration.

Somehow this apparition was making use of Vera in an unjustly manner, and took full advantage over her existence. Vera started dancing and humming a strange tune, then she grabbed hold of me, and started to swirl around, causing me to stagger and stumble like a drunken hobo. I pulled hard to try and separate us, but her grip was too strong and I couldn't break free, so I pretended to play along with her as she danced. Sally and David just stared at her with big dollar sized eyes, but she didn't pay attention to them and kept on dancing. I struggled more and finally broke free stepping backwards, stumbling over my own two left feet and fell to the floor landing on my butt. Vera started to come towards me, but stopped dead in her tracks and placed her hands on her cute little hips. She gave me her best evil eye that looked the same way in which that other bully Sally did on the playground at school.

Sliding backwards a couple inches I propped myself against the wall. She kept coming at me with that mean gaze in her pretty big dark brown eyes, knelt down beside me grabbin' me by the throat and began to strangle me. I gasp for breath and tried to call out for my friends to help me, but all they did was stare even more. I gasp harder as the tears started to stream down my face, it was turning redder and redder as her hands got tighter and tighter. I struggled harder but couldn't break free; finally Sally and David rushed toward me. David grabbed me and Sally grabbed Vera and at the same time they both pulled real hard breaking me free and I fell backwards laying on the floor in horror, shaking real hard gasping for breath, coughing and crying all at the same time.

"V-Ver-a, what the H-Hell are you (cough) d-doin' (cough)? What did I d-do, step on your feet or somethin'?" I expel more air from my lungs, gagging suddenly with the release of irritation once more, David just stood there like he was outta breath, Sally only stood in her tracks as still as the night was dark and just kept a prolonged gaze fixed at me and Vera. "What in the hell are you doing Vera, are you crazy or something?" My voice took on the frustration of a two-edged sword., but I didn't say anything, neither did Vera as we both sat there on the floor looking up at them, Vera shook her head from side to side a few times and coughed as well from the dust that had infiltrated our noses and mouths.

"I-I-I, (cough) what are you all starin' at? What's wrong Eddie? Are you ok? What are you doin' on the floor?" I slid myself to the side a couple inches along the wall as Vera approached me crawling on the floor. She then grabbed me and gave me a big hug. I thought I was gonna be strangled once again by a mad woman, but she just held me and started kissing me on the cheek so I wouldn't be afraid of her.

"All I really wanna do is to tell you all what happened to me just now. Something seemed to be inside of me, it was that darn little ghost girl and she told me things that were just awful, I couldn't help what I was doin' but I just wasn't able to wobble her out of me but while she was still there she told me, and believ e it or not I remember every word she said…. Well her goes, she said: "All I'm doin' is showin' you what happened to her here in this y'here dungeon of my farmhouse mansion when she was alive and there was this renegade Indian that stayed here for a couple weeks and was about to leave, but needed some previsions for his journey back to the Dakota territory where he lived, so he ask one of her six mommies and her to help him get what he needed from the basement, so he followed us down here, but when we got in this room he closed the door and locked it so neither of us girls could ever leave. My name is Maggie, this savage he raped my mommy, making me watch the whole sexual act, then he grabbed me and began to strangle me, I gasp, trying to escape, but couldn't get free and then fell to the floor and the man took what he wanted and ran out thinking us dead, but we was just unconscious, but by the time I opened my eyes and reached the upper part of the house the man was gone and my mommy was dead, chained to the big mechanical thing mostly naked, that's her in the other room, her body stretched and torn apart. It was awful."

Vera stopped all the sudden and looked at me and the others as her thoughts began to flow back to her like she had always been and then said. "All she was doin' was telling me and all of you in her own way what happened to her and one of her six mommies, there was gonna be more, but I shook her out after you slapped me in the face Eddie, but I forgive you, I wasn't myself, and knew it, but there was not a thing I could do, please believe me, please." All she wanted to do was have me and my friends forgive her for making them scarred, crying and peeing all over themselves.

I grabbed Vera and gave her a big hug and started kissing her on her cheeks, she just held onto me as tight as she could, I thought she was gonna attack me again, but she didn't, she just kissed me back several times on the cheeks as well. We sat there for a few minutes to dry our tears trying to pull ourselves back together raising ourselves to the upright position so we could walk hand in hand to our friends, we tried to give them a hug, but they just backed off sayin' no way that we were too strange because they thought that it was just way too yucky to get things like hugs and kisses the way Vera and I were doin' to one another. "I forgive you Vera... hows 'bout you guys?" I ask with a somewhat red blushing tint on my face.

"Yea I forgive ya Vera" Sally said as did her brothers all at the same time. All seemed well once again and we continued our journey into the unknown realm of insanity and death deep inside the chambers of horror of what was once a residence of good and not a residence of evil.

Soon we were looking at still another doorway, but none of my friends wanted to go in after they seen all the atrocious scenes of death before their pampered eyes. I couldn't help but think of all the various ways that people had been killed in this creepy 'ol mansion farmhouse, and every time I came up with a new scenario, my blood ran as cold as a block of ice. I'd felt the presence of an entity inside me once in awhile; it wasn't a good feeling either 'cause they take over your whole being and twist it in all sorts of directions when inside a body, its lock stock and barrel and the only thing that can make it go away is good thoughts, or to have someone slap the dang 'ol ghost and maybe a little crap right outta ya. All the sudden the door swung open as we passed it, a voice seemed to be calling to Vera and she stopped in her steps, turned around and walked into the room as though she belonged there. A light was peeping through one of the walls, but it also seemed to be moving in different directions. I couldn't help notice the look on Vera's face, it was a cold pale glow, like frost on a window during a snow storm at night once more, she called to us to come inside to play with her for a little while and as I watched her act really strange most of the time she was in the dungeon, my worst nightmares seemed to be happening right before my eyes, and man oh man that was scarier than bein' in that 'ol spooky place all the while we were exploring it.

Well sir, my friends snuggled real close to me as I walked towards Vera who was playing with her hands in mid air, they were stretched outward as though she was holding someone or something and rubbing it in the back, just the way I'd seem some of the adult fold do when they were dancing to a slow song at a barn dance. I walked over to Vera and ask her if she was ok, but she seemed not to be paying attention to me whatsoever, then she looked at me and told me that yes I could have this dance with her and she grabbed me once again flinging me back and forth as we moved in a round about fashion she slowly moved her hand down toward my butt and squeezed it slowly a couple times, trying to look at her was sorta hard under the extenuating circumstances and predicament she had me in and moving wasn't an option'cause she held me so dang close it sent goose bumps over my whole body causing a strange tingle below my waist and down my legs. Vera grabbed my hand pulling me hard as we ran out of the door and down the hall as fast as we could. I couldn't break free, not that I really wanted to because of my love for her, but I wanted to in the other sense that she was scaring the hell outta me allot.

David and Sally came running after us getting turned around just a wee bit they quickly recovered their global positioning systems, and their radar directed them back on track. Sally was much faster than her brother David, making him fall about six or seven feet behind of her, and soon Vera and I were out of their sight heading down a different hallway, up a winding stairway that had lots of cobwebs all over it, brushing some of them away from my nose and eyes with my left hand as we entered a room that had a real big bed in it that was still as tidy as if it were just made. I could hear my friends calling us, but couldn't see them, I called back trying to attract their attention, telling them to go to the winding staircase and follow it up to where Vera and I were at, but Vera quickly let my hand go and slammed the door closed, then locked it with a rusty skeleton key that she'd picked up from an old night table beside the fancy four poster bed in one corner of the dark room. Silence was not as close as Vera wanted it to be, but maybe it was close enough for her to do what she had intention to do, I knew it was that ghost girl inside her, but my mind didn't want me to slap her ever again, so I just let it all play out like she was herself and not a half and half creature and human.

As we stood there in the dingy room that had appeared to come back to life right before my eyes, I could faintly hear my friends coming up the staircase still calling to us, but Vera told me to hush, then she pulled me toward her and we both fell on the bed, dust flew into the air causing us both to cough, and Vera came out of the spell she seemed to be in once more.

"Eddie. What are we doing here? Where are Sally and David? Why are we laying on this big 'ol dusty bed?" Vera had a confused look in her eyes, and was about to cry, but I gave it my best shot so she wouldn't cry and get us both all soaking wet.

"Don't you remember Vera? You were dancing with me in the dungeon then pulled me out and brought me up here and locked the door. Now where is the key for the door so I can let Sally and David in?" She looked at me and ask me what key, I started to get mad, but didn't out of respect for her, knowin' that shed been possessed by some dang 'ol ghost girl once again.

"Now look Vera, our friends are real scared and so am I, but we must get out of here and head home now ok. Now where is that key so I can unlock the door so we can go?"

"Eddie, I said I don't know where the key is. Can't ya believe me?" She started ta cry, but my sympathy kicked me in the butt once again… geesh what a feller wont do for love.

"I believe you Vera, but we must find it, now help me look for it, OK!" My emotions ran high.

"Come on YOU TOO, Open the door OK, please open it and let us in." My friends finally found where we were, Sally pounded as hard as she could and was pleading desperately outside the huge wooden door with a brass lion head door knob on it. David had just come up the stairs breathing real hard. I heard him tell Sally that he almost got lost in this creepy place and that he wanted to go home now, that if Vera and I wanted to play this kind of game, he just didn't want to have any more to do with explorin' this mansion with any of us ever again. Big mouth Sally shouted and told him to just button his lip or he'd be in trouble when they got home, that is if we would ever go home.

We were so far inside the place that we really didn't know where we were. Yes, the inedible had happened, we were finally lost inside the big mansion. All the twists and turns along with Vera' strange behavior had caused us to be more afraid than we were in the beginning of all of our explorations a month or so ago. Yet deep inside me, I was not gonna show my total fear forno one. I knew we had to find our way out of here and real soon, or we'd all be in deep cow manure that was one thing for certain.

"Vera, please look in your dress pocket, maybe ya put that dang 'ol skeleton key in it." I said and without delay she slid her dainty long black fingers into her left pocket, and nothin', then placed it in her other pocket, and bingo, it was there. She didn't say a word for a couple seconds, and then told me it wasn't there either. I gave a sigh, and wondered just where the hell she'd put it. Vera looked at me with her big dark eyes, and a slight smile on her face, then blinked her eyes and gave me a wink and giggled a bit.

"Vera, are ya pullin' my leg or what? Well do ya have it in your pocket or what?" I was startin' ta get upset, but at the same time I didn't want her mad at me. Maybe it was because she may get possessed again and really hurt me next time or worse yet, she ma try to kill me or somethin'. I didn't want to find out so I just gave her a big grin and told her to just come on and let me have the damn key so we could get the hell outta here and get our little butts home.

"Ok Eddie, I have it, but I just wanted ta see if'n ya would get mad at me, but since ya didn't, well I suppose I can let ya have it." Vera sortta smiled outta the corner of her mouth. She smiled really big as she pulled her hand outta her pocket, then reached for my head, I pulled back in a slight jerkin' motion and gave her that look of discontent, not knowing all she wanted to do was give me a big kiss on my lips since we were all alone at last. I took the kiss with joy, but was frightened at the same time, then she took her hand from the sides of my face and placed the key in my hand, man was I ever relieved when she did.

"Here Eddie, sorry I pretended that I didn't have the key, can you forgive me this time." Her attitude changed with each passing mood moment that gave way in her soft ravishing body.

"Well, I guess so Vera, but please don't do that to me again ok." I took the key and turned toward the door glancing' over my shoulder at Vera as I tried to place the key in the door at the same time, I kinda missed the key hole a couple times and fumbled about the big brass key hole in the 'ol wooden oak door. She smiled at me and I at her as she giggled a bit, her giggle made me uneasy as well as embarrassed at the same time, my face turned beet red and I turned my face toward the door tryin' to place the key in upside down, that made me blush even harder, but I didn't show my face to my princes Vera as I turned the key over placing it in the right way tuning it to open the door for my friends who were just standin' there gazin' at the door in wonderment if I was gonna ever open that door or not.

"Ha, ha, ha, we sure had ya both scared didn't we? Bet ya thought we were gonna leave ya here, but ya know we wouldn't do that, we just wanted to scare ya just a little more, now lets find our way outta here ok pal" David blurted out with his crazy and weird cry-baby attitude.

"Ya mean we're lost Eddie." Sally said as she glared at me with her mean, but frightened blue eyes poppin' outta her head.

"Yea, fatty- fatty two-by-four, did ya go and get us lost in this creepy 'ol place? I wanna go home too, but first we gotta find our way back to the broken window ok scarry-cat." I tried my best ta make her mad enough so not to be afraid and maybe even smile for once, but she just cried like the really big baby she was, and I wasn't gonnna let her get my goat any more. David also glared at me and pissed all over himself, man did he stink. How was he gonna explain his pissy pants to his folks, and why he didn't go pee behind a tree or something when he was playin' in the woods, he knew better than go to the outhouse in his pants cause he would be spanked royal for doin' it.

"I- I have to go home and change my pants, please get us outta here ok, I'm gettin' really scared, and besides I have to climb up the tree beside my house to sneak inside so I can change my pants, so my mom and dad wont know I pee'd myself." Sally said as the Crocodile tears flowed down her fat Nile face.

"M-Me t-to." DAavid agreed in tears as well as being totally soaked with piss.

"Yea, let's find our way back to the main hall so we can get outta here, besides I'm gettin' hungry." Once again as usual I took the lead, and with Vera holding my hand this time it sorta -kinda made me feel some-what at ease and as we headed out the door, and it slammed behind us making us scurry down them windin' stairs almost to the point of just tumblin' down them head over heals. One of the steps broke under Sally' foot and she let out a scream scaring us even the more as we reached the bottom of the stairway we turned left and took off lickety-split down the long hall way and dashed up the other staircase to the top floor. Light shown in through the windows with all its glory and that made us all start to laugh and giggle.

Knowing that we were almost outta there, we plopped ourselves down on the plank wood floor lookin' at each other as though nothin' had ever happened except for the smell that was comin' from David' pissy pants. Soon we were on our way back through the other rooms, out the kitchen and back down to the basement area of our entry just a few feet below it. We glanced at the rubble and there was even more than before, and was the only one that, and I wondered just who was piling up more and more dusty-broken things in a haphazard fashion. David climbed out first then pulled his sister out, she was a bit heavy standing on my back, but I tolerated the pain. I then lifted Vera up to the window exit, her dress flung over my face once again and I got another whiff of her sweet behind as she went through the window that thing smiled at me.

Vera and I walked hand and hand the whole time we walked from Spooks-Ville, through the cornfield, the woods and all the way to her front door. David and Sally went to their place across the street where David started climbing the tree beside his house and Sally started to play out front for a distraction so her brother could sneak inside to change his pants and climb back onto the tree as though nothin' had ever happened at all. I snuck a kiss off Vera as we stood outside her door, then I ran to the back of her place jumping the fence and ran as fast as I could down our path towards Luke's place so I could finally eat dinner.

Chapter 16

Lost in the Graveyard

 ein' at home with a full stomach sure felt real good to this tired little boy, but I just couldn't wait till we went back to explore that farmhouse once again. We sure did have a lot to explore yet and cause I was getting a bit anxious. I guess it was because it was almost time for me and my Aunt Mary to move back to Muncie, but I sure wasn't ready for that to happen just yet.

I got a good night sleep even after all that me and my friends went through yesterday. I was all rested, rearin' ta go once again, but Luke had different ideas for me, and when he told me he wanted me to help him dig a new outhouse hole, I got mad at him real good, and boy was he shocked.

"Boy, don't you run away from me, how dare you sass back at me, I should tan yer hide a good one, but there ain't no time fer that right now, I'll deal with you on this later boy." Man was I shakin' so hard in my shoes that even my shoe laces were tryin' ta hide from the fierce voice of 'ol Luke Dillon. He glared at me with his big dark piercing hairy eyes and told me to go fetch his friends from down by

Mr. Fulkler's place. Immediately my skinny 'lil butt fled from his sight as fast as my little long legs would carry me and in a couple of minutes I was at 'ol man Thompsons place and fetched him, then I speed to David's to get his dad, but he wasn't there, he was in his pasture that mornin' at the but crack of dawn, so I had to rush to Mr. Cash's place to fetch his son Johnnie, who was sort of a lazy bumb of a fella that only sat around and told his stories to those who'd listen ta him, but none the less they were the only ones I could get for Luke's outhouse dig.

"Come on Johnnie… Luke's a countin' on ya big time." I pleaded with him for my very life depended on him, well at least my butt and I was anyways.

" Yea… ok I recon, maybe a little work won't hurt me any, and besides Pa's been telling me ta gets off-n my dead lazy ass and start doin' things, tht my lyin' ta folk wasn't gonna gets me any where in life less-n I did." I was as happy as a lark in a meadow I was, and ran back to tell Luke who I was able to get at least two of 'em, then I flew in the house ta I eat my breakfast so I'd have the strength to help move some buckets of dirt as well as to fetch their water, and the heavy tools they'd be a needin' from the shed.

Time flew by so fast that it was lunch time; I sure was hungry once more, so much so that I could eat the whole Frigidaire if'n I was able ta eat one.

I shoveled my food down faster than the others bein' a wee bit more quiet than usual, as the men folk ate like a bunch of pigs, chewin' and a talkin' at the same time; it sort of like watchin' a gory cave man flick on the TV late at night, and kinda nasty just watchin'.

We soon finished our big hardy lunch that Aunt Mary had fixed; and wanted ta ask if I could go play for awhile, but thought I'd best leave well enough alone for today, and maybe if I worked even harder, just maybe I wouldn't get that whoopin' that Luke told me he'd let me have later. My mind was also in hope that I would be able to go see my friends for about an hour or so in order to plan out the next exploration of the mansion of horror.

We all worked so hard that mornin' and the whole was over half done, so Luke decided that since I was such a little fellow that I could get cleaned up and not have to do any more for him. I reckoned I had been punished enough, and as far as that whoppin, well I never got it at all. Boy was my butt glad too.

I ran as fast as my tired little body could carry me into the house; grabbed my clothes and placed them on my feather bed at the foot, Aunt Mary already had my bath water drawn, heated up and in the big round shinny metal wash tub that she also used to wash our clothes in with a scrub board at times just ta help keep the electric bill down below five dollars a month. When I was finished I asked her if I could please go play, and as usual she said Ok. She was such a nice woman and everyone liked her allot, and that made me feel good inside.

"The rest of the day is yers since ya worked so hard this mornin' Eddie, have fun, and be back by five as usual for dinner ok." Her tone was soft, sweet and low and filled with a gentle nature.

"Oh boy, ya mean it… thank ya-thank ya." My excitement gave me such a rush that my energy had been replenished to its fullest and soon I was perched in front of Vera's house waiting for her to come to the door.

"Hi Vera wow don't you look pretty!" My smile was as big as all outdoors when she came to the door, and she looked more beautiful than a new born puppy, all dolled up in a tight pair of pants. Which she'd never worn before, and it was a real shocker to the both of us, 'cause in those days it was unheard of for a 'little girl' ta wear pants let alone any women folk. Her hair was in some sort of bun in the back of her head with the dread locks popping out from all around it, but the amazing things was that she had a little eye and lip makeup on her face. I couldn't help but to repeat myself. "Wow wee, Vera you-you look very pretty today."

She smiled really big, as a blush popped from her blackish brown cheeks that was just slightly visible to the eyes. "Thank ya, your sweet Eddie, real sweet my prince. Hehehehehe, you look real nice too, hehehe." Vera then asked me to go fetch Tommy, Sally, and David and that she would wait at her house 'cause she had to do one more chore before she could go play, turning around at the same time I headed down the steps, my two left feet caused me to start tripping all over myself while still looking at her instead of what I was doing. Vera giggled as she went back into her house and I took off for our friends' house as fast as I could go after I picked myself up off-n the ground.

When I knocked on the door, David answered telling me his brother Tommy still had to stay home for a couple more days to work off some more trouble he'd gotten himself into. My feet were fidgety and I paced back and forth in front of their big 'ol house. After about ten minutes or so, Sally and David came outside. Sally too was in pants, and that really shocked the hell outta me. I looked at her with puzzled eyes then at David.

"What's up with your sister, she's wearing boys' pants just like Vera is?" My shook head shook itself a few times really hard and caused my eyes ta flutter like a girl all at the same time.

David just shrugged his shoulders and cocked his head to one side giving a funny face. "Ya got me Eddie, I can't figure out girls anyway let alone this."

Her big butt stuck out like a fist full of swollen pumpkins ready for Halloween, or maybe that pregnant wolfs belly was more like it… "Hahaha." I couldn't help but laugh a little 'cause it struck my funny bone like a sledge hammer had hit it. The very thought of it made David chuckle just a bit as I looked at her big butt protruding in the outback well beyond her waist.

"Hey butt hole what ya lookin' at, don't I look good or not." Sally blurted out with a killer mean look in her pissy - baby blue eyes.

"Let's go Ok; hahaha… I wanna get to the farmhouse as fast as we can so we can have all afternoon to explore it."

Vera was just coming out of her front door as we approached her place and she still looked as pretty as before even though she'd done one extra nasty choir, splitting like wood we took up root and fled through the treed as fast as our tiny feet would take us, but this time we went down alongside David's pasture to the cornfield and it somehow seemed to be a much shorter way than taking the usual route by my place, but we still had to run along Buck Creek to get to our bridge, but that didn't matter much to us kids, we never paid that much attention to things like that at our ages.

We soon approached the mansion, but from a different side than usual and ended up next to the graveyard that lay on the other side of it once again. We kids knew it was there because of all the tall trees, bushes, and weeds couldn't hide it since we'd been in it yesterday by accident, it sure was much bigger than we'd thought, but wasn't too afraid any more.

It was so cool, but scary at the same time as we paced our way between the tombstones that surrounded us like a bunch of wild Indians on the war path. Coming to an abrupt dead stop, we were standing next to a tall metal fence with spiked poles extending to the sky with a cobblestone road that stopped in front of the fence, but there wasn't a gate to go inside, and that seemed stranger to us than the cemetery itself.

"What the?" I started to say, but couldn't finish my sentence.

Vera grabbed me by one arm, but looked at me with a secure feeling inside her; although she was shaking a little she looked at me and smiled sayin' "Why's this fence inside the graveyard, shouldn't it be on the outside instead?"

Sally on the other hand threw her arms around her brother. David pushed her away telling her to get her dang ol' cooties off of him. Naturally Vera and I laughed and then she started teasing Sally about bein' a scary-cat and she blurted out in a wicked tone. "I aint no dang ol' scary-cat, ya take it back now, ya hear".

She let go of David and pulled Vera away from me, at the same time she shook her fist in her face. "Ya take it back dang it, you're a pussy-cats butt hole, na-na na na-na, just shut your big pussy cats mouth or I'll shut it for ya". Sticking out her tongue, Sally gave Vera the raspberries and wanted to slap her in the face, but didn't for the obvious reasons of not wanting m y sweetie pie ta kick her big fat ass; cause she sure would've if-n the bickerin' hadn't of stopped the way it did all the sudden.

David and I thought for sure the two girls were gonna tear into each other and have a good ol' cat fight right there in front of us, maybe we'd see some of them besides their faces, maybe their behinds or something, but I couldn't let that happen. The thought of seeing something other than Sally's puss face just made me sick at my stomach, but Vera, well that was a different story, cause I wanted to do some more exploring, and if they would've had a fight and got down to the nitty-gritty of scratchin' each-others eyeballs out, then we'd have at go home, face the folks and be in real big trouble, so I pulled Sally away from her telling her to just knock it off or I would make her eat a chicken poop sandwich. Sally let go of Vera, and turned around toward her brother.

"Ummm, the nerve of some folk." Vera was pissed off, but she maintained her composure cause she didn't wanna get her new jeans dirty so she avoided the fight, but

I knew Vera would get Sally someplace, sometime, and sooner or later that was for certain, and knew her expression wasn't a bit pleased, but she'd get over it once we started our adventures inside the Spooks-Ville mansion and now we had a graveyard to play in as well.

In the night, more-so than in the day time, ghosts walk the grounds outside the house. One of the caretakers was killed there sometime during the early 1900's, and his spirit lingers in the cemetery all the time just like all the other apparitions for some dang reason? It is said he appears to folk who go inside the graveyard forcing them to leave the grounds immediately. Haunting' in this grim place were common occurrences, but we kids didn't know it outside of that which we'd heard grown-up folk tell.

Through-out the past hundred or so years that this place has stood, all of it's inhabitants have been buried in the cemetery and haunt not only outside, but inside the mansion as well and everyone who ever worked on, lived at, or visited the farm died on these very grounds, making it a sort of legend, still other stories say that several men who worked here quit after they saw a woman stroll through the cemetery across grave after grave and enter the house without opening one solitary door or window to get in, she just disappeared right through the walls, but the spookiest of all was the one about several children disappearing while exploring the mansion and never came back out alive during the past century; and, at least two of the girls appear just before bad weather, and immediately after the bad weather starts, they float towards some windows on the upper floor, peering inside with their hands partially covering their faces.

"Come on let's find a way inside and look around OK?" I grabbed Vera's hand and started walking along the fence, but David and Sally just stood there starin' at the hundreds of graves that were haphazardly placed around the entire mansion but more-so at the few on the inside of the spiked fence inside the confines of the cemetery.

"Hey wait up Eddie, don't leave us here, I would rather go inside the house and look there instead of this creepy place." David leaped toward Vera and me leaving his sister standing on the cobblestone driveway.

"No ya don't, I aint gonna stay here, not me, wait up guys." Sally jogged toward the rest of us as we slowly walked beside the fence, pushing our way through the weeds and bushes that covered the whole place as far as we could see, we finally found a small gate with a broken padlock and a rusty chain dangling from its one broken hinge'.

Bein' the brave one I pushed the gate to one side and then slid through sideways so as not to tear my clothes, and then the others slithered in right behind me. The gates of Hell seemed to open right in front of our eyes. The sky above the cemetery appeared as lead, with the glow of the faint sun turning our faces to a crystal red shade, cold winds taunted our skin, and seemed to fill us with some sort of ritualistic spirit, dust flew up in our faces from the loosened and driven winds inside the graveyards ragged metal barrier with a misty fog drifting down on us from Heaven in a fire-laid sheet of red dew droplets that seemed to burn our flesh with millions of tiny goose bumps. The smell from moss covered grave stones penetrated our nostrils, turning our stomach with the trifles on which it was driven. I felt heavy hearted as my soul drifted upward in the dusty sheets of fog; but all the sudden the fog broke from my skin and was gone with the winds on which it came, and as I glared right at a big stone, I seen that it had an inscription carved in it that read: "Voodoo Princess 1862, manner of death, yellow fever." Moss covered the stone from top to bottom, but it was still readable. My friends looked all around as they stood in one spot pivoting their bodies in a complete circle and their eyes popped outta their heads the size of silver dollars as we slowly crept further inside the cemetery.

In the days around the Civil War time there were a lot of disease killing lots of folk all over the country as well as bein' a time of great hardship for most people, hunger was also a major cause of death, but here at the mansion, most of it was from some sort of murder in one manner or another. The Voodoo Princess hailed from the neighboring town of Selma about twenty-five miles away, and at that time but was originally from some place else far away; she was the local doctor so to speak and her voodoo magic could cure most anything there was, and people didn't mind having a witch… doctor them up, 'cause most of the doctors were either in the army or dead from being killed in war, or from the outbreak of yellow fever, cholera and other diseases that were a plaguing the territory.

One day she was called to the mansion to take care of one of the women who was married to ol' man Maxifield. Charlotte, a black slave was his fourth wife, and the one he liked best out of all of them; any how, Charlotte was dying from the fever and lay in her golden room weathering away piece by stinky piece, the room wass so called because it had lots of real gold things in it, all the bedrooms were named for one reason or another, but this one was a very special one indeed. Three days later Charlotte died and the Voodoo Princess was locked in the dungeon, being accused of killing ol' man Maxifield's beloved Charlotte, three days after that the witch somehow escaped, but while in the dungeon she contracted Yellow fever and caused the disease to spread like a wild prairie fire.

Some say that the spirits of both Charlotte and the Voodoo Princess get together in the golden room on the very same day Charlotte died, and all of the other days throughout the years they wonder the cemetery; Charlotte crying, the Princess chanting and dancing as if nothing ever happened that January day of 1862.

"Amelia is buried here, she was one of my, uhmmm, the mommies who lived in the mansion with a half dozen other women." Vera said as she started to cry. "Charlotte too was another one of my mommy's, I sure loved them all." Tears streamed down my beloved Vera's face and dripped on her white blouse, but as each tear drop hit it and dropped red spots and made a face on the green moss covered floor, I just couldn't make it out; as well as not bein' able ta figure out how she knew all of what she just said, maybe it was because she was afraid or something and the whole time Sally and David glared at her in amazement, but only shook their heads like she was crazy or something.

"What's that Vera?" I asked. My eyes crinkled almost to a close as I glanced at her then the gravestone, it said the woman's name, the date, how she died, and that she were one of six women who was married to ol' man Maxifield. I knew then that she had read the inscription from the stone 'cause the ghosts spirit had interred her once more, but somehow she'd goofed in her speech, I knew what was happening, but David and Sally still couldn't figure it all out. And I sue wasn't gonna tell 'em either... hahaha."

They were so dang stupid sometimes, b ut I never told 'em that; and, all I could do was chuckle a little, telling them to just keep walking so we could get to the house and look around inside some more.

Little did we know that David had stepped behind a large tomb structure to take a pee, and just kept on walking; about a hundred yards or so later, I looked over my shoulder, and saw only Sally tailing me like she was attached to my butt, Vera was beside me holding my hand, but where was David? He was lost inside the graveyard someplace.

"Hey where the heck is your brother at Sally?" My eyes pierced Sally's, and then I glared into Vera's dark eyes with much question as well?

"We need ta find my brother and quick Eddie; I'm scared and wanna go home now." Sally pissed her pants staining them, but since she was so afraid… that she didn't even notice the wet spots on her pants that streamed all the way to her shoes, nor did she notice she'd even peed herself in the first place. This time I knew she'd get her hide tanned really good when she got home, but that wasn't the big issue that we were faced with, all we knew was he'd disappeared and needed ta find him before we went on. Having to trace our steps back and look for him as fast as we could took away some of out time, but if we didn't find him, man would all be in deep shit trouble that was for sure.

Step by step we paced ourselves from one grave stone to the next in a haphazardly pattern, none of us had any idea what we were doing, but nothing else mattered except to find David now. I had in my mind that as soon as we found him that I would tell him and Sally to just go on back home and leave Vera and me here to finish the exploration of the graveyard and house, that they would be able to come with us another time. After about an hour of looking we found him cowering behind the tomb where he took a pee and of course we were all glad to find him as fast as we did knowin' that it could have been worse if we hadn't found him, and who knows what would have happened to pee-boy David, as I nick named him after this incident.

"Hey why the heck did ya go and scare the daylights outta us? Next time, tell us you have to go pee Ok pal?" I wasn't having any mercy on him in the least, and proceeded to tell him to take his sister and go on home, that Vera and I would be alright here without them.

"A - are ya s-sure b-buddy, I, I, I didn't mean to d-do that, I, I w-won't do it ever again." David and his sister the blabbermouth Sally started to go toward the gate., and we'd also gave Sal the nick-name of pussycat pee girl, and boy oh boy did she hate us for it too.

"Hey Sally, you better not tell anyone a single thing, y'hear, or ya know what'll happen to ya, got it?" Vera blurted out at her like her dad or mom would have done when they really meant what they said to her and her brothers when they were told to do somethin' or misbehaved by goin ta places that they shouldn't be in - in the first place. Vera and I turned around going in the same direction that I came from to find pee boy. Sally and David didn't hesitate to scurry themselves to the gate and out of our sight.

"Wheeew (I wiped my forehead) thank God they're gone at last. Now we can continue our journey." I leaned forward and gave Vera a kiss on her shivering cheek. She grabbed me giving me a great big bear hug, and planted a bigger kiss smack dab right on my lily white lips so tightly that it almost made me faint from lack of oxygen. Her kisses were always sweet, and filled with the juices of a sugar-cane, but this one made my blood almost boil over causin' some sorta strange feelin' to slither through my body like a bunch of blue racers.

Soon we came upon another large tomb structure that had a cross planted on its top steeple and its door on the front was partially open;

we slowly crept up to it, taking a peek inside with some steps leading downward just on the inside and that drew my curiosity; and knew that I had to explore this place no matter what, even if I had to go in by myself leaving Vera outside in the graveyard all alone. I knew she would cling to me like she was pasted to my insides with flour clue just like the good 'ol country gravy my aunt Mary made for breakfast and dinner all the time.

Looking at the inscription on the front gave me an indication that this place was older than we initially thought it was; 1720 was the year inscribed on the door and the name was just a little hard to read. I couldn't tell if it was a man's or a woman's tomb, but we would soon find out as we entered the dreary dark domain of the crypt. It was in ruins after years of neglect., while outside was the gloom of a once beautiful day, but there was still the horizon, sun, and sky - nothing more than a lead colored haze of cold-heat infiltrated the cemetery's unpleasantly cold rustic realm. The earth shook as we crept deeper inside the crypt's sphere of influence where the dead lay as if in a state of apoplexy.

Not all strange happenings are related totally into one particular scenario, there are some that have more bizarre stipulations behind them than meets the eyes; and, I knew that this was one of those times if things were to go wrong on our adventures of the farmhouse mansion and its creepy ol' graveyard, this would be the one for sure that may make us never come back here ever again.

Since the 1720's, something unusual has always happened on these grounds in the months of November and December of almost every year no one had ever been able to figure out why, or learn the significance of those months? One chilly morning, early, before dawn, on November 23, 1720, George H Maxifield lay awake in his room thinking about his accomplishments of building his dream mansion in the country. He was an odd man in his early 20's, and had become very wealthy when he stolen millions of the King of England's gold, and had it transported to a waiting ship in the harbor where soon he would be on his way to a different land, but he did not know exactly where he would end up, it just didn't matter to him. The journey abroad was a rough trip as the ship tossed and turned in the turbulence of the ocean and about a month or so after he left his home land the ship landed in the new world. Shortly after they set food ashore, George had come upon a Native tribe known as the Abenaki Indians. Well as it so happened to be that these savage Abenaki Indian people had been native New Englanders for millennia and knew not only their own lands, but also all the lands for two thousand miles to the west and all the tribes along their routes of travel for trade purposes.

George was a lucky man when he was taken in by the tribal chief's shaman, who had a beautiful daughter named Waity. George immediately fell in love with her, but for a price that he would regret for the rest of his life and his future family for generations to come, because the ways of the Native American Indians wasn't nothing to be foolin' around with in these treacherous times and it so happened that he had to drink the shaman's herbal potions and smoke his horrible smellin' weed in a long pipe and become a true man of the tribe in order to take Waity for his wife. The effects of those potions gave him weird feelings of being transformed into some sort of mystical being or creature, as legend has it. No one to this day has ever figured that out just what it was that he was possessed with.

Once he became a man and married the shaman's daughter, the shaman had his people escort them to their own country's land in a town that George later named Hyde Park, in the territory of Indiana near the Muncie Indian tribal village. It was there that he took all his gold and constructed his dream mansion for himself and his new bride.

One night as he relaxed on his bed he drank a glass of goat milk concoction that his wife had made for him before they retired for the night. Little did he know it was laced with a white solid substance from a poisonous garlic smelling root known to the native people as Kwai Kyoli Oleomed and when it is lignified it becomes highly toxic, but the Native American Indians didn't know that at the time. Waity had put way too much of it in his buttermilk to help him sleep because she'd never been told how much to use so it wouldn't kill anyone, and in the middle of the night George felt strange and had became nauseous heaving up blood drifting into a deep, deep sleep. Unfortunately he died during the night and needed to be buried that next morning around 4 a.m., before anyone in the household woke up so Waity dragged his body to the front yard to be buried it in a very deep grave, and had woke up their most trustworthy servant to do the honors of putting George to rest properly. She'd told their half native Indian and half black servant Jamal Spotted-foot not to tell anyone else and leave his death up to her to tell how it happened or he'd die as well.

After he was laid to rest, Jamal got a few other laborers to help construct a crypt to mark the spot of his burial place as a tribute to all who came to their home and was more than right to show respect to not only the dead, but to the widow as wll according to the native peoples in Waity's mind at least.

She and George had two sets of twins before he died, and poor Waity knew she needed a new husband to take George's place on the farm as master and overseer; and, to also help her raise the children, two boys and two girls one from each set. They would be the ones to carry on the Maxifield name after she passed. Six months later Waity

Anna Maxifield married George's younger brother and had another five kids on top of the four she already had and it was lucky for her that her belated husband left her his entire estate including the hidden gold that was left after the construction of the big mansion. Waity and her family never had to worry about money, 'cause they sure had plenty to spare for at least a hundred years or more.

Some thirty-five years after the death of George, Waity passed away when the yellow fever caught her one all the sudden one day and it was beyond what any shaman was able to cure. She was laid to rest in the same crypt where her husband's weary soul was placed along with his curse that Waity's shaman father placed upon him in early January 1699, so legend has it.

Anyways doc, this place might be even older than the indications from this crypt, and I really didn't want to discover what evil lay beneath its confines, but Vera and I kept exploring, and we wasn't aware as to the bizarre things yet to come.

As we pussyfooted about the crypt a feeling of being buried alive came over me as we walked down the stepped path-way filtering deeper, and deeper into the earth to what looked like the very pits of Hell itself. Plastered to my arm Vera dangled herself to me as if she were my testicles so tight that her grip was starting to make my arm tingle and go numb a little. Trying not to tell her to let my arm go so I could recover the feeling in its now paler - than - white goose bumped flesh, it just hurt way too much and I finally had to say something to her, she was so dang scared and that made it even harder for me to say a word, but I had to nonetheless; and, I guess that's where we got the phrase… "More scarred than any paleface I'd ever seen."

"Hey, V-V-Vera, m-my arm is falling asleep, can I h-have it back for a few minutes, p- p- p-please cutie pie?" I smiled at her and rubbed her hand in the process of trying to rub feeling back into my half-dead arm. She looked at me and smiled back.

"Oh, E-Eddie, I, I, I'm sorry, am I h-hurting your arm sweetie?" She let my arm go allowing me to rub the flow of warm blood back into it till it wasn't in such paleness. It felt so good to have my arm back with some feeling in it, and as soon as I had the feeling back, I took her hand in mine and we crept along the slimy moss covered steps. Soon we came to what looked like a dead end, but it was a door and next to it was a lantern hanging on a rusty nail. It had plenty of fuel in it still and luckily for us, I had a box of wooden matches, that me and my friends were gonna use to smoke with when we had some of those nasty 'ol cigarettes when David was able to snith some from Cash's store. Thank God I had those matches in my pocket, now I could light the coal-oil lantern so we could see where the heck we were.

Holding my sweetie by the hand, I turned slowly around, while the lanterns flame flickered to and fro from specks of dust blowing in its path, there on two separate slabs lay the bodies of George and Waity Anna, he was in black and she was all in white, and they lay there amidst the dust, cob-webs, and moss-covered walls of the tomb and as cold as the clay from whence they'd come and it looked as though they were getin ready to me married once again, but with that thought in both our minds, some how neither one of us was afraid any longer? I don't know if it was because we now had light to see with, or what, but those creepy feelings fled both our minds at the same time for some unknown reason.

They looked so nicely dressed and all that we began to smile and laugh a little, and talk more like adults than kids. It looked like we were no longer lost in the graveyard, but where the heck was we now were the only thought in my head at that particular moment, and bein' suspended in time amongst the dead wasn't my idea of havin' fun, that was one apparent thing I knew for certain. I grabbed Vera's hand once again, turned towards the door, opened it and started to walk up another flight of stairs still chit-chatting away and laughing as if nothing had ever happened to us at all. As we approached the upper part, it looked as though we were entering the ol' farmhouse mansion from the tomb of the departed George and his wife Waity Anna it looked like one of the lanterns had a light glowing in the upstairs, but the rest of the house was as black as our old coal and wood stove in Luke's small living room.

Coming to the top of the staircase we spotted another door, with the light inside illuminated, and a small shadow of what appeared to be a little girl in a full-length white dress standing there as if she wanted to greet us upon our entry into her room, but she didn't say a solitary word, her dress flared outward from the large hoop in it like one from the mid-evil period; the girl vanished in a flash of an eyes bat vanishing into thin air, but as she departed, she seemed to be laughing and so was Vera at the exact moment the apparition left the room.

When we went into the room where the light was coming from was a fireplace in one corner with a different lady standing by it and she too was dressed all in white, but this lady was a black lady of about eighteen years of age, and the little girl was a dark- white in color. My beloved Vera approached the woman, but before she had a chance to say anything to the her... she also vanished into thin air just like the little girl had done. This room was in more of a mess than the rest of the house and was full of cobwebs, but it was still a lovely room in spite of those eerie webs. It had all sorts of fancy mirrors, dressers, night tables, and the biggest-fanciest bed I had ever seen in my life. Vera went and jumped on the bed and dust flew high in the air causing her to cough a few times. I started to laugh as I approached the bed as well and sat down gently so as not to stir up any more dust, my eyes slithered around lookin' at the walls with many fancy things all around them, and only had a couple of paintings on one wall, one was of the ghost lady with two little girls all in white, and they looked like twins but who was the other one of?

When we had first come into the room only moments before, there was only one little girl waiting by the door. I wondered why only one girl was waiting by the door when there were two of them in the painting with the lady. The other painting was of a tall man dressed all in black; he had very pale skin, and sure didn't look very friendly. Turning towards my sweetheart Vera, I leaned over on the bed and began kissing her with a passionate sensation I'd never felt before, man it felt good, and at the same time I was afraid, maybe I was outta my mind for doing it, but I couldn't hold back any longer. Vera tried to make me stop kissing her so passionately, but it was hard for me to stop\, all of a sudden she pushed me real hard causing me to almost roll off the big bed onto the mildew and mold covered floor and the dust flew once again making both us cough vigorously.

"I told you Mister Ed not to kiss me that way now didn't I?" Vera looked furious, and had an evil glare in her pretty dark black eyes; it was a look that could kill on contact if it had a weapon to do it with, feverishly I shook my head a few times still coughing and rubbing my eyes at the same time trying to look at Vera who was still laying there as if she belonged in that room.

"Vera, Mattie or who ever you are, we can't do this, we're just kids and don't have the strength to make love like adults do… p-please lets go ok." I pleaded but she held me down and tried to take my clothes off, but I was able to pull away before she had the chance to go any further than unbutton three of my buttons and start ta unloosen my belt.

Four years after, a young woman that had been in the near by town of Selma for the better part of her fifteen years moved into the mansion with the Maxifield family and was a distant relative by marriage whose father and mother had died from hostile Indian attacks on their village near Selma town back in the year of our Lord, 1703., she was a talented artist for an Indian girl in those days, and had been paid by George to paint all their portraits. One night while she was asleep, George went to the girl's room and raped her. She ended up pregnant and wanted to kill herself, but Waity showed pity on her and pleaded for her to not to do it to herself, but stay to with them and bear the child and had managed to calmed her tears and agreed, because only 'cause she liked Waity as a mother figure, and not just as a friend who took her in as an orphan.

Now, ol' man Maxifield had four wives to contend with because of his sudden lust for women, and it didn't stop there… no sir, he wanted still more wives and even more children, and by the time he died he had six wives and a house-full of kids and they all had their individual rooms to suit their personal needs and personalities just to keep the peace, or so he thought anyway. They all worked very hard in the big mansion as it was an ongoing project of being constructed on a daily basis and Waity was in charge of the whole place alongside her new husband, their kids and the other five women and all their kids, it seemed like a mad house of insanity most of the time, but they seemed to manage…why I' never have been able to figure that one out to this day.

The third wife of George liked Waity's new husband Alexander and had sex with him on many occasions still furthering the house not only grew, but the family did also. It was getting way too crowded and something had to be done and soon now that there wasn't much more room to build anymore' cause of the cemetery also getting bigger.

Waity didn't like all the goings on and started to eliminate most of the children one by one in various manners. Some she drowned, saying they went swimming in the near by lake and swam out too far, others she said ran off and never came back because they didn't like all the hard work and were ever found. The family presumed Waity's stories to be true, but the real truth was that she poisoned them the same way she did good ol' George, and buried them way out in the property where no one would ever find them. She had her faithful servant Jamal Spotted-foot place markers where she buried the kids in the middle of the night with different names on them so that no one would suspect her of any of the killings.

Well; like any town as time passed the community beyond the mansion was starting to grow more and more every day, and soon it was well established and called Hyde Park officially, by the new town proprietor at one of their annual meetings. They had no real rule of law established yet and when a person died, they just buried them and moved on with their lives in stride and pride like it was nothing outside of keeping the population down to a minimum.

After Mattie passed, the beautiful fifteen year old half black and half Native American Indian girl finished her portraits of the family members; she added a partially opened rose to her own self portrait to signify her untimely demise. All of her paintings were done in charcoal, and in black and white, but as time went by, they ended up being beautifully colored pastel paintings, but from a significant others distance they appeared to be a charcoal grays, black, and white because life was in reality nothing more than a colorless one with no future what-so-ever, at least not to her anyways.

Her name Nellie Matilda Sarah Sue Cleavage Maxifield usTuss\y (pronounced in the native Cherokee language it sounded like this: u-s-ti u-s-ga a-s wa-ya). She liked to be called Mattie, short for Matilda because it was much easier to say, and her last name meant little bad wolf in the Cherokee language or werewolf if you were from a European descent. She always signed her name Mattie usTuss\y, and everyone in the family knew that she was one of the most mysterious girls ever born, she had a behavior like none that I'd ever seen before, even though she was a ghost all those times I seen her when I was a kid.

Mattie always spoke a different language, and of course me and my friends made fun of her gibberish 'cause we just didn't understand a single solitary word she spoke most of the time that we played with her in the basement. Mattie sure was a fast runner as I recall, and man could she leap over things with such delicate skill, almost as though she'd floated over them. Some times Mattie would chatter up a storm in her native tongue just to be mean to everyone around her especially when she was furious about, well almost anything and everything, just because she didn't understand the white man's ways, or their language very much, and it aggravated her to no end.

But like most all people back in the old west days and beyond; she was named after some other relative, all except her last name, and that was Indian all the way. Yea, I know that lots of people get confused when others down along the genealogy line have the exact or similar name as another person, but that's how things were done way back then, and even dates and places get mixed up in transcriptions and translations along with the name similarities just like people, so if-n yer confused, well, welcome to the club med of so called humanity along with me ok folks.

Mattie had hung her portrait above the fireplace in the main den of the lower floor and close to the front entry way, which to this day I never found.

As we left that room which my sweetie tried to seduce me in; Vera and I heard tiny-faint sounds of a single chanting women coming from down the hall. Not knowing what to think, we went to investigate the chatter.

"Hello," I called out. "Is anyone there?" No one answered, and a few seconds later the chanting started again.

"Hey is anyone there?" Vera echoed my call immediately, but no one answered her call either, and again the chanting started up and we crept toward another room near the end of a hall and looked at another door; Vera took a hold of the knob and as she did the chanting stopped once more and all of my goose-bumps came back very quickly as she opened the door to the room. It appeared to be another a den of some sort and there on the wall was a painting in living color of a very beautiful teenaged half black and half Indian all dressed in her native attire, and in the painting was one single rose, which none of the other paintings had in them, only this one and my mind wondered.

Inside that room it appeared to be getting late in the day as I peered out of a window on the upper floor, and then I knew where we were inside Spooks-Ville mansion, we'd ended up in the same hallway as on one of our previous explorations of the mansion.

I told Vera that we best go home now so we wouldn't get into any trouble, and besides I for one wasn't about to be late for dinner, or I wouldn't be allowed to play any more till me and my Aunt Mary moved back to the big city of Muncie, so we headed out the door and the chanting started in for a third time… Our feet wasn't about to fail any more as the tinny voice cried out in a loud and strange native tongue: "a/Esfl usTuss\y u4h=v o<n e! aU/" (Pronounced in English)

(a-ni-tsa-s-gi-li a/ u-s-ti u-s-ga a-s wa-ya u-do-hi-yu-i o-tlv- na e-hu a-ha-ni) and then we realized what was going on and took off down the hallway lickety-split and n one stop. Soon we were back at out basement entry place and climbed out, heading back home once again as fast as our legs would take us as far away from Spooks-Ville Mansion as we dare to flee.

Later on, I ask some old Indian that lived near by us what it meant. He told me a/Esfl usTuss\y u4h=v o<n e! aU/ meant: Ghost of the little bad wolf is my name, please make home here? The old man thought me strange, and asked me why I had asked him such a strange thing and then he said that he heard of the name usTuss\y when he was a small boy, that the name was very one of evil like no other had ever been before him, I dare not tell him one single word of anything that happened to me and my friends or he'd have me as well as my friends put away in a loony bin for a very long-long time.

Chapter 17

Night Screams, and the Crackling of Flaming Arrows

From beyond, to escape for an instant from the pitiful… where miserably the intrigues of an impoverished native peered in a window beside the front door of the mansion. He had left the cholera - stricken camp site of his people to look for help any place he could find it. He thought about his surroundings and came to his demise for the conclusion of where he would most likely be able to get the help he really needed. My half-breed sisters' husbands' place would be the most likely than any other place in the territory. At least he'd be assured his people wouldn't find him in the most obvious place, he thought, at best not under the terrible circumstances of this horrible ailment.

He knocked on the front door as hard as he could. As soon as the maid, Cloe' answered it, he collapsed at her feet. She let out a blood chilling scream that caused Calvin Leander Maxifield, the grandson of ol' George M. Maxifield, and the son of Calvin Sr. and Matilda

Maggie as well as Kent Haltersmen Maxifield to run to the door to see what was wrong. During this period they helped as many people as they could because of the War between the states and the Indian wars and on top of it all was outbreaks of Cholera. He was a tall slim man about six foot three or so with a big mustache, and always wore suspenders to hold his trousers up well over his big belly, because he was so skinny. His trousers seemed to bag just a bit and when he walked it looked as though he always had a load in them, and people always laughed at him, especially his comrades in arms in the army. He had just finished his supper, and just wanted to relax for a spell when the maid screamed.

"What the Sam Hell's goin' on now, who the hell is it at the door at this time of night Cloe' are we bein' attacked by them damned yanks or somethin'?" Calvin yelled just loud enough to make the housekeep Cloe poke her head out the door and whewn she seen it was a wounded man she called for Calvin to come quickly.

"Damn it, now what, can't a fella get some sleep?" He mumbled to himself... "Crap." He said as he headed down the winding staircase that George had build all by himself several years back.

It was during the Civil War in the year 1863. Calvin was a Corporal on the Confederate Army, and had just come home on furlough to visit his wives and all the kids for a spell and take break from the war, but for him there wasn't no escape, and at the same time most all of the native tribes were in small skirmishes all over the territory as well as bein' in the process of removal from their lands. Times were hard for everyone because of the war, poverty and from the fever, but more-so for the poor Indian tribes were the ones sufferin the most, and they were after all relitives of the Maxifield family in spite of everything else that was happening back then. The outbreak of Cholera was spreading like wild fire all over the place, people were dying like flies on diseased cattle, and this too had people half scared to death. No one wanted to die from war let alone this horrible affliction of the Cholera and its deadly fever like symptoms.

Calvin finally reached the front door, but Cloe couldn't hold the man up, let alone drag his butt inside to be tended to.

"Well woman, don't just stand there lookin' at the poor soul, help me bring him inside to the polar and go fetch Mattie and Maggie, they'll know what to do for this poor Injun feller, now go woman, quickly ya hear." She scurried as fast as she could up the stairs to fetch the two women, and by the time they reached the poor cholera-ridden Indian man 'cause he was almost gone and all he was able to do was to tell them a little about his tribe and the terrible inflictions on him and his people, but as far as being able to pronounce his name, that was impossible for all of them after all he needed to be buried with a name marker.

Everyone felt for the poor soul, because they too were part Indian also, and all they could do was to watch him lay there and die a horrible death. They took him to the front yard, which already was a huge cemetery with very little room left for those who were dying all around them, and the only thing left that they could do was to pile up a mound of dead trees, bushes and bunches of dried leaves, then they took the Indian man and lay him on the pile, lit it on fire which was the only true way to get rid of the disease was to burn the dead persons body so it wouldn't spread and kill them all

After they burned his body they proceeded to place bones, ashes, and the other debris from the fire in a box, then buried it deep in the ground where upper crust vermin wouldn't knawel on the diseased ashes and spread the famine to them. Their servant, Wilber spent all night making a marker for his grave and placed it on the spot he was burned at. There was no name on the marker, because he couldn't spell it the way it was pronounced, so he just carved Cholera-ridden Indian man, June 15, 1863 God rest his poor soul on it and went back to his quarters and wash himself the best he could so he wouldn't get it and die too.

The next night while they were all snuggled in their beds all cozy and warm they were attacked by a band of renegade Indians who had fled from both the Union and Confederate Army's. Flaming arrows pounded the mansion and started a fire on one side of the front porch and the smell of smoke woke Calvin and the others up once again, and they ran down stairs as fast as they all could in order to extinguish the blaze, but when they saw that it was Indians attacking and they quickly pulled down their rifles from the gun racks and began to shoot killing all but one of the renegade Indians, but he took off as fast as he had arrived and fled deep in to the cold blackness of the woods out of sight.

When the battle was over the blaze had grown bigger than what they could handle, and the smoke spread towards Hyde Park. People all over started to wake from the smell of fire, and gathered down close to Buck Creek with plenty of buckets to help put out the fire, luckily for everyone they had a bridge to cross over, and an hour later the fire was extinguished and everyone was safe., but had left major damage, so the town folk volunteered their services to help them rebuild the burned out portion of the mansion the best they could under dyer circumstances of war and disease.

The war was drawing further away as was the Indian feuds and the Maxifield's were very grateful for some of the town folk helping them rebuild as best they could, so they threw a big party, none the likes of Hyde Park had ever known, or seen before.

It was finally the weekend and me and my friends moseyed back to the mansion, but this time we went our normal route, through the basement so we could avoid that 'ol cemetery. As we approached the ol' house' basement window, I swear that I seen a different little girl standin' next to it. This wasn't no dang ol' ghost girl, and as we kept getting closer, the girl was still waiting there she was in an old fashion white dress and as I got close enough I reached out and touched her to seee if-n she was for real, a living, breathing real little girl. I asked her what she was doing here at this spooky place by herself, she didn't tell me and my friends, but did tell us her name.

"Hi, my name is usTuss\y, but you can call me Mattie for short. Do you wanna play with me?" She said with a sort of saddened smile on her face and I almost let out a scream loud enough to make us all run away like a greased pig caught in a lightening storm, but didn't 'cause she sure felt real ta me.

"Do you live around here? I never have seen you before?" I was curious, and wanted to know all about her for some reason, but I guess it was 'cause it seemed really odd that after all these months of me and my friends exploring this ol' spooky place that we'd ever seen this little girl in our neighborhood, or any place near by before, especially at this scary place; and, besides, she sure didn't go to our school that was for certain. Somehow it didn't matter who or where she was from' cause we had a new friend ta play with at least for that day anyways.

"Come on, let's go play inside ok." She sure seemed anxious to go inside Spooks-Ville mansion for some reason, but I and Vera paid her no never mind and at the time it didn't dawn on me that she too was another relative of that Maxifield family that once lived here, 'cause we only wanted ta play since summer was almost over.

"Hey, wait up kid. Where did you come from in the first place?" I started to show some frustration with her, maybe because I was always the one in the lead and not some dang bossy girl like she appeared to be.

"I live really close to here, and I seen all of you playing around her lots, but was afraid to come to play with all of you, because I didn't know if you would like me, but I just had to come introduce myself to you all after seeing just how much fun you were all having here by this beautiful big house... hehehe," She giggled and sure did like to talk lots in particular to us boys; it was irritating to no limit, a dang chatter box girl that's what me and my friends just didn't need or particularly like was a bossy-talkative girl, yuck, I justt turns my stomach at the very thought of it sometimes, well all except for when Vera does it... "hehehe."

We all looked at her like she was crazy or something', imagine her thinking that this place was beautiful, how dumb can a kid get, beautiful indeed... geesh., what the hell was this kid thinking and what strange planet did she get off of in the first place. I reached out to pull her back away from the window, but Vera slapped my arms outta the way before I could even come close to touching her, I belonged to her and that was that.

Vera told her that that I always went inside first so I could help her down from the windows ledge, then Sally, David, and Tommy, and then her last... she looked furious at Vera then smiled at me, man if looks could kill, 'cause my princess Vera sure wanted to slap the piss right outta this kid that was for sure.

After we were all inside the basement, the girl seemed both happy and sad at the same time; she started twirling, laughing and sayin' wheeeee at the same time, and her voice echoed throughout the house shaking and shattering the small pieces of glass that were still left in a different window as well as some of the ones that was leaning on a wall in one corner, glass flew out of its frame and shattered all over the floor making Vera and Sally jump and screamed at the same time, but David and Tommy just stepped back a couple steps.

"Wow, how did that happen?" Tommy said, his big blue eyes shown the whites more than the blue parts, and almost popped outta his eye sockets. David stammered and stuttered something in a real soft whisper that none of us really heard let alone understand. All we knew was that it was strange for that window to break like it did after all the times we all came in here, and didn't break till that girl joined us.

Sally and Vera was holding each other for the first time in one corner of the basement, not paying attention to the strange girl. She came toward me and whispered something in my ear, but I was so shook up that I didn't understand her let alone really hear what she said, her breath was cold, like ice-cycles, and as she leaned forward touching my shoulders, her hands also seemed like ice and sent shivers all over my frail body causing me to tremble vigorously.

When Vera seen what that new girl was doing she let go of Sally and walked toward me, and by the time she was standing beside me, the girl was way off in the opposite corner of the room and seemed to move as fast as that train going under Hill Street Bridge. All the sudden she ran towards the door laughing aloud. She ran up the stairs and stopped at the top.

"Hey, come on; let's play up here for a spell. Come on now, hurry. Bet ya can't catch me na-na, na na-na yer it… HEHEHEHEHE." She laughed even louder than before and her laughing sent shivers all over not only me, but my friends as well. Vera and Sally both wanted to climb back out the window, and go home and forget this exploration all together, but I convinced them that we should just start playing with this strange little girl and show her our friendship, no matter how strange she was.

We all ran up the stairway trying to catch up to that usTuss\y girl, she was way too fast for any of us, but we could still hear her laughing during the whole pursuit. We looked all over the main floor for that girl, but she seemed to have vanished into thin air all the sudden like all those dang 'ol ghosts had done. At that point we were all scarred to just forget the whole day and try again tomorrow, but my stubbornness wouldn't allow me to leave this house till I finished looking around for this day, and besides I had only two m ore weeks till I had to move from Hyde Park back to Muncie.

"We can't leave this kid in here, you all know that them spooky 'ol ghost' will do something' to her now don't ya, guys we have to find her and fast ok." I wouldn't let up on my chicken friends, not for one moment and hid my fear inside myself the best I could, my nerves were almost shattered the way it was, but I dare not let on now or I'd never in a million years live it down specially with Vera.

"Yes." Vera said, "We have to do like my prince Eddie says and find this poor little girl before something bad happens to her… come on lets go ok."

We looked in almost all the places her laugh seemed to be coming from, but still we couldn't find her. It seemed hopeless. The next thing I knew was that we were in front of two doors in a single room. There was one door on each of the opposite walls across from each other. I had a choice as to which door to take to find where that kids laugh was coming from, but which one. I must choose the right one or I'd be laughed at by not only that girl, but my friends as well. Sometimes hide and seek was a hard game ta play, but we were all pretty darn good at it, but my heart beat so fast that it felt as though it was coming outta my chest, I was confused, tired, and a bit frustrated all in one at the same time, and making up my mind confused me all the more, so I ask Tommy ta choose, since he hadn't been her too much in the past.

"What's goin' on inside ya Eddie?" Tommy asked with a slight shiver in his voice.

"I don't know pal, but I need help tryin' ta figure out which door to go through, 'cause Confucius has infiltrated my mind." At that point I didn't know what I was sayin' and all my friends just starred at me like I was an idiot, ' I guess it was 'cause of the new words I'd said or something.

"What ya mean buddy, all we have at do is split up and go in both doors, that way we can cover more territory that way." Tommy tried to be the smarter of us two, but I just pretended and went along with what he said.

"I guess your right Tommy. You, David and Sally take that one on the left, and Vera and I'll take this one here on the right ok." They agreed and went in the door to the left, closing it behind them. Vera and I were alone once again, but this time we had more important things to do than googol-eye at each other, we needed to find that girl, and send her packing back home where she came from, 'cause we had better things to do than play her silly games right now, or any other time either.

Vera and I had the lantern with us the whole time, and it was a little dark in this room, so I lit the lantern in order for us to see where we were really at and just what was in the room if anything at all, we hoped there wasn't anything bad behind door number one.

Once in side I lit the lantern, and as the light started to glow brighter and brighter people began ta appear outta no where, and right there in the midst of them was the little girl. I stood frozen in terror; too petrified to move or turn around and leave the confines of the room. There in the midst of 'em all was a soldier in a Confederate uniform, and several female figures and the Soldier had a hold of that girl's hand, her disfigurement started to appear right before our eyes, and she was older than what she looked like before in the basement. I turned toward Vera, grabbing her in my arms and buried my head in her small boobs for comfort and reassurance. I was in hope that if I were to raise my head and look, the apparitions would be gone, and Vera and I would really be all alone, but when I peeked from her chest, the ghosts were still in the same room as we were.

Vera stood frozen in time, I pulled myself free from her arms, and took her hand in mine, and pulled her backwards toward the door, reaching' back with one hand to grab the door handle, I felt a chilly-clammy hand touch mine, it was all I could do ta try and jerk my hand free as hard as I could and fling it around Vera's body once again, slowly I reached for the handle once again and succeeded this time in opening the door, and under the shock of the moment; Vera and I walked out backwards into the room that we'd came from and then the door slammed behind us all by itself. Little did we know that our friends were standing right behind us? We turned around, and as we did, Vera screamed, "AHAAAAAAAH, SH-IIT." I almost jumped outta my pants, and shouted at my friends for scarring us almost half ta death.

"WHERE THE HELL D-DID YOU GUYS COME FROM? Ah the hell with it, lets get outta here now."

We had succeeded and discovered where the girl was at last, but she wasn't human any longer and she sure wasn't that dang weird little girl, but the woman's ghost from the torture rack in the dungeon far below the mansion that we discovered a week or so before, her clothes were still torn to shreds, blood seemed to ooze from each lash mark, and her skeleton had hanging pieces of flesh dangling from the confines of the torn blue dress in every direction, her arms and legs were clung to her torso in every direction imaginable her throat was slit from one ear to the other, her tongue hung out of her black lips, and her nakedness shown red with fresh blood.

Departing the double door room faster than anything a person could possibly imagine inside their minds eye , me, Vera and our friends the Fulkler kids stumbled and tripped each other as we fled the main floor and not paying any attention to where we were goin' we ended up in a totally different part of the mansion than we had ever been in before scared totally outta our wits, we huddled together in one corner of that different hall-way so we could be somewhat safe and secure under the circumstances we had just left behind us. Now we were really lost, and this time in the mansion, and not the graveyard. I couldn't believe what I had just saw; my body trembled so fast that even my friends were shaking in their shoes, Sally was flooding all of us with her tears from being scared outta her mind, Tommy crapped a bit in his pants from bein' scarred so much and David had pissed all over himself as usual, but Vera started to calm herself down a bit and seemed the bravest of us all, especially more than I was at that time.

"Where the sh-shit are we." Vera asked in as calm a tone as here lips would let her do.

"E-Eddie, A-are w-we s-s-safe n-now? E-Eddie, hey E-E-Eddie!" David was stuttering more and more all the time and didn't say as much as he normally would in just plain everyday living, and Tommy was tried hard to wipe his runny nose at the same time he wiped his tear filled eyes on his shirt sleeves, it was one of those smear campaigns I recon?

After a few minutes and no noise beyond our own fear movements and the ever-so slight whispering conversations we had in our wind, we poked our heads one by one up and down the hallway to see if anything or anyone was there with us, it looked like all was as bright as a clear day and knew that the ghost' that Vera and I seen were all pleasantly right where we'd left them, at least I hoped so anyhow.

Stopping for a couple minutes I briefly told my friends what Vera and I seen in the room, but all they said back was that they didn't see anything in the room they went into and all they heard was I shouted at them and we took off like a bat outta hell and was twisted around like a bunch of grape vines dangling from those big 'ol trees we swung from when we played Tarzan, but now we were in the land of the lost in this Spooks-Ville mansion. Getting up from our tight huddled nest, we crept down the hall to a dead end, no doors on either side and none in front of us. Vera looked up at the cobweb covered ceiling and there was a door, the kind that ya had to pull down in order to get to an attic. None of us could reach it, and all we could think of was finding a way out of this sorry looking hallway and make our way back down stairs to our basement entry window so we could head home once more.

Tommy thought that he had a brilliant idea for him to get down on his hands and knees, then me get on his back the same way, then have Sally climb up to reach the door, but Sally was way too heavy and would break both our backs, so I ask Vera to climb up to reach the door. It was difficult, but soon we were all piled on top one another under the attic door; Vera made a gallant effort and since she was just tall enough to tip toe an inch further upward to reach the rusty handle a big spider shimmied itself down in her face, she pushed it away and almost fell down on top of us, but was able to hold her Elvira's pose from off the TV show with the same name.

"Hey, it's locked…. David, Sally, there has to be a key someplace near by, look for it ok." As we looked for a key, our bodies were to the point of collapsing, but we held on as if our lives depended on it.

"Can ya please hurry up, my knees and back's a hurtin' really bad." I said with a pain in my butt from them takin' way too much time ta find that damn key.

"Yea, ya two butt faces, finds that dang key wills ya." Tommy was really feelin' the effects of the dog pile ladder we formed to reach the attic door.

"Here it is, found it, on this ledge." Sally shouted with glee like she done something so fantastic that we'd all praise her like a hero… ha, that happenin' just wasn't gonna happen not in m y lifetime anyway.

"Well, damn it, give it at me ok." Sally handed Vera the key, and once again she tip toed upward to unlock the door. As soon as she had it unlocked, and pulled a foot down close to where we could reach it, we all come tumbling down in a mingled pile, Vera landed her cute butt right on my face; her dress draped it giving me a good whiff of her little pee-pee, I almost sneezed, maintaining the tickle I held it real tight, but as we came down from our dog pile my nose let loose, and the spray went all over Sally.

"Hey, butt head what did ya go and do that for, ya sprayed your snot all over my blouse, YUCK, BUTT HEAD?" Sal was so pissed off I thought for sure she was gonna slap me, but she knew better, Vera would of tore her apart limb from limb like that poor lady in the torture chamber that had also scarred me and Vera outta our wits makin' us end up in this awful location.

"Do what, big mouth Sal." I said and just smiled at her as we all stood up. Vera and David just laughed, then the rest of us joined in, all except mean ol' big mouth, big butt Sally, she was still trying to wipe off the slimy-snotty spray with her hands, and that seemed to maker her madder at me, but I just didn't care.

"Shut up, just shut up or I'll tell." She cried, but I just ignored her threat and jumped up grabbing the door handle, pulling it down while I hang onto it. The door was sort of heavy, and David grabbed me by my pants pocket and helped pull me and the door all the way down, but in the process my pocket tore half off.

The door squeaked, swooshes of air brought dust migrating down upon us as we looked toward the opening and the ladder that was part of the door was full of cobwebs and still more dust that made us all sneeze and cough, even mean ol' Sally, but she didn't apologize as she returned her sneeze right back at me. Her spray hit me in the face and I felt mad enough to just slap her down to the dirt an d make her a part of the floor, like the dirt she was herself, but I maintained myself and wiped off the gooey substance from my face with my hands, then flicked it at her with a big looking possum killing grin, thinking to myself, girl, you'll get yours one day, and when you do, I will be the happiest kid on this planet, that is if we ever found our way out this time, and when we did, I'd let her have my full wrath, both of 'em, pow right in her big pussy prune-shaped, fat ugly mouth, but went part way up that ladder and asked Tommy to hand me the lantern so I could see what the heck was up in this dreary attic. Taking it in my right hand I proceeded to climb the ladders ragged rungs, the lantern light illuminated brilliantly towards the opening and as I looked, my friends bugged me to tell them what I saw.

"Eddie, is this our way outta here." Vera yelled at me with a sort of whispering voice, it sounded so sweet, that the tone of her voice made me sit the lantern down and take a deep breath of her wonderful affection for me. Looking inside once again after a moment of silence inside my head, I turned looking down at them as I climbed inside and sat on an old wooden box of books.

"Hey, ya guys gotta come on up here and see all this bunch a cool stuff, there's a ton of things in here and plenty of room ta stand too." Since David was the closest to the ladder, he came right after me, and then Vera, Sally, and Tommy last. Upon entering the attic, they were amazed at all the stuff before their eyes. It was a real treasure chest of goodies, and at the time, getting out didn't seem to matter any more. We all wanted to search every box, chest, dresser and piles of old books and clothing that had been hap hazardously hewn about as though someone else had been also looking through all of it to find maybe something important? Vera walked across the piles of dust covered clothing stirring up puffs of the rotten stuff into the air, it settled back down as fast as it had gone into the air. She came to this trunk, opened the silver latch, then gently the lid. Scattering things about she pulled out a pretty off white dress and held it up against her body, smiling.

"Ya think this would look pretty on me Eddie." She gave me a wink along with a giant sized smile, but I was way too busy looking at some ol' books for clues as to who lived here and anything else I could piece together.

"Huh, ummm, Oh yea, it would look real pretty on ya Vera, once ya cleaned it up a bit." I glanced at her for a brief moment smiling, then drew my attention back to what I had been doin'. My mind just wasn't really on Vera, or any of the things she and my friends were doin', all that really mattered to me at the time was to look for clues in all the books and scattered papers.

The dress had an awful smell to it the minute that Vera took it out of the trunk, in fact, the whole trunk smelled bad with a very distinct odor of fire. Vera noticed it too, but wanted to keep the dress for her own anyway. I took a couple interesting books from the pile, and folded a few papers, placed them in one of the books, and walked to where Vera was still holding the blue lace, and ruffled dress in front of her, she began twirling just like the little girl had done only moments before we ran from her and ended up in this place.

"The dress, the dress, she repeated several times. It used to belong to that little girl we seen down the hallway. She loved this dress and she wants me to have it now. She said that it was stitched by hand with love for her by her favorite maid, Cloe' shortly before her timely departure to the other world." She hesitated for a minute or so then started to cry for no real apparent reason.

"Hey Vera, are you ok princess?" My facial expression was one of wonder and confusion at the same time. "Vera, what the heck are ya talking about? That girl didn't tell ya anything like what ya just said." I tried to say more, but she interrupted me before I could utter another word.

"Yea." She said, "The dress is mine now, and no one's gonna take it away from me this time." She held it closer to her body and spun around one more time. It rubbed up against her nose, and the smell of dirty ol' smoke made her sneeze a couple times. Vera looked at the dress, then at me, and dropped it on the floor in front of her. "Hey, what ya lookin' at Eddie, are ya alright sweetie? What's that God awful smell in here?" She seemed confused as she looked at the dress on the floor. "Why'd ya throw the dress on the floor for Eddie?" Her eyes were poppin' outta her head a little and the whites of her eyes shown more than the middle did and for a minute I felt guilty, but then why should I, I didn't do anything wrong and let her know that I didn't either, bending over the dress, I picked it up, handing it to her with a smile, telling' her sorry, but had no real reason to. Say sorry in the first place.

"Keep it my princess, but ya better have a good explanation ta tell your mom as to just where ya got it ok, I'll try and help ya think of something ok cutie pie." I was tryin' ta lay on the honey real thick so I could stay on her good side. After all we were an item together.

"Eddie. What the heck's goin' on?" Vera was still confused, but when I told her what happened, she immediately held the dress to her face telling' me she's wash it when her mommy wasn't around, and tell her Sally gave it to her. "Sally, ya better stand up for me if my mommy should ever ask you about the dress, and I know she will too. If ya don't I'll help Eddie put chicken poop in your big mouth and make ya swallow it, ya hear." Vera meant every word of it too.

"Ok Vera, but not because you like Eddie, and not because of what he said either. But because we were friends before meanie Eddie seen ya ok." Sally really wanted to tare into both Vera and I, but knew we'd do exactly what we said we'd do and had no doubt in her little pea brain and neither one of us seemed to care what she said or done, because we knew she'd be in even bigger trouble if she ever blabbed to anyone what us kids had been doin' all summer long.

"Yes, this dress is mine now, cause I found it here in this trunk, in this dingy ol' attic among all this rubble. This is my treasure and will always be my memory of exploring' this dang spooky ol' place all summer. "Mine." She said as she held that dress closer than she'd ever held me, or so it seemed, but I knew she really cared about me more than that damned ol' dress ever would.

"Hey, guys, we'd best figure out how at get outta here so we can go home now ok, 'cause I don't know what time it is and besides I don't know about all of you but, I ain't a goin' ta get myself into any trouble for bein' gone too long." My monologue took a straight and narrow path to their ears, they agreed and we headed down the attic steps entering the dead-end hallway, of course I went first holding onto my treasure real tight so I wouldn't drop any of it. As soon as I was down, I laid the ol' books down gently so they wouldn't fall apart any more than they already were. Sally came down next, and I didn't offer her any help whatsoever, then Vera, and I was more than happy to give her a hand, both of 'em', right on her cute little butt. One hand went under her dress startling her a little, and it touched her private part just a tiny bit. She stopped on the third rung from the bottom of the ladder, and looked at me dropping her treasure dress in my face.

"Yucky, why'd ya do that for Vera?" I pulled it off my face as fast as it landed tossing it on the floor beside me.

"You know; you naughty boy." She looked at me again, smiling as I pulled my hand out from under her dress and placed it on her waist where it should have been in the first place. Vera climbed on down and stood beside me, and then slapped me in the face as a reminder to be nice, not naughty all the time. The rest of our friends finally came down and joined us. Sally stood there giggling with her hands over her big mouth, almost peeing herself once again.

"What ya cackling about big mouth." I said as I turned toward Sally for a brief moment like I wanted to just pound her in her nose a couple times, but didn't. "Vera, now why the Sam Hell did you slap me, OUCH, that hurt." She leaned toward me and whispered in my ear not to do such things in front of our friends ever again, that if I ever wanted to play doctor with her it would have to be in private.

"Come on; let's find our way outta here." My ego was hurt some, but I pushed it aside and moved on with what me and my friends were supposed to be doing, and that was to try and find our way outta the Spooks-Ville farmhouse mansion and go home once more.

As our identical dimension passed before our eyes so did the time, which we had no clue as to what time it really was and then we'd reached still another hallway a short pace beyond where the basement stair door was and started to walk down it, not very long after that we came upon another bunch of doors, one on the right, one on the left and one right in front of our noses and once again I had another decision ta make as ta what door to take again, I asked my friends to help me make the choice once more, but when they did, each said different doors, naturally, and I told them to put their heads together and just pick one, that it would be the door we'd take this time. I thought: "Why should I always be the one to decide? They have some brains, I think." But when they told me they couldn't make up their mind. I blurted out in a moment of frustration: "What mind?" and then said. "Ah dang it, never mind, guess I'll always be the leader of our group for the rest of my life hun, we" then... come on." I turned toward my cute little sweetie Vera and asked, "What door should we take?" I was giving her a real big chance to not only prove she wasn't afraid, but helping her to show our friends that she wasn't just another pretty face, but had some brains as well. She looked at me, pointed to the door right in front of our faces, and asked me to open the door. I reached my hand out to grab the handle, and hers went right on top of mine. I remained silent and we all walked into the dark-dark, dusty room, around a stack of books and turned toward a broken window on one wall. I was surprised when I looked and seen we were standing in our basement entry room already.

"Hey guys, this looks awfully familiar don't it?" I said before any of them opened their traps. "This is our entry room; don't ya recognize all this rubble? Look there is the ol' wooden dresser we placed in front of the basement window." My friends were ecstatic that we were finally going to leave the house once more and be able to head home and not be lost any more in the big ol' mansion that contained many weird things as well as past secrets that we dare not tell ta anyone, not now or ever for sanity's sake if-n we had any still left inside our 'lil pea brains from runnin ' head long into such things as ghosts and the likes.

Bein' a gentleman always, hehehehehe, I let my friends go out first, leaving me and Vera last in line to climb outta the basement window to the real world again. My imagination ran amuck as I helped Vera up on the dresser. My eyes were looking right up her dress again, and I wanted to place my hand where it shouldn't be placed, but knew better, placing my hands on her nice tight little cute butt instead.

"Hey Vera, ya satisfied sweetie?" I looked at her as she peered inside the window watchin' me climb up on the dresser in front of the window. She smiled at me real big, still holding onto her treasure dress. I handed her the books I brought out with me, pulling myself out with her hands in mine for help.

"Eddie." She whispered toward my ear as my body emerged through the window pane and onto the weed stubbles. "Yes, that pleases me very much my love." She then kissed me on the lips real fast then on the cheek causing me to blush a little, but soon I turned my normal pail white color and not the beet red that I'd been the whole time we were inside the mansion.

As we walked away from our entry place, she looked back over her shoulders for a second, and there outside of the window was that little girl once again, this time in a different dress altogether. Reachin' her hand behind her, Vera waved good-bye to the little girl drawing my attention back toward the house and Vera at the same time.

"What ya waving' at Vera?" Puzzled by her actions, I just shook my head as she told me.

"Ahhh, never mind Eddie, ya wouldn't understand if I told ya anyway. It's just one of those girl things ya know."

Holding her hand in mine, we walked toward the bridge over ol' Buck Creek, back through the newly planted corn field. She turned her head one last time and the little girl waved back at her then disappeared into thin air. We all walked on home; outta sight of the mansion for another day of fantastic exploration; knowing that I would have just three more weeks' before I had to leave Hyde Park and my friends.

Chapter 18

Vanished Into Thin Air

Three days went by. Me and my friends had another weekend free from choirs, allowin' us our freedom so we could go back to explore that big spooky house once again.

Aunt Mary Belle went to Muncie with one of our neighbors in their ol' pick-up truck and took some of our things to the house on Cornbread Road so when we did finally make our move back to the farm, we wouldn't have too many things to haul all at once. While in town she went to Se'ers Rosebuck and Company and bought us a new wood stove for our kitchen, and bought me a new shirt and pair of real nice jean pants on our charge account. Then she went to the discount pay for less shoe store and purchased a brand new pair of Buster Brown shoes for me. When she got back to Hyde Park, she surprised me with all the new stuff and told me about our new stove for the house on Cornbread Road.

I sure was happy to get all those new things and could care less about the stove, but acted real happy about it anyway, knowing that I'd have to work all the harder to bring in more and more wood as well as coal for the big new Dutch Oven wood stove.. My mew clothes made me feel like a new dollar bill all full of self worth and pride. This would really make a great impression on Vera, as well as my other friends.

After lunch, I asked my aunt if I could go and show my friends my new things. As always she said yes, cause in her eyes I was the best boy in all Hyde Park and deserved everything I got, cause I worked so dang hard all the time for everything, and I knew I was worth it all.

Speeding down the road on my bike that Luke finally got around to fixin' after my accident on Hill Street a few months ago, I was all shined up ready to strut my stuff as adults would say when they got all duded up like show horses and such.

Tossin' my bike on the ground next to Vera's steps, I hurried up them to knock on her door as fast as I could, tripping on a couple steps in my urgency to ask her to play.

"Hi Ms. Capturesme, is Vera able at come out and play for awhile?" I was always as polite as I could be when talking to Ms. Capturesme or any other adult as that goes. They liked that in a kid, and especially when I gave them the utmost respect at all times, even if I argued with an adult a little once in awhile, I was still always polite to 'em in a mean sorta way.

"Vera your boy friend is here ta see ya." She yelled toward the back room where her daughter was, and then looked at me smiling. "My daughter will be right here in a minute, would ya like to come in for a few minutes Eddie." She asks in her deep southern black drawl tone of voice.

"N, no maim, I'm fine waitin' here Ms. Capturesme. I sure thank ya though." Smiling real big and batting both my eyes at the same time as if I was flirtin' with her just a little, well that's what it seemed at me at the time. She smiled back and fluttered her big brown eyes right back at me, giggled, then turned, walking in the house to hurry Vera up.

"Are ya sure Eddie? I just made a big batch of sugar cookies for later, hehehe. Well mercy me what's keeping' that girl, VERA I SAID YOUR FRIEND EDDIE IS HERE TA SEE YA. Sorry 'bout that Eddie, I'll go an see what's a keeping' her, just a minute I'll fetch her and bring ya some of them delicious sugar cookies for you and my show poke daughter Vera ta munch on. Be right back." She headed inside yelling Vera's name once again, but before she got to the back room, Vera flew by her and almost ran her mom over in the process. Usually at home Vera was a real slow and lazy sortta girl, but not this time and her mom didn't quite know what came over her daughter all the sudden.

"Mercy me Girl, slow yourself down now, ya hear." She told Vera to wait right where she stood, that she'd be right back in a minute, that if-n she moved then she'd just have at stay in and not get any of her cookies.

Vera looked at the open door where I was waiting, and waved hi to me with a big smile, and blew me a quick kiss before her mom came back her way. She giggled, covering up her mouth for a second as her mom came out of the kitchen holding a small sack that contained those fine sugar cookies she'd just made. I could smell 'em all the way outside.

"Here Vera, I just made these this morning'. There should be enough sweet delicious sugar cookies for you, Eddie and your other friends. Enjoy 'em ok. Ya be sure ta share 'em now, ya hear child." She handed Vera the bag of cookies, smiled and told Vera at go play, but for her to be home by supper time around 5:30 p.m.

It was only 12:30 p.m., and we had plenty of time at play and explore the house again. I really didn't want Sally, Tommy, and David to come with us this time and made my wishes known to Vera as soon as we walked around the side of her house. She agreed that we should be alone this time, especially after yesterday when they made me and Vera a little mad at them.

I told her that we needed to make up a whopper of an excuse to tell our friends so they wouldn't get mad at us, cause our friendship really meant a whole lot, and loosing it wouldn't be the best thing for any of us right now.

Goin' to my friends house who were playing in their front yard, I told them that I had way too many choirs to do, and that I wouldn't be able to see them for a couple days or so. Sally asked me if Vera could play or not, cause she seen me at her place from her bedroom window.

I got smart with her, and told her to ask her for herself, that I was too mad right now to say one way or the other, and for her to just keep her big mouth shut if she knew what was good for her. She didn't say another word, turned her back on me.

"Huuum, boys! Go figure?" She just walked away from me, stompin' the ground with both feet as hard as she could.

Her heavy thumps almost caused an earthquake. I smiled at her brothers just because she was to dang angry at me, that I just couldn't help myself. I said bye, and ran off towards the our entry into the woods that was right beside Vera's place and ran off out of sight, knowing she was there waitin' for me so we could be alone still one more time.

"It worked cutie pie." We both started laughing as we ran off into the thick of the woods. We never got lost any place in our wooded playgrounds, cause we knew every inch of every tree, bush, leaf, and stick that there possibly could be in there.

Approaching the creek, a really creepy and -eerie feelin' came over me causin' me to double over in sharp stomach pains; it filled every pit, nook and cranny through out my small intestine belly. I fell to my knees in agony forcing Vera to kneel down beside me asking me what was wrong.

"Eddie, ya ok babe." I looked deep into her eyes with such pain, that it sent shivers all up and down her spine so much she stood up in fear as if I wanted to kill her or

something.

"I, I d-don't know Vera, I guess I'll be ok in a few minutes or so, just let me sit here for a few more minutes ok." While sitting on the ground, I kept looking at Vera. The more I looked at her the more she got scared.

We continued on our way, the uneasy feelin' was still on my insides and felt like a freight train came right inside of my stomach and was rumbling its way along the tracks of my intestines, drawing heat from its huge rusty wheels slithering down the track as fast as it could go.

Soon we were beside the basement window, and the near by bushes that Vera once took her first pee after bein' scared almost to death. I felt the need to go potty this time, and excused myself and headed behind the bushes.

"Vera, I really have to go poop, my belly is hurtin' so much. I'll be right back." I excused myself as politely as I could wabbling my butt behind the bushes just in the nick of time too.

"I'm really afraid Eddie." Vera started to follow me behind the bush, but realized that I was gonna take a crap, so she stayed real close to the bush for safety.

"You'll, AAAAAAAAAHHHHHHHH, damn, I have the runs, aaaaaaaaaaaahh, I'll be ok. I, I'll be done in a-ahhhh-ahhhhhh couple more minutes." Man this stinks, I thought to myself. " I sure hope Vera don't smell this crap."

"Eddie, Are ya ok baby." She poked her head through the bushes; as I was startin' ta wipe my butt with a bunch of leaves, but I quickly pulled up my pants and came from behind the bushes.

"Wow, I feel much better now, I don't know what I ate to get the runs like this." I glanced at her, and she just looked down at the ground, not sayin' a word I just smiled as if I hadn't seen her, knowing that she'd seen my lower half. She pulled her head back outta the bush very fast, but I seen her and she was a holdin' her nose and her breath for a couple minutes, as soon as I came from behind the bush Vera looked pale like she'd held her breath for hours. I knew all along she had watched me poop in the bushes, but kept my big mouth closed as tight as a whiskey barrel.

"Eddie lets go inside and sit for a little while ok, I want you to feel better, and if ya sit for a spell, I know you'll be ok." She smiled as I entered the basement window and waited for her to come through backwards as she usually did. I had anticipation of getting her dress over my head once again so I could maybe see her smooth little piece of flesh next to her cute black butt.

The dress draped my head again, and as it did, she wasn't wearin' any under panties, and I got a good full view of that odd lookin g thing she kept close guard on, and I had to smile even bigger as I helped her down from the dresser to the floor. She looked at me as if she knew I'd seen her private part real good this time and I somehow had the feelin' that she seemed to like me lookin' under her dress a whole lot.

We sat there for about a half an hour then proceeded to go about our further exploration inside the mansion. This time, neither one of us seemed scarred like all the other times, after a few minutes of resting, we went down the same steps we descended from whence we'd came the day before, it was dark, and had a damp smell to it this time. Vera held her nose and my hand at the same time as we filtered our way back into the depths of the very pits of hell again journeying still deeper than what it seemed before, we both felt uneasy like someone or something was with us the whole time, but we never seen anyone. Soon we stopped at the bottom of the steps, where we'd left our lantern the day before; I took out the matched and lit it and as I looked at the fuel inside, I knew we didn't have much time to use the lantern, and besides where would we get more coal oil for its further use.

The glow from the lantern drifted in and out from a slight cool breeze that flowed its way over the globe, and I prayed that it wouldn't blow out any time, a cloud like mist hovered above the lantern, and began to take on the shape of a female woman, it kept getting bigger and bigger with each breeze that drifted over the lanterns flickering flame, then settled down onto the floor below our feet, but the shape of the woman was gone as soon as it touched the damp moss covered floor beneath out feet, and so was the mist that it came in on with one last flicker of the lanterns flame blowing in the breeze.

Now we were in the dark, cold, and frightened once again. We turned around to head back to the stairway so we could gather some papers, wood, and what ever else we could to build ourselves a small fire so we could see the room we'd just entered. Vera went ahead of me a couple steps with me behind her to catch her incase she slipped and fell, but as she ascended upward, the opposite happened and I slipped, falling back down the stairs to the damp slimy floor below, thud, my head bounced off the last step and banged hard against the floor and I didn't see Vera anymore.

Unconsciousness took hold of me, and I was all alone deep inside the house and with no Vera or anyone else as far as that went; a few more minutes passed, and I stood up like nothing had ever happened to me at all, walking slowly to keep balance I went back up the steps to the exact same spot where I last seen Vera, but she just wasn't there, I had finally made my way back to the basement window my head still throbbing with a deep – deep pain in the back, like someone had hit me on the head with a baseball bat or something. After I climbed back out, I made my way partly back to where the bridge was so I could cross to the other side, not knowing quite where I was, I looked for a way to cross the creek to make my way back to my pickup truck, and horse trailer, but I must have collapsed, falling once more to the wet ground just a short distance from where the mansion stood and as I fell flat on my face I looked toward the ol' place, but it had seemed to vanish into thin air. As I lay there not realizing it, somehow I knew that I'd soon be back in a place where time stood still; yes a place that almost felt like home to me for some reason, but I couldn't quite put my fingers on it.

"Hey Ed, wake up, come on now, I know your in there some place wow sweetie you sure did have one heck of a fall, lay still ok, I have to change your bandages now." Vera was a good nurse, and I knew I was in good hands with her.

What? UUUUMMM, Where am I? What happened?" I was in pain, lots of pain and for a few minutes I didn't even know what my name was, or who Vera was. As she changed the bandages on my split open head, I started telling her everything that happened to me during the past three or four days, she sort of laughed it off, and continued patching me up.

"All I knew is that I was riding my horse in this field, and she bucked me off when a snake spooked her, and you should have seen all the strange things that came into my mind, they were incredibly unbelievable that I couldn't wait to tell you. Yea, yea, I know Vera, you're probably thinking I'm went crazy, or maybe I'd bumped my head awfully hard when I hit the ground, well darlin' I'm telling you the truth, all of this really happened to me. How, I don't know but here is all I have as proof? What I just told you really happened to me over the past few days... honest to God it did. Ya do believe me don't ya." I showed Vera an arrowhead, and a pink bow that I stuffed in my pant pocket sometime during the course of bein' un-conscious, and laying on the ground. "My horse was eating grass when I looked at her a couple times and I drifted back out of reality I guess. He must have came back sometime during the night. You believe me don't ya? Honest to God. Aweeeeee. Dang that hurts. What ya using on me now Vera, pure alcohol, snake bite oil, or what? Aweeeeeee, crap that hurts baby, please don't push on it so damn hard ok princess."

"Will you just sit still Ed, let me fix your wound ok, and maybe I'm your baby, and maybe I'm not hehehe. The gash in the back of your head should have stitches put in it. Are you sure you don't want me to take you to the infirmary and have stitches put in your head?" She turned her eyes toward mine and smiled really big.

"No, I'll be alright. Tell me again where ya found me, or better still just take me, Aweeeee, there OK. Please." I was still in pain, but that didn't matter, all I knew was that I had to know if what I told her was real, or just a bunch of bad dreams from being knocked out for several days and my head pounded with thousands of throbbing beats per second or so it seemed.

"Lets wait a couple days to see how your feeling." Vera always is directly to the point and just don't like to go someplace that really wasn't necessary at the time. She had a good sense of things and when the time was right, or when something had to be done, and then it would be done in a timely manner. Vera bein' a nurse and all, worked so dang hard all the time. My fiddle-fuddle nonsense wasn't of any interest to her in the least.

My anxiety was setting in, maybe because I was serious most of the time, but once in awhile I liked to tease her just for the fun, of doing it and most of the time she didn't like to fool around and this time was no exception to my rule either. She was busy taking care of lots of other patients, not just me and just didn't have lots of time to chit chat and loll-e gag about like a dang little school girl.

Well, several weeks went by, and things seemed to be getting back to normal. I went to bed that night around eleven-thirty or so, but just couldn't sleep for thinking about everything I told nurse Vera.

The next morning when I got up, took my shower, and after I ate a hardy breakfast, I wondered the corridors of the hospital ta find the nurse in charge for the day, and low and behold it was Vera, thank God, she must have pulled a double shift and was ready to go home to get some rest.

"Hey, Vera, hey come on, wait up a second, please wait. I have ta talk to ya, please wait." I shouted, begging her to slow her pretty little self down just a tad and stopped next to the main hall entry and waited till I caught up to her.

"What do you want Ed? Can't you see that I am about to go home. I worked all night again, and I'm tired and need to get some sleep. Thank God, I'm off for two days at last. Make it snappy ok. AHHHHHUUUUM." Her eyes showed red streaks in their misty black colored glow as she rubbed them a couple times while tryin' to focus on me at the same time.

"Please, I couldn't sleep last night. I thought about everything I told you yesterday, and I was wondering if, well ya said you were off for the next two days." I was stopped short of my sentence by her tiredness.

"Yes, I am off, but need to get my rest too. Well?" She asked abruptly out of haste not want or need, and certainly not outta need.

"I was wondering if you could possibly take me to that field I was found in so I could see it for myself. Please, it is so important to me, please, please do this one favor for me and I will never bother you about it ever again, please, I'm beggin' ya." My eyes drooped like a puppy dogs eyes and my lower lip puffed out quivering like the heart beat in that poem I'd found in the mansion as a kid.

"OK, OK, stop your groveling, gee wiz... men, they are such pains in the neck sometimes aren't they? I guess, well I will have to ask the doctor if your well enough to take the long trip to the country or not. I'll let you know tomorrow, but right now I have to get some, AHHHHHHAAAAMM, some sleep Ok. See you tomorrow." She yawned one more time and headed out the front lobby door of the infirmary. I yelled thank you to her as she was out the door and walking down the sidewalk to her car, boy was I excited that she said a partial yes and it sent goose-bumps up and down my spine like Porky pine quills saying that she take me, and I headed back to my room so I could wait patiently for tomorrow to come.

Vera showed up the next afternoon to talk to the doctor, even though she was off work, she must really care about me and my well being enough to take time out on one of her days off to please me. I really do love that sweet-wonderful woman.

About an hour passed when Vera walked into my room and told me the doctor would be in to give me another exam to see how my head injury was doing. I couldn't wait till he examined me and I prayed he'd tell me if I was in good enough shape to take the long ride from the hospital in Muncie to Old Hyde Park. The excitement was building so much it started to bring tears to my eyes as he walked into the room.

"Well Ed, everything looks real good, I suppose it will be alright for you to go on this trip I heard so much about from Nurse Vera." His tone was pleasant, but stern, and he sure seemed like he wanted me to recover quickly so he could finally release me from the health resort so at speak in a moderate term.

"Thank you so very much Dr. Kindofgrins." I blazed my teeth real big and they shown like a roaring wild fire as if there were no tomorrow. After about fifteen minutes in the exam station, I went to my room to prepare for the trip the next morning and was totally anguished by all the excitement of finally getting out of this awful hospital to travel back in time so I could finally put my mind to rest.

Morning came quicker than my anticipation; finally me and Nurse Vera were on our way back to the country where I grew up as a kid. I couldn't think about anything but seeing the old home town and the big Secluded Mansion and wondered if it was still there after all these years.

We had a long way to drive from Melmont which is 4 miles from Carbonado, Washington to Hyde Park, Indiana, and it would take us about eight or ten long-hard solid days of steady driving before I'd finally be back in my home town once more before I died of old age, not knowin' before if I'd ever see it once again as long as I lived.

Time flew by and we were getting closer and closer. Seven, six and then five hours passed by, my anxiety grew with every mile, every telephone pole, every cornfield, and every bug that splattered on the windshield of Vera's almost new car. It flew like the wind that brings with it the sands of time, father time and yes even good ol' Mother Nature had her hands in this journey as well. It had been the best trip that I'd ever taken in my entire life. I was so happy, and so excited that she got a two week vacation instead of a few days off.

After five days of long hard and almost constant driving, we soon reached the outskirts of Muncie where we stopped for an early dinner, a place called Melvin's Country Hometown Buffet, it was an all you can eat for the low-low price of $7.95. We both ate like pigs till our bellies almost burst wide open. Once we ate we relaxed at a near by park which I'd recognized it as McCauley Park... one of my old stomping grounds as a kid way back in the day, and much to my surprise the big long soapbox derby hill and derby building was still there right where it has always been, way up high on a hill, where the runway track for the derby cars use to be set in motion while racing as fast as they could for about six or seven hundred feet of speed and excitement man did that place bring back memories looking at it within my minds past eyes and saw people having picnics, and good times, children playing on the big slide, man it don't look as big as it did way back when I was age seven and eight years old, but back then it seemed like it was a hundred feet tall or so, but now, well it's only about maybe seven feet tall at the most.

"Gee." I said to Vera with a child like smile.

"What, what's that Ed." She looked at me with her beautiful dark black eyes and sortta wrinkled her cute little nose in wonder as to why I said Gee?

"Let's go on the slide ok." I smiled from ear to ear.

"Are you crazy, whoops, bad choice of words?" She smiled and covered her mouth like she aid something bad or something.

"Yea; yea lets you and I go for just one slide down it, it'll be fun, and besides its been way too many years since I went down that thing." I said as I stood up from the picnic table bench and looked at her with child like eyes once again.

Vera just smiled. "Well, why the heck not, let's go." We both took off running, and by the time I got there I was outta breath. Vera was in real good shape and since she came from Africa and used to run allot; she wasn't a bit tired. She went up that tall ladder and slid down it like shed done it a million times. I took my time climbing the ladder and stopped near the top in hesitation and started to come back down.

"Hey, Ed aren't you going to slide down too, after all it was your idea, its fun, come on slide down it like you used to do, come on show me you still know how to do it." She smiled really big and her encouragement meant a lot to me and I took the last step, plopped my big butt down on the cool steel slide plate and down I went.

"Wheeeee, this is fun, just like I remember it being, wheeeeeee." I said as I flew down the side and it was like I remember it being, so much fun and all. When I reached the bottom I flew right off the end and landed on my butt on the soft green grass that swept the whole park like a huge green blanket of velvet, like a big green wool carpet, it went on and on for what seemed like miles as my child like mind drifted in and out with the many memories of that park. I came back to my semi-senses, and stood up, brushing my butt off with both hands. Vera laughed so loud that what few people were there at the time just stared at her and me like we were both a little strange. I joined in and laughed as well.

"Hey, you people should do it too, hahahahahaha. What ya all looking at? Hahahahaha." I just kept on laughing, and Vera couldn't help herself, she laughed just as hard as I was, and as we both walked away like a couple school kids and sat down on still another bench near by the slide, there was also that big swing set I use to play on, and my thought was to go swing on it as well, but Vera said no way, that was enough and besides we had a mission to go on, the thought kept entertaining my mind, as I was having lots of fun and felt like a kid once more in my child like mind from the times long past. After leaving the park we headed out toward county road 32 on the other side of Muncie, as I looked around me it seemed like not very much had changed in that part of town since I lived there as a kid. The day was still in its morning rise and was only about 9 a.m. with the warm summer sun shinnin' brightly as it usually did in Muncie in early June. The humidity was at 100% and around 70 degrees like it had always been, birds were chirping, people taking life nice and slow as they usually did in the country, and that made me have a sense of peace once again, not because I was outta the hospital, but because I was back home where I really belonged.

Vera and I went for breakfast at Danny's Lil' Café' on the way outta town towards county road 32, but the food wasn't all that good, but at least we got enough nourishment from it to sustain our strength till lunch time anyway. It seemed like I was always hungry for some unknown reason, and I just couldn't figure out why, nor could the doctors. I never got too fat, and held my own pretty well, not to exceed the 190 mark on the old scale at the hospital that looked like it was from centuries long past.

Man was I starting to get ecstatic and could hardly wait to see Hyde Park again after all these years, my anxiety grew more and more with each mile we put behind us as we speed down county road 32 toward my old stomping grounds. Since my mind was as a child at again and acting like one as well, I even played a couple good childish jokes on Nurse Vera from time to time and was having a blast doing it too.

The country air felt refreshing to my nostrils and the slight moisture was almost like breathing in the winters furry from 1957 when time was innocent and so was I.

"Hahahahaha." I chuckled out of sheer emotional expression and Vera just looked at me as if I were a fruit cake at the Christmas table. More and more smiles filtered from beyond my jaws, outward, and deep into the fields, streams, trees, and oh the houses, so many of them since I was a kid and the longer I looked, the more the surroundings felt like the city instead of the country, even though it didn't have the theme of a city, well sir it sortta felt like in between the two, with a mix of both outer and inward spaces that had been tied with hundreds of ropes that contained millions of loose ends left to dangle in the breeze along with the sands of time.

When we reached the outer edge of Hyde Park across from where we was supposed to make our turn a different community named Woodland Park poked up like a new forest of trees right next to where the old folks home stood like another big mansion out of la la land on the other side of 32, and the old bridge had been rebuilt too, all shinny like a freshly minted silver dollar. As we crossed over what use to be called Hill Street, was now called 400 South Willard Ct, what strange name was this I thought? I couldn't believe what my eyeballs were a lookin' at, the old corner store was standing just like I remembered it, and as I look back to the other side of highway 32 before we entered Hyde Park, the old folks home was even right where I remember it being too. I couldn't help but rub my eyes and shake my head several times at its different shape… how weird they had refurbished it from its rustic style to a modern one.

"Vera, do you see that." I looked at her with puzzled eyes, my brow began to sweat just a little and I didn't know if it was because of the heart, humidity, or what, but my whole body started to shake like leaves blowin' in the warm summer breeze, and chills took over my entire being for a brief moment.

"See what Ed? Ed, what was it you seen, well, come on tell me. What was it, an old building, or what?" Vera pulled over and sat there staring at me as I stare at the ominous surroundings from my past. The parking lot of the corner store was the same, but the store had been abandoned for many years and I quickly turned my head from the store toward the ol' folk's home, and shook my head once again.

"I-it hasn't changed in all these years, the people are still sittin' on the porch of the old folks home, and there's old man Cash goin' into the corner store, but he has his own store down closer to Luke's place, as we started to pass by him I rolled down my window just a little more and yelled: Hi Mr. Cash," Waving frantically for him to notice me, but in a flash he was gone.

"Ed snap outta it, there ain't anyone there." Vera kept staring at me over her shoulder with her beautiful big black eyes as she continued to drive past the store.

"Huh, w-what's that w-what'd ya say Vera? Oh I thought I seen ol' man Cash goin' into the corner store?" Puzzlement still plumaged from my wrinkled eyebrows, and I wiped my forehead once again.

"Are you going to be ok Ed? The store is all abandoned, boarded up with planks and particleboard, and the door is chained with a padlock on it." She started showing more concern for my well being, and was ready to turn around. "I'm taking you back; I don't think you should be here Ed." Her face seemed strange to me for a second.

"I'm, I'M OK, Lets just go on, I have to do this, please let's just go on into Hyde Park now okay. Please let's go." Pleading like a little boy I smiled real big at her with my puppy dog hazel eyes as she put the car back into drive and headed once again back towards the bridge.

It was all she could do to keep the car on the road as we headed over the bridge because all she did was look at me almost continuously, but I was in a different world or so it seemed. She took her concentration back toward the road just before we went onto the bridge, and it was a good thing too as another car was coming down the hill. I waved at the car as if I knew the man driving, but all he did was shake his fist at us and gave me and Vera the middle finger, or the bird as I used to call it when I was a kid living out here in the country.

We were soon over the bridge and even everything on that side of the bridge was also exactly the same as I remember it. Every tree, house, bush, and rock hadn't changed one iota. Not one stone was turned over in my mind and was amazed at how things on this side of the county road remained intact for the past forty-five or so years. I was home at last and the kid in me came back to life once more and I was in high spirits, laughing and giggling as I used to way back in the mid fifties.

Vera just kept looking at me with her beautiful big black eyes as if I really was crazy. I knew she had doubts in her mind as to what my reality in truth was, factual fact or true fiction. Puzzlement kept reflecting off her face in an adverse sort of way, but I paid her no real never mind 'cause I was way too busy looking at my old stompin' grounds, tears of delight filled my whole being as we approached the end of the road close to Luke's ol' place, but the road didn't end, it kept going on and on and on and not too much beyond that spot looked the same any more. The long dirt road beyond his long driveway was now paved, and lots of new houses spread out as far as

I could see, my mind raced in and out like a time machine had been placed deep inside it; images kept appearing as though they were still the same as when I was a kid and as I glared towards Luke's place, it appeared to be still there; nothing changed… man oh man nothing whatsoever, the ol' place was real, and not just a vision from my past as some things seemed to be appearing in the realm of my wondering spirit that cheerful day.

"Ed, hey Ed, is this the place you told me so much about? Is this Luke Dillon's old house or not?" Vera seemed a wee bit in a state between confusion, and sanity in her speech pattern.

"Huh. Oh, yea, stop here we will have to walk down his drive way, he don't like anyone driving any car down it since his fence was hit by one of his drunk poker buddies when I was a kid." My monatomic voice was full of excitement, my mind was filled with a feeling that is so indescribable, so much wonder spread through my mind.

"Ed." Vera started to ask me if it was Luke's place once again, but I interrupted her.

"Yea, yea this is Luke's place, will ya just look at it, wowzers, it hasn't changed one iota, not one?" As Vera stopped the car, I jumped out and started to run down the drive, but before I had a chance to make one single solitary move, Vera crabbed a-hold of my arm.

"Hey, Mister Ed, wait just a minute ok, there are two people here, remember me, Nurse Vera?" She turned me around so I could look at her directly in the face and as I turned around I caught a glimpse of a tall man with a full brimmed ol' brown hat on his head just like the one Luke used to wear, Vera grabbed my head and tried to make me look at her, but since my mind was totally on my old friend so strong, she wasn't able to force it towards her, and turned my head back toward Luke's house and yelled:

"Hey Luke, it's me Eddie. Can me and my friend come visit ya for a spell?" Vera took hold of my shoulders and gave 'em a good swift shake or two.

"Ed, snap out of it will you? I'm just a little bit embarrassed ok. You have to stop yelling at people here, they may call the cops on us for disturbing the peace."

"I don't care, um-a, oh yea, um I'm a -really-really sorry Vera. I - I'd sorta forgotten for a minute or two." I came to my senses and we both walked down the ol' cinder driveway toward the white gate, and little house that stood behind it.

"Hello is anyone there." I shouted, "Hello, hey Luke, it's me Eddie, remember, Mary Belle Holman's boy?" I looked real hard at the little house; it hadn't changed one single bit in over these past forty-five or so years. All the sudden a tall figure appeared at the door.

"Yea, what the Sam Hell do you want, and what are you doing on my property in the first place." He looked through the screen door at us as he yelled with his rough tone of voice.

"Sorry, so sorry to disturb you sir, but is this Mr. Luke Dillon's place?" Vera shouted in her tiny voice.

"Who, Who are you looking for Maim'?" He yelled back. "Please come in, I'm sorry for being so dang rude, please just come on in, you and your friend. I won't bite, at least not too hard, HAHAHAHAHA." He yelled back as he stepped out his door to get a better look putting on his glasses at the same time, and as we walked through the gate his tone changed to a more mellow and pleasant sound letting out a deep pitched melody the exact same way it did when I was seven and eight years old.

As me and Vera approached the front of the little house, he introduced himself as the grandson of Luke Dillon. He sure looked a whole lot like good ol' Luke, but was a tad shorter, much more muscular than he was and not as scruffy as Luke used to be either.

"Ahhhhhhh crap, dang-it, that isn't Luke." I whispered under my breath with much disappointment.

"Hi, I'm Vera… Vera U. Capturesme, and this is Edward H' Wolf, but just call him Eddie ok." Vera reached out and shook his huge hand and smiled after the introduction.

"Aaaaaum." I cleared my horse throat just a wee bit… "Hi Mr. Dillon; you said you were Luke Dillon's grandson?" I smiled just a little, but was sad that it wasn't Luke himself, but how could it be, he was an old man when I was a kid of seven years old.

"Yep, that's right… my grandpa told me a little about you and your Aunt Mary… grandpa talked lots about the old days before he passed away in 1975 at age seventy-five. Won't you come in and sit a spell, please. How 'bout some coffee? I just don't get many folk visitin' me y'ere lately these days. Please sit."

"I'm sorry, but what did ya say your first name was." I looked at his living room it was a little more modern than when Luke, me and Aunt Mary lived here.

"Wayne… Wayne's my first name." He grinned just the way I remember Luke grinning when he was in a good mood right before one of his poker games.

"I'm sorry; I had my mind in the past, its been way too many years since I been out in this neck of the woods, please forgive me, but its all amazing to me, my how things have changed around here Wayne, may I call you Wayne?" I asked with deep sorrow.

"Yea, go ahead, Wayne's fine, and can I call you both by your first names?" He headed for his small kitchen and glanced back over his shoulders at us. "Excuse me, please, would you both like for your coffee… cream, sugar?" He said and he so much reminded me of his grandpa Luke in many ways, I was beside myself with amazement.

After the long introductions and several cups of strong black coffee; I still wasn't satisfied with how things were goin', but what the heck, at least I found out some things that happened to Luke after me and my Aunt Mary left Hyde Park for Muncie way back in 1958. My curiosity was still floating in and out between other realms; drifting back and forth from present to past as though my mental state was getting worse as time went by. I had to see more of my old stomping grounds before something else bad happened to me. I just had to, there was no doubt in my feebly unstable mind's eye, and as I stood up and told Nurse Vera that we'd best get on with our exploration on the other side of Ol' Buck Creek.

Wayne looked at me with worry in his eyes, but Vera didn't see his immediate facial expression because she was looking at me at the time when I said it. She turned thanking Wayne for all his hospitality; his facial expression changed miraculously from worry to like I'd not said anything about going over to the other side across Buck Creek.

"You're both, welcome back any time, any time at all ya hear." He shook Vera's hand then mine. As he stood in the doorway of his place, Vera walked out toward the gate, but I stood there staring him right square in his deep set eyes, and I couldn't help but notice how much he seemed to change right in front of me. Luke had appeared within Wayne. I turned, stumbling over a brick that was loose next to his porch and walked backwards toward the gate where Vera was waiting for me.

"Thank you so very much Wayne, It was a real pleasure to meet you, take care ok." She smiled a warm and friendly smile and then looked at me as if I was the one possessed with a different spirit, and as we walked down the long cinder driveway to where Vera parked her car, I couldn't keep from turning back toward his house, and every time I did, Luke's face appeared in my mind, and then a stranger thing happened to me. I started to ask Vera if Wayne was on the level about all that he told us, but she turned toward me with a strange look in her eyes. She is after all a psychiatric nurse with an RN Nurses degree on top of it and I do so very much admired her, and her opinion always meant a lot to me; Vera is a very trustworthy and beautiful woman, and I'd never dispute her opinion, maybe out of the love I had inside of me for her was the main reason for me not doubting her, but my mental state was a bit on edge lately.

"Eddie, it's amazing that this little house is still standing after all these years, too bad no one lived there anymore; it would have been nice if we could have talked to someone, but that's life sometimes. We best head on out to the other place that you wanted to see, it's down this street isn't it?" Her voice was soft as she told me that no one lived there and it was all boarded up and ran down. A little disappointment peeked outta her pretty black eyes as she got into her car.

"What do you mean; too bad no one lived there anymore? We just finished talking to Luke's grandson Wayne, didn't we?" I pulled the door open like a raging mad man as I too got into the car; my thoughts were racing like the locomotive that was speeding down the tracks in the distance blowing its loud whistle as it passed under what used to be called Hill Street, but my tone went from a raging bull's voice down to a mild mannered mouse in just a few seconds.

"Yes Ed, no one lives there any longer... who is this Wayne you mentioned?" She was almost as confused as I was in a matter of minutes. "No one lives there anymore, didn't you see the run down condition of the little house, the fence was rotting away, shingles and boards were falling off it, and the doors were hanging from their rusting hinges. It was a real mess." She drove down the hill and was almost to my old baseball field when I looked over at her and said:

"Mess, what do you mean a real mess? What's happening to me am I dreaming? Pinch me, please! Wake me up, I must be dreaming. Where am I?" I didn't know what way to turn, and my thought patterns were adrift like logs on the open ocean of time. More and more confusion filled my head with things from the past and I just wished I was back at the hospital for a few minutes, and then I shook my head, or was it Vera shaking me, I can't quite remember, but all the sudden I was back in reality as Vera drove down the winding street to our next destination.

"Look at the time Ed, are you getting hungry, I sure am?" She changed the subject so I could take my mind away from past events and people from a time when my youth flowed through the meadow and woods that was hardly around any more.

"Yea, yea I am getting' a little hungry too, hey there's a Mexican restaurant on the right side about a half block up." My stomach started crawling like that mean Ol' Gray Wolf was a chasin' me once again, but my thoughts were on eating and not on that spooky wolf in that spooky Ol' Secluded Mansion that hopefully was still standing another mile or so up the road, but without all the ghost that have taunted me from a kid to now. The restaurant was an authentic Mexican setting as we opened the door; the atmosphere had most of the old world style, and even an authentic mariachi band was playin' in the background. Not very many people were inside, but what few there were, was all of Hispanic nationality, and one black couple at a booth in the far left corner of the place. Lights were low, tables were patterned with cacti legs, and table clothes made of green, brown and red hand woven materials just like in Old Mexico. There were many paintings of bull fights, hand painted pottery made of clay sitting on shelves and even the walls were also painted and were of the adobe tradition in construction material. It was indeed a very pleasant and quiet little place to sit, relax and eat a hardy meal that was fit for a king or even a president and his cabinet.

"This is a real nice place Vera. The prices are good and the servings look like more than any one person can chuck down into their belly in one setting, but ya know what, I just love a heaping plate full of food, and what you can't eat, I will ok." I held the chair for Vera and the people in the place just glared at me, because they didn't seem to understand that was how a gentleman should act. Vera looked at me and smiled real big, she always did when I held her chair for her the way it should be. I guess that folk here 'bouts aren't mannered like big city folk are, but that's ok, I'll just keep on bein' the gentleman that I am no matter what other people think.

"Thank you Ed." Her smile stood out amongst all the other patrons that were dinning at the time. She picked up the menu and began to look to see what was good. I done the same, but I already had in mind what I wanted my usual, smothered burritos; yum-yum I could taste them now, hot, spicy, and full of meat, refried beans, topped with sour cream, cheese, and hot sauce with a side of Spanish rice and more refried beans on the side and a coke. Vera ordered the Tilapia fish plate with no refried beans and extra rice and a medium coke.

"I'm stuffed. How about you Vera?" I asked as I put my napkin on the tray and pushed it aside. Vera was still tryin' at finish her plate, which had way too much on it. She had me ask for a take out box so she could munch on the rest of her fish and rice later in the evening. She always does that when she orders at almost any restaurant. I was more than happy to oblige her and went to get her take home box for her food, and at the same time I took my tray to place it back on the shelf with all the other trays, after putting my trash in the disposal receptacle area.

Anyway... Vera packed her box, closed the lid and we both headed out the door with cokes in hand and full stomachs enough to tide us over till way late in the evening. I knew Vera wouldn't eat all of her left over' later and I was lookin' forward to a snack before I retired to bed. Plopping ourselves in the car we set there for a few minutes to relax our bellies that we'd stuffed full of good Mexican food and then drove off to our next stop, the creepy ol' haunted mansion that I so longed to see once again in my old age before I got too old to even travel to the bathroom in a wheel chair or something later on in my life as a senior citizen in some nursing home in the smoggy, crowded suburbs of the city near Melmont, Washington on the west coast of this beautiful country. Gee, I sure would like to retire in the country instead of the big city that is if God grants my prayer before I bite the dust so to speak.

Approaching the area where the field of the mansion was, I could see Buck Creek from the windshield of the car; it looked like it did when I was a lad. My excitement grew more and more as we got closer to where me and my friends had placed the footbridge over the rippling waters of the little creek. It somehow looked smaller than it used to, but I paid no never mind cause I was back in my youth once again. Off in the distance behind me I could hear the old farmer driving his tractor to plow his corn field. A baseball game was going on at the field just up the road and I could see Tommy and David running down the hill yelling for me to wait up, but Vera and I had already crossed over to the other side of the creek, but I just kept walking toward where Spooks-

Ville Mansion stood years ago and it all of the suddenly appeared outta no where just like it stood when I was a kid as well as for the past two hundred years since it was constructed by George Maxifield and his wife Waity A.

I went close to where the window to the basement was, Vera just stood back in the distance like she was afraid of the big spooky ol farmhouse, but my mind's eye was focused on the Mansion only because I was a kid once again; and, I just ignored her as though she'd never been there in the first place. As I knelled down to look into the window, I heard my friends yelling at me to wait for them. I stood up and looked behind me, and there was Vera, Sally, David and Tommy who had never changed in appearance or age. We were all together once again and ready to explore the mansion as usual. I lead the way inside and then I helped Vera down to the inside like I had always done, wow... what a gentleman I was, and then came David and last but not least, my best bud, Tommy. I knew that nurse Vera was a grown woman and not a little kid like she's use at be, but my mind had went all the way back in time to see Vera as a little girl and my childhood sweetheart. Man oh man, she has always been a beautiful girl back then and now a beautiful woman. My mental state seemed to have been brought out of reality for a brief time and drawn back to Hyde Park and my friends. I knew that good ol' Dr. Kinfofgrins was someplace near by for some strange and odd reason and I could hear his voice. I looked around and no one else seemed to be near me, but I couldn't place my finger on the reality of my mental state of bein'. at that brief moment in the space that I was inside of.

We held onto each other in a big group hug and then started to laugh just the way we'd always laughed. Our reunion had finally taken place inside our playing field. As I turned around toward the piles of rubble, the little girl Nellie Matilda (Mattie) Sarah Sue Cleavage Maxifield usTuss\y appeared outta no where and we all began to play and explore the Mansion as usual. Vera looked toward where I had stood at one time next to the place that she could never see in the first place. She called my name, and I could hear her calling me from beyond, but for her not hearing and seeing me was so shocking, and so scary that she took off running back toward her car. She ran as fast as she could tripping a couple times to hobble across the footbridge and cross Buck Creek to get into her car as quick as she could and drive off leaving me in the great beyond of time, space, and another dimension of the imagination where I always wanted to be when I was young; in my Secluded Mansion Nights, looking out from the tower chapel and my final home of peace and rest at last.

Vera drove back to Washington all by herself that day, and was so much alone with me not pestering her the way I did as a kid. The two days she had off was much needed after having to deal with the likes of me. By the time she reached the asylum where she worked as a Nurse, she was almost exhausted to an obliterating pulp. She walked down the long hallway toward my room with tears streaming down her cheeks like the flow from the old artesian well alongside Buck Creek in Hyde Park, Indiana, but when she went into my room, much to her surprise I hadn't been released yet and there I was laying back against the head of my bed watching my TV as I have always done. She could hardly believe her own eyes. She dropped down on her knees and prayed to God, thanking him for me still being alive and well after the terrible car accident that I'd been in... loosing my memory for a couple months, but while she was away, I'd recovered and regained my memory totally. Vera got up as fast as she'd dropped to her knees and flew to my bedside and gave me a bear hug that almost killed me. Laying her head on my shoulders she cried for several more minutes; thanking God in my ear that I was alive and told me how much she loved me over and over and that she'd never leave me alone for the rest of my life.

I soon recovered my imaginary creative illness of writing for the time bein' anyway, and a wonderful thing happened that winter in February 2002... Vera and I got married and are living happily ever after in a cozy little house in the rainy state of Oregon.

In any existence, all the senses in the wonderment of creativity that is drawn from the imagination bring with them the vastness of truth that lay beyond the visual imagery far beyond the outer reaches of what one would want to expect from this life or the next. Not just a mere simple thought, or word that is thrown into page after page of people, places and things, but all that is put together with them come the major six senses drawing a sense of genius to either fact or fiction, truth or lie.

Literature flows like a beach filled with billions of grains of words like the sands of time in the realm of space, imagination, and genius. All we must do is place ourselves in such realms, look at their proper perspective as if we were a particle in its vastness as Mother Nature and father time that has done to every living-breathing, and every non living and breathing thing that our Great Spirit (God) has created, then just distinguish between reality and fiction. The choice is yours to command at will. Have un-pleasant dreams and happy nightmares. Hahahahahahahaha... Let your imagination flow with thoughts to fill page after page full of wonderful words, no matter how big or how small, there will be no end until the end of time itself. Oh how I miss those days long since passed, my friends, my aunt, most are more than likely gone by now; but like myself, somehow I know some may just be still alive that was one thing I knew, and then again maybe not… who knows, but life must go on as I will also some day depart, but till then I will continue to write what lay inside my imagination where fact meets fiction…

The End

"Awooooooo." Says the Gray Wolf